About the Author

John Bishop was born in Heswall on the Wirral and now lives in Codsall near Wolverhampton. Originally an English teacher, he was for six years a College Principal in Birmingham. For longer than he cares to admit he has attended weekly Greek classes at the Brasshouse Language Centre in Birmingham, where Roula, Lina and Eleni in particular have laid the foundations for his deeper understanding, and enjoyment, of the culture and language of Greece.

This novel derives from a fascination with Crete that began on his first visit in 1982, since when, interspersed with trips to over forty other Greek islands, he has been back several dozen times, traversing many parts of the island on foot, often to the amusement of the locals.

Love, Freedom or Death is his second novel. The first, *The Chinese Attack*, was published as a Vanguard paperback in 2011. A third, dealing with the frenzy that in 1914 led to a war no one wanted or whose consequences they could imagine, is due out in the summer of 2014.

Website: www.johnbishopauthor.wordpress.com

Love, Freedom or Death

JOHN BISHOP

Matador
9 Priory Business Park,
Wistow Road, Kibworth Beauchamp,
Leicestershire. LE8 0RX
Tel: (+44) 116 279 2299
Fax: (+44) 116 279 2277
Email: books@troubador.co.uk
Web: www.troubador.co.uk/matador

ISBN 978 1780884 646

British Library Cataloguing in Publication Data.
A catalogue record for this book is available from the British Library.

Typeset by Troubador Publishing Ltd, Leicester, UK

Matador is an imprint of Troubador Publishing Ltd

Printed and bound in the UK by TJ International, Padstow, Cornwall

For Jeremy Sheldon
who always believed in Kiwi from the start
and whose empathy and expertise drove him on.

Late May 2011

The Road up to Omalos, Western Crete

Was there guilt in the shiver that rippled through the standing crowd? From the priest's reminder of debts to the past they'd too easily forgotten, perhaps?

It might only have been the cold. This straight stretch of the road, below the white marble slab of the memorial, gave no shelter. And at a thousand metres the wind coming down through the gap in the mountains could still chill.

The schoolchildren wearing national costume fidgeted or gazed with incomprehension at the New Zealand flag beside their own. From time to time they slipped a glance at the handful of wizened figures in the official party. The fierce eyes of the one upright old man, resplendent in black-fringed head-kerchief, baggy trousers and polished high boots they tended to avoid.

Beside the monument the tall, dark-robed priest softened his gaze and gave some the hope to his small audience that he was about to conclude.

'Finally,' he said, 'when we remember here today those who undertook the fight for our freedom seventy years ago – their sacrifice, their achievements, their unconquerable will – let us not forget that, in the end, their struggle was driven by love, a love that will always endure.'

One

Late May 1941, Galatas, Western Crete

'God, I hate this bloody place, Danna.'

Acting Corporal Dudley Watkins (New Zealand Artillery) flung his rifle and himself down in the dust under the olive trees. Shade at last. And on a reverse slope where no enemy sniper could pick you off. But Danna's laughter made him glare up at the Maori. 'What is there to laugh at?'

'You, Dud. No bugger's on our tail for once, so you could smile. But I reckon you're only happy when you're getting stick. Never mind, from the sound of it back there, you won't have to wait long.'

'Very funny, Danna. This time, I've had my fill. First Greece, now Crete. Every bloody step backwards. Is this what we joined up for?'

'I thought you did it to get away from your Ma?'

'A big comfort, you are, mate, you know that?'

'Yeah, I should have been a vicar like your dad. You know you need a firm hand to keep you in check.'

'Sod off.'

He rubbed the three-day stubble on his cheek and closed his eyes. That only brought back the nerve-shredding shriek of the stukas, the heaving earth of the trench and the constant spatter of bullets in the olive branches. Above all the gut-hollowing sense of helplessness… From somewhere close by, his dad was shouting at him.

'You men, on your feet!'

He jerked awake. The light was fading. Around him shadowy figures struggled upright. He wondered how they'd offended his dad. Then he realised where he was and went to obey but his body felt too heavy to lift. He sought for the source of the order, in case it was one he could ignore. Instead Danna was lugging him up. 'Come on, hero, shift your arse, it's Kip.'

He blinked alert. The slight figure of Colonel Kippenberger stood a few yards away, arms crossed, a pipe glowing in his right hand. The memory of the tongue-lashing Kip had given them for ceding ground two days ago shot him to his feet. After their latest collapse a repeat performance was on the cards.

Over Galatas white flares and the orange flash of mortar shells lit the violet sky. The picture deepened his depression. As Danna had said, it wouldn't be long before the German advance caught up with them again. If Kip wasn't going to bark out a dressing-down, he knew all the next order could be. More retreat.

The elation of boarding the troopship in Wellington harbour as they left for Egypt was a sick joke now. How could you face people back home after this?

Colonel Kippenberger was pointing with his pipe up the hill back towards Galatas, whose village streets they'd only too recently scuttled through with indecent haste.

'Do you want to stand up for New Zealand, men?'

He grunted like the rest from surprise as much as from reluctance. Kippenberger seemed to take their muted response as a refusal. And a personal insult, by the sound of it. 'I said, do you want to stand up for New Zealand? Or are you going to let her down again? Do I have any volunteers for a counter attack? With the bayonet.'

His own doubts were lost in the huge cry. Kippenberger raised his arms for quiet and eased the men a little further back. 'For a moment I thought I must have gone deaf,' the Colonel said. 'Spread yourselves in two columns behind the 23rd. When the tanks come back, we're going up the street and into the Square.'

Two battered light tanks chugged round the corner from Galatas village and lurched to a stop. One had had a bad time. He stopped to watch a wounded corporal being dragged out of its turret until Danna punched his arm and pulled him away. 'Happy now, Dud? I think retreating had its advantages.'

'Go on, you're the one who loves a scrap.'

'A scrap's one thing, machine gun bullets are quite another, thanks.'

He didn't need reminding of that. Fixing his bayonet he let Danna shove him to the left of the road. They squeezed past the damaged tank where two kiwis, replacements for the wounded occupants, he guessed, were listening to shouted instructions from the first tank's commander. The idea of being cooped up in a boiling sardine tin made him shudder even more. That's all they were. Panzers they were not. Then he remembered how exposed he was going to be.

'I hope Jerry's not expecting us,' he said, more to himself than Danna.

Danna snorted. 'And I hope he's as full of shit as you are, Dud. But on the evidence so far, there's no chance of that.'

In the dusk he scoured the tense and grim faces around him for reassurance. A counter attack. Something new for all of them. His throat was dry and his insides churned. He swallowed. Did the others feel as scared as he did?

The crowd was growing by the minute. Word must have spread. A chance to get even. Some of his companions stamped as if to keep warm even though the night was hot. Many were bare-headed. Several walking wounded had joined them. From the village came confused shouts and occasional shots. Someone muttered 'stiff with Jerries'.

When he glanced at the sky, not quite dark, the stars were out. Nice night for it, he told himself and knew he was trying to avoid thought. Crouching behind a field gun, behind a wall, in a shallow trench, had never seemed especially safe. Until now.

'I'll let your mum know you gave all for the greater glory of New Zealand,' Danna said. 'Charging the enemy.'

'Make sure you say I was wearing clean socks.'

The racing of the tanks' engines cut further reflection. The little tin boxes clanked away, spewing dust and smoke. Some spearhead and protective shield, they'd be. He felt himself moving, too. The Colonel called after them:

'This is for New Zealand, men. Don't let her down.'

The walking pace quickened to keep close to the tanks. His legs protested at the steepness of the hill but at the first bend the road flattened out and by the second he'd caught his breath again. The narrow street forced both columns to merge.

The swaying mass of bodies gave an illusion of comfort. As did the delirium of attacking, a change from the last two cowering days in the dense and undulating olive groves, waiting where you couldn't see ten yards ahead. Until he remembered that an illusion was all it was. And the enemy would definitely see *them* coming.

The tanks veered left and he tried to recall how many bends there were before the Square but they'd scarpered down here too fast to notice.

Another slight rise. Through gasping breaths he cursed to see the tanks were pulling away. Weren't they supposed to provide some protection? That racket they made was only forewarning the Germans of their approach.

He felt his exposure again. The men around him seemed an insubstantial shield. Others must have shared his doubts because at once everyone broke into a trot. He glanced at Danna to his right but saw the Maori's eyes were fixed on the clattering boxes ahead.

The leading tank disappeared to the right. Another bend though still no hail of bullets. He wondered how much further. The pace continued to increase. He began to pant though once more the ground levelled. The tanks appeared again, fifty yards ahead. The first began to turn to the left. As it did so a blaze of fire erupted over it. So they'd reached the Square. His chest pounded.

The crowd carried him on now. He found a second wind. Around him men began to shout. A Maori bawled the challenge of the haka: 'Ka mateh! Ka Mateh!'

Someone in the darkness answered the call: 'Ka ora! Ka ora!'

Many voices picked up the chant. It beat the rhythm as he raced, faster and faster now. Its roar filled his head, swelling on the rolling tide he was part of, lifting above the thunder of gunfire ahead.

They swung round the last bend. Flashes of flame lit up the tanks. A white wall slid past. Still he could see no enemy. An explosion rocked his stride but the chorus rose back over it, building to a howling crescendo. As they entered the Square he tightened his grip on the rifle and lowered his bayonet. He was flying. On fear.

Then all seemed to stop. For a moment he thought he was hit. He could hear nothing. He hung in a maelstrom of smoke and noise and stumbling figures. A huge scream of fury broke from the throats beside him and the flood surged on across the square, men going down all round but the mass no longer checked by the hail of fire.

He careered by a burning tank, knocked onto its side and caught from somewhere, in the din, an improbable English voice shouting 'Come on, New Zealand, clean 'em out. Clean 'em out, New Zealand.'

A block of grey uniforms swarmed from the smoke. He fired at the wall and everything became a frenzy of collision. A helmeted face loomed at him. He jabbed with his bayonet. The impact swung him round and the bayonet jammed. As he fought to free it a body cannoned against him and tore the rifle's stock from his grasp.

A bare-headed German flung a helmet at his stomach. He clutched it and felt the breath rush from him. The crowd swept Bare-head off. Dud stumbled backwards over a body.

A huge paratrooper stabbed down at him with a spike. He parried with the helmet. The spike skewered it. He strained to hold the point from his chest, saw the Para grinning and felt himself forced back. The man's left hand clamped his throat. He struggled but the grip tightened.

He was choking. He let go of the helmet with his right hand and tried to pull down on the throttling arm. With a grunt the Para ripped the skewered helmet free. At the same time the man released his throat and he was falling.

He glimpsed the helmet being swung aloft, a leer of triumph on the broad face. Then a dead weight drove him down and crushed his breath again. His ears roared.

Everything went black.

'You wanna be more careful, Dud.' Danna's voice echoed. 'You always were too bloody reckless.'

Reckless? Terrified more like. On his hands and knees, he coughed and gasped for air. Danna must have pulled the body off him. He tried to mutter thanks but Danna dragged him behind the other wrecked tank. The clatter of grenades and rifle fire had receded. The Germans had vanished.

'Jesus, Danna,' he got out at last. 'What did we do?'

'Just don't expect more miracles,' Danna said.

He struggled to his feet and blinked at the carnage. Medics were already tending the injured. He bent to pick up a rifle and only then noticed that Danna was leaning against the tank and the dark stain on his friend's thigh.

'Danna, you're hit.'

'Hope so,' Danna winced. 'Or something's gone a bit wet down below. At least we sorted out the buggers.'

Danna sagged. He shuffled him across the square and sat him on the church steps. All around them wounded were being patched up. A sergeant was carried past on a door used as a stretcher. Apart from the cries of injured men and the occasional crump of a mortar off to the west, a hush had fallen on the Square.

He helped the medic strap a field dressing on Danna's thigh, surprised no longer to feel tired. Was it numbness or relief? For once he'd done it and come through. A piercing shriek to his right brought him out of his daze. The wounded man's agony shamed his complacency.

Cretan women and girls were moving among the troops giving them water. A young girl who couldn't have been more than twelve or thirteen offered a bowl to a bandaged kiwi. He felt humbled. At that age, in the presence of death, his reaction had been very different.

They eased Danna to sit and the medic slipped away. A mortar shell landed close by. Maybe, as usual, the job wasn't done. He frowned at the Maori. 'I thought we were supposed to have cleared them out?'

'Plenty more of the buggers waiting back there, I reckon,' Danna said. 'Just reminding us until the stukas roll up in the morning.'

'Then why aren't we doing anything to dig in?'

'My fault, Dud, sorry. I'll start now.'

'You know what I mean. We've beaten 'em for once. And we're not bloody taking advantage of it.'

Another mortar dropped. Someone had found the range. The familiar rage of frustration was surging back. Danna must have picked it up because he heard him laugh. 'That's probably because nobody has a clue what's happening, Dud. They never have so far, have they?'

Angry shouts made him turn to his left. Men were standing up, with protests and curses. A New Zealand captain threaded his way through the crowd. Whatever he said drew the same response.

'Sorry, men,' the captain said. 'Orders to pull back.'

'Pull back? Why?' he asked.

'Orders, that's all.'

Dud glared round the shattered square. At the clumps of bodies. The pair of wrecked tanks. So it had all been for nothing, once more, had it? No different from the past... Merely another futile gesture in the dark.

His dad would have come up with a fine sermon for that. The wages of pride. Vainglory. For once he'd have agreed with him. He shook his head at the strewn corpses. 'Come on, Danna, let's get the hell out. They're dead. What's it matter now if we've bloody betrayed them?

He heaved the limping Danna the final few yards to the summit of the pass. If the sea lay below, they might still make it.

Something made him stagger. At first he couldn't grasp what it was. Danna grunted in alarm but he regained their balance. He told himself to get a grip. The updraught had almost made him faint. What was it – honeysuckle? Lemon blossom? His mind couldn't sort out which. Its pungent sweetness had stunned him. The smell of death and dust and filth he could cope with: a sudden breath of life was almost too much. He gritted his teeth and told himself to stop being such a bloody girl.

To his left, the grey sky showed streaks of orange. Behind them, the valley was in darkness but from the plain beyond came sporadic gunfire. That meant dawn raising the heat of the German advance on the rearguard. How long it could hold hardly bore thinking about.

From nearby the groans and curses of fellow stragglers punctuated the gloom. He peered ahead through it. A rounded hill, topped by a square block, filled his line of vision. He wasn't sure what it meant. Except that it wasn't the sea. He let out a heavy sigh, stumbled off the track and lowered Danna against the gnarled trunk of an olive tree. Disappointment should have come as no surprise but it had.

Where the hell were they? To the right of the round hill seemed to stretch a low flat plain. With mountains still to either side. No glint of water. Shit.

He threw himself down beside the Maori. All they must have reached was an upland plateau. An extensive one. How far beyond the other side the sea was, he daren't guess.

So it wasn't over. Nowhere near. Damn the war. Damn the whole bloody place. Damn Crete. He lay back and closed his eyes. A sudden longing to give up swept him.

The retreat had been one long trail of disillusion. And pain. How his mate had managed to stagger this far on his wounded leg amazed him. Was it five nights now since Galatas? Five shambolic nights.

He could no longer separate them after the first – when they'd begun an orderly withdrawal. It had become one relentless crawl in this mob of filthy, thirsty, cursing desperation. The days, too, a blur of huddling in ditches from the cannon fire of the unremitting Me 109s.

The petty debris of retreat they'd stumbled through – gas masks, rifles, cartridge boxes, webbing equipment, kitbags, blankets, and burst baggage with its contents strewn to the wind – had been a constant reminder of the ignominy. They'd even abandoned their pride. Except for a few companies of Australians who marched on still bearing rifles, the army – he included – had become a rabble.

Last night's endless uphill slog had seared every nerve, until only exhaustion blunted his bitterness. Now, resentment flared back. The thought of capture, after coming this far, after all the failures and betrayals, stung him to his feet. 'We need to move before it gets fully light, Danna, it's too exposed here. We're on the crest of the ridge.'

Danna opened his eyes and squinted up at him. 'Aw, let's stay here, Dud. Won't watching the sun come up remind you of home?'

'No – Messerschmidts.'

'That's your trouble, Dud. You lack soul.'

The word again conjured up his dad. He shut out the memory. He didn't want lectures about his immortal soul, he wanted a bloody ship. And if they didn't reach one soon, he might end up joining his dad. The prospect of the scorn that would bring made him squirm.

In the growing daylight he could see a line of dust snaking into the distance across the plain. The main body of the retreat, keeping going as the sun rose. A perfect target for the fighters. So somewhere close beyond there must be the navy and a way out of this hot, dusty nightmare. What the hell. Just get away. Let the fighters come. Escape was all that mattered. Why care about the risks any more? He bent and pulled Danna up.

For two hours no fighters had come. The cloudless blue sky remained empty. The sun beat off the stony ground and, with the dust, parched the mouth and cracked the lips. The first wells they'd come to had already been sucked dry. Danna showed signs of delirium and he himself felt the heat starting to play tricks on his eyes.

Especially when he saw an oasis ahead, off to the right of the road. A clump of dark, erect cypresses. Other trees, lighter and more stunted. A building near them. The biggest puzzle, and why he thought he was seeing things, was the orderly line of men at the well. If there was no jostling crowd fighting to quench their raging thirst, it must be a mirage. Until he saw why not.

Australians with fixed bayonets surrounded the well. Two helped a Cretan man haul up the bucket and dole out water. He blinked at the sight of a barefoot girl in a green dress run off balancing a pot from which liquid sloshed. An Australian Officer waved another man forward from the queue with his revolver. Dud lumbered from the road with the groaning Danna.

Dust- and sweat-streaked troops sprawled everywhere around the house and well. He eased Danna to lie on the ground and slipped to his knees beside him, bending forward until his forehead struck the spare, spiky grass. Even that breathed hot dust. He closed his eyes. The thought of joining the queue was too much effort but he knew he had to. He just needed to rest a moment first.

Something poked his right arm.

'Hey, Dud, am I seeing things?'

Oh, God, he should have brought Danna water straight away. Yet opening his eyes seemed to require too much of an act of will. And as for moving... He'd stiffened up.

'Come on, Dud. Will you take a look at this? Am I seeing things or am I in heaven?'

He groaned and rolled onto his left side, squinting at Danna through the sudden brightness. Danna was grinning. And nodding upwards somewhere beyond his feet.

He looked. The sun blinded him. He shifted his head and a halo of golden light swathed the girl and the blue dress. Another mirage? His mind tried to register. Hadn't he seen a green dress? The slight figure bent forward and the sun dazzled him again. He caught a word. 'Nero?'

Water? He shuffled so her head blocked the glare. She was offering him a tin helmet from which water slipped. Her dark, searching eyes and the anxious concern in her face stunned him. Then she moved and the sun forced his eyes away. He pointed at Danna. 'Not me. Him first.'

She knelt, lifted Danna's head and held the helmet to his mate's lips. Dud drank, too: drank in the deep, uneven blue of her dress, the black hair glinting in the sunlight, the pale down on the brown arm supporting Danna. She could only have been seventeen, eighteen. He sought for some Greek words but mind was empty. He realised she was offering him the helmet.

'Ya sas, tora?'

He took it, staring into her eyes. She looked down. He splashed water everywhere and then gulped it in. She stood up and he clambered to his feet and handed her the helmet.

'Efharisto.'

He'd remembered the word for thank you! She smiled and nodded. He pointed to her. 'Your... sas name?'

Shit. Why had he forgotten so much from the Ancient Greek class in Christchurch? Or not picked up more from the locals since landing here? She seemed to understand.

'Eleni. Me lene Eleni.'

'Efharisto, Eleni…' That was about all his Greek. It had to be English. 'You just saved the lives of a couple of Kiwis, here.'

The amusement in her puzzled frown made his heart bump.

'Ki-wis?'

He couldn't find the words. She went to move off. He felt a gust of panic. 'Wait… Kiwi.'

Pointing to himself and Danna, he dropped to his haunches and flapped his arms in desperate imitation of the national emblem.

Danna laughed. 'What's that, Dud, a kiwi mating dance?'

He glimpsed embarrassment on the girl's face. His stiffened legs gave way and he toppled back in a heap.

'Or are you telling her we're headless chickens?'

His cheeks burned. He cursed his stupidity. But a warm smile flickered about her mouth and in her eyes. 'Ah…' She waved her arms like a bird. 'Kotopoulo?'

'Yeah, you got it, a chicken,' Danna grinned. 'But only where women are concerned.'

He clambered to his feet, sure his face looked the colour of beetroot. Danna's face was creased with laughter. 'Lucky she didn't think you needed the toilet, Dud.'

Her smile, however, showed no contempt. She inclined her head to him in thanks. He still had no words.

A girl's cry of panic made her swivel, frown and dash off, pushing through a group of standing troops. Straining to see the source of the shout, he lumbered after her. Another cry came, more shrill.

He heard the laughter and saw the semi-circle of kilted Scots at the same time. Glimpsed the green dress half-hidden by a broad back and Eleni hurling herself at the assailant. The Scot staggered. The girl in green slipped clear of her captor's clutches but the impact knocked Eleni back.

She fell, her head banging on the ground. The big Guardsman whirled in fury then chortled to see his dazed attacker. 'Well, well, thissun looks more ripe for pluckin'.'

'No, she's not…'

A red, bloated face glared at him. No lack of drink there. Or muscle. He tried to sound off-hand. 'Where's your manners, Jock?'

The Scots sergeant stepped by Eleni and towards him then stopped and looked him up and down. With a toss of his head he turned back to the girl.

'Ach, wait your turn, sonny,' the Scot called over his shoulder and grabbed for Eleni's blue dress. At that, something snapped. Five days' pent-up anger burst. He took three steps forward, seized the big man by the collar, hauled him back and in one movement kicked him with the sole of his boot sprawling at his mates. 'And pull your skirt down, Jock. Your brains'll catch a chill.'

The Scots' faces swelled at him in fury. The dishevelled sergeant staggered to his feet and swung round. Eleni stirred on the ground. Dud snatched up a discarded rifle. He waved it at them, hoping they thought it was loaded. 'Go on, get. Now!'

They stared at him. He worked the bolt. Muttering, they pitched off onto the road. He watched them go, tossed down the gun and took both Eleni's hands to help her up.

She disengaged one hand to feel the side of her head. He held on to the other. She gave him a shy smile and worked that one free, too. He peered at her face but there was no blood. Still he couldn't find the Greek.

'Whyn't you ask if you can kiss it better, Dud?'

Danna limped towards them, supporting himself on a rifle. Before Dud could tell him to get lost the younger girl rushed to Eleni and hugged her. He stepped back. Eleni gave him another diffident smile. He felt a thump in his chest.

'Efharisto ya tin aderfi mou.'

He shrugged acknowledgment at what sounded like thanks and tried to smile back. His facial muscles wouldn't move.

'In New Zealand he does that all the time,' Danna said. 'It's his only mode of conversation.'

Eleni brushed and straightened the other girl's green dress and glanced from Danna to him. 'Ah, Neo Zealandes?'

'See, it's my grasp of their language you need, Dud,' Danna put in. 'She probably understands Maori, too.'

14

He glared at his mate and indicated himself. 'Ney, New Zealand. Kiwi.'

Eleni smiled and pointed at him. 'Ah, ney, Kiwi?'

'I think you just got a new name, Dud.'

Groping for some words to detain the girl, he gestured at the house then at her. 'Sas? Yours?'

She nodded and a sudden fear shook him. Jocks were the least of it. The Germans would be here within a day. He indicated, in frantic dumb show, that the girls should come with them towards the sea. Her eyes flashed, in anger, it seemed. She turned away. He waved his hands.

'No, ochi, ochi…' Thank God words were coming back. 'Not like that.'

He pointed to the north, mimed shooting a rifle.

'Germans. Bad, Germans coming…'

'Ah, Yermanni. Ney…'

He tried again, with gestures, to convey what he meant. She shook her head but this time with a ghost of a smile.

'Then berazi. Tha eimaste endaxi.'

Troops came pushing on past them, faces shot with anxiety. There were shouts behind. He couldn't tell why. Surely the rearguard wasn't already upon them?

'Tonight's the last night the Navy's here, they reckon,' a man flung at him as he rushed by.

He gaped at the messenger. At the girls. Once more his old sense of failure bit into him. He directed the girls' gaze to the mountains above. 'Up there. Get out of their way. From the Yermanni.'

Eleni shrugged her shoulders. He cursed that he had no words to urge her. He could only stare into those dark eyes. Her gaze wavered. Danna's voice broke the spell.

'Come on, Dud. We gotta go.'

Danna was pulling at his sleeve. Eleni looked down.

'Yeah, I know, I know,' he said.

He took Danna's arm on his shoulder and steadied him.

'Efharisto,' he said to the girls. 'I'll come back. One day. I promise.'

Eleni looked up and again gave him the concerned frown. Had she understood? Probably not. But what more could he do? Didn't his helplessness just sum up his life and this whole bloody futile Greek escapade?

'Your love life'll have to wait till the war's over, Dud,' Danna grinned at him. 'Anyway, your ma'd never approve of her. She's too young. And too pretty.'

'Oh, sod off, won't you?'

He jerked Danna into step and glanced back. Eleni raised a hand. Her face still held the frown. The sister gave them a wave and a smile. He tried to keep looking at them but couldn't manage the angle. The grin on Danna's face forced him to bite his lip. When he did twist and look back there was no sign of the girls. He sighed and trudged on. Typical, that on his last day in this damned place, someone had lit it up.

It wasn't to be his last day. Only the following night did they stagger into Sfakia, the little embarkation port on the south coast. What he'd taken for the plateau's exit to the sea had proved merely to be the lip of one saucer of upland that funnelled them into another. After that they found to the bottleneck of the Gorge.

Endless delays in the rock- and debris-strewn path down this had made progress slower than ever. There were long, stationary queues. Others pushed past them.

Even when they staggered at last from the Gorge they were still not at the sea. The land sloped away for a mile or more. The port lay further off and out of sight to the right. All they'd reached was a holding area for what seemed thousands of men.

He tried to argue Danna's needs but embarkation officers, or so they called themselves, held him back on flimsy pretexts. Not until these guardians suddenly vanished were they able to join the stumbling charge for safety.

But when, in the dark, they limped onto the quay it was clear they were too late.

A pale moon illuminated the bay and the dark outline of a destroyer. Beside him on the dock a signals corporal dismantled a radio and, with surly grunts, tossed the pieces one by one into the sea. Turning away from a splash he glanced at the gutted buildings behind him. In the dark he could make out immobile clumps of men. Left behind like them. Asleep on their feet or stunned into silence by this last piece of foul luck. Every so often someone would scream a curse towards the ship. And others would grumble complaints at being woken up.

The sound he was expecting echoed across the bay: a clatter of anchor chains being drawn up through the hawse. The destroyer's shape started forward and turned away.

'Goodbye from the navy, eh, Dud?'

'Guess so. Seems I might keep my promise to those girls, after all.'

'Unless Jerry shoots us first. I wouldn't get too excited just yet.'

Excitement was the last emotion he felt, after two days when he'd never felt so empty, sitting and waiting to become a POW. For the Germans to corral them like apathetic sheep. What an inglorious end. Or was it the just reward for his pride? That's what his dad would have called it. He shrank from the shame of that memory.

They began the trudge back up the line of their retreat, with the evidence of their failure all around them. In the burning sun, up the steep ravine to the plateau while the few guards fumed at them to hurry, lugging the now-drained Danna took all his strength. So that when the ragged column blundered past the blackened shell of a building off to his left, he didn't connect it to Eleni's house. At first.

He looked again. Stopped. The man behind stumbled into Danna and swore at them. Someone, held up further back, shouted threats. One man took the chance to dive out of the line and rummage in a heap of tins. Others swooped after him. The scramble turned into a brawl. Angry voices screeched. His eyes were on something else. Dark shapes lying in front of the house.

He offered his burden to an English private. 'Here, mate, support Danna a bit, would you?'

Eyes fixed, he forced his way through the mob, a sense of foreboding clutching at him, drawing him to a sight he only wanted to avoid.

Then he was on the ground. Crouched from the crash of a shot. Whirling thoughts in his head fought with the echo from the hills. He glanced back at the line and managed to focus. Other prisoners also hugged the ground. He saw a skinny German guard still with his rifle pointed skywards. The shot hadn't been at him. From further up ahead an older guard stumped into view and he heard gruff orders.

'Moven! Ein die reihe! Ein line! Schnell! Schnell!'

The older guard reversed his rifle and began to club those who hesitated or persisted in their scrabble for food. The younger one followed his lead. The air filled with screams of pain and anger.

The distraction gave him his chance. He scurried towards the house, keeping low, stumbling. Then he stopped. And saw.

The charred shapes *were* bodies. A heap of them.

The stench of paraffin swept at him. His stomach heaved into his mouth. He fell to his knees, eyes gaping. A thin, blackened arm, its hand splayed palm upwards, protruded from the foot of the pile. He crawled forward and touched it. And shrank back. It was cold. His whole body screamed but no sound came out. Tears blinded his eyes. The image of the girl in the green dress and bare feet flared across his brain.

He forced himself to squint at the burnt mass and pleaded not to see more. The heat had fused it together. He could make out no detail. For an instant he hoped.

Then saw it. Blown slightly apart from the pyre. A fragment of blue cloth. Deep blue. Singed at the edges. Unmistakeable. He reached for it and pressed it in his palm, squeezing his eyes shut, too, to deny, to wish undone, to close out the anguish of realisation.

Something hard jabbed his left shoulder. A wave of pain seared. His face thumped into the dusty ground.

'Raus! Raus!' boomed through the din in his ears.

He couldn't move. More shouts echoed. Someone dragged him to his feet. He forced his eyes open.

The skinny German with the rifle was gesturing at him to move. He stared back, unable to obey. The youth reversed the rifle into a club and raised it as a threat. From somewhere rang distant shouts of abuse.

The throb in his brain steadied. He gazed at the German. A growling rage welled out of the pain. The cowards. The vicious, inhuman cowards. They had done this. Perhaps even this one, here? This cowering boy. What right had they? And what reason had any one of them to shout at him? All they deserved was to be damned in hell.

The young private nodded to him to move and flicked a sneer at the mound. That did it. He launched himself.

He'd forgotten how weak he was. The swinging stock caught him on the right shoulder and knocked him to the floor. In a haze he gathered himself for another go. The youth was fumbling his rifle to fire and he knew he'd be shot. He didn't care.

But the shot came from elsewhere.

He stared past the youth and saw the older guard lower his gun from two standing POWs. One clutched at a bottle the other held aloft, then went limp and, as the owner let go of the bottle, slid to the ground with it. The survivor spread his arms out in a plea. The older guard worked the bolt, gesturing him back in line. For a moment all was silent.

'Raus! Raus!'

He was yanked up and shoved forward. A rifle butt jarred against the middle of his back. A kick drove him on and several more blows battered his shoulders. They meant nothing any more. He stumbled and fell.

'Liften sie! Moven! Schnell! Schnell!'

Hands grasped his arms and pulled him upright. His bruises screamed when the helpers took his arms across their own shoulders. The agony tore open his eyes.

Ahead of him Danna twisted back and frowned a question. His eyes steered Danna's gaze to the fragment of blue cloth clutched in his right hand. Danna's face stared at him in horror. He shook his head. 'Killed her, Danna… Killed… and burned them all. Even the young kid in the green dress.'

Danna wrenched away. The column lurched into motion.

'I said I'd come back and I did, didn't I?' he called. 'I promise, too, that they'll pay for this. One day.'

The jolting made him scream. But that wasn't the real pain. Inside, the real pain, the screaming, went on and on.

'They'll pay for it, I swear, Danna... I swear... Even if it takes for bloody ever.'

Two

Two years later. Egypt, July 1943

It did seem to be taking for ever. He tapped his foot on the quay as he waited for the pinnace to chug across from the anchored sub. At least, at last, he was now going back.

Danna's words, when he'd proposed escape from the prison camp on the north coast of Crete, reverberated. 'Just crawl out under the wire, Dud? Sure, that's the easy part. Then what? This is an island, you know.'

'So's New Zealand.'

'Ha, bloody ha. You going to swim all the way back to Egypt?'

'There's bound to be boats. In the south.'

'Yeah, fishing boats. Egypt's a hundred miles.'

'That all?'

'You're crazy, Dud.'

'Look where being sensible's got us.'

'Dud, it's a lunatic's errand. We've lost. And the girl's dead. Whatever you do won't bring her back.'

'I made a promise.'

'You don't owe anything to anyone.'

'To myself.'

Danna had been right. Slipping under the joke of a perimeter fence – as men did all the time to forage for food – was the easy part. Followed by the year it had taken to get off the island. That's why the Germans weren't bothered about the wire.

Thirteen months. Days of heat and cold, illness and hunger, fear and frustration. Yet the same day always haunted him. The one, the exact date a blur but it must have been in early 1942, when he broke…

21

He sat down in the snow. Who did he think he was? Emaciated, burning with fever, a scarecrow without the strength even to shake his fist at a German. And the future of the war lay in his being back in it?

He fingered the patch of blue cloth and began to sob. So he'd also come at last to betrayal? Yet the thought of an end to all this had a delirious appeal. He dragged himself shivering to his feet. There was no choice.

He hesitated. Not here. He had one shred of decency left. It was too close to the village. The Germans would draw their own conclusions. For the villagers his own abject surrender would mean far worse than that: reprisals. It had to be the main road. If he could make it there he'd at least avoid betraying *them*…

The shout from the boat made him start. A seaman was shaping to throw the mooring rope. He waved that he was ready. Now the time had come at last his head was a swirl of thought. Would he have given himself up, back then, if the shepherds hadn't found him unconscious in the snow before the Germans did? Maybe he'd just have frozen to death. As it was, three weeks later his will – or a sense of shame – had returned with his strength.

He dropped his kitbag into the pinnace, climbed down the ladder and settled on the bench in the bow. From there the grimy bulk of the *Eleftheria* loomed large and grey.

The prospect of days in its stale air, with a ban on smoking and the claustrophobia took the edge off his impatience. And stirred up forebodings: of his childhood panic if they were attacked and depth-charges put the lights out; of being unable to land and so stuck on board for two more weeks before a return here; of having to face Dancy again.

His fists clenched. Yes, that would be the worst of it. An aborted mission would see him back before Major Dancy. He exhaled loudly. One humiliation at the hands of the Head of Liaison, Special Operations Executive, Cairo, had been enough to last him for ever.

Dancy's first words set the tone. The Major made a deliberate show of perusing the folder open on the wide desk. An office-wallah, by the look of him, only early forties but already gone to seed. After what felt like several minutes of studied indifference Dancy looked up at him with a smirk. 'So, Watkins, after the surrender…'

The Major let the last word echo off the panelled walls. '… you spent a year wandering about on Crete?'

His gaze remained rigid on the wall map of the Mediterranean behind Dancy's head. A trickle of sweat ran down behind his left ear. He heard a chuckle. 'Must've taken a fancy to the place, eh? Since you can't wait to get back. Your third request this month. Not got a bit of stuff on Crete, have you, Watkins?'

His chest tensed. 'No, sir.'

The Major sank back into the dark leather of his chair and flashed a complacent smile. 'Feel you owe them something, do you?'

Consciousness of the blue cloth in his breast pocket made him catch his breath. 'They were good to me, sir… in my year on the run.'

Dancy glared at him as if suspecting insolence. 'Were they really?'

This time he met the glare. Dancy looked away and picked up a paper clip. The smirk returned. 'Well, Watkins, isn't life full of surprises? Brigadier Keble has decided to take a chance on you.'

He kept his gaze level. He wanted to whoop but his mind checked. Was this a trick? He heard Dancy sniff. 'You are off to Crete. The South West. As Fielding's number two. The Brigadier wants some hell raising.'

The last phrase brought his churning thoughts up short.

'Hell raising? To what end, sir?'

'We're fighting a war, Sergeant. That not enough for you?'

'Yes, sir, but…'

'The Brigadier isn't interested in buts…'

Had the fool no idea what he was proposing? 'No, sir. But if all we're doing is raising hell, there'll be reprisals…'

Dancy cut him off with a flip of one hand. In the other he twisted the paperclip with his fingers. 'You sure you're suited for this, Watkins?'

'Yes, sir. I just like to know…'

'You don't need to know. Except that we're all working towards the opening of the Second Front…'

'The Second Front? Sir? Not in Crete? You're kidding?'

Dancy shot upright. 'No, Sergeant, I'm not "kidding". And I'm not giving away secrets. Your only requirement is to do your job. Oh, and steer clear of the Communists. Our next problem, that lot, after the war.'

His confusion deepened. So all they wanted was to use him to raise hell? To provoke reprisals? He'd spent a year avoiding doing that. Danna's 'headless chickens' swept into his head. No, this was worse.

Dancy twiddled the paperclip and flicked through the papers in the file. Had the interview finished? Was that it? The Major looked up. 'Just trying to find what you did in New Zealand, Watkins, before you were called up. Anything useful, was it?'

'I wasn't called up, sir. I volunteered. The day war was declared.'

'Indeed? Couldn't have been a top-hole job?'

'I was at university.'

'A student? My word. Weren't you rather old for that?'

'Twenty-five. Sir.'

The throb of the punkah above beat on his brain like an inflamed nerve. What was all this dragging on for? To put him in his place? Sort out the grubby colonials? The Major smirked at him again. 'Hmm. And I see OCTU didn't rate you officer material?'

'No, sir.'

'A high-flier like you? After all, you'd been a sergeant for, what – a whole six months? Being turned down must have been a disappointment?'

'Not really, sir, no.'

'Too bolshie, eh, Watkins?'

'No, sir.' He paused. 'Bored.'

The paperclip dropped. He kept his eyes fixed on the map. He could feel Dancy glaring up at him. 'SOE's officers on Crete are all young men. Alec Fielding, i/c West, is early twenties. You'll be taking orders from him. Obey orders, do you, Watkins?'

'I think so, sir.'

'Your job isn't to think.'

'No, sir.'

Dancy eased himself back in the chair. 'After all, we don't want a repeat of '41, do we?'

He swallowed but stayed silent. He knew what was coming. 'I said, do we, Sergeant?' Dancy repeated.

'No, sir, we don't.'

Dancy closed the file and gave him the supercilious smile. This one a broad beam. 'No. Not another New Zealand balls-up.'

The pinnace bumped against the hull of the submarine. Damn Dancy. He'd let the bastard get under his skin again. Feeling belittled made him shrink back to childhood. Would he never be free of its shadow? So far, coming halfway round the world had made no difference at all.

When he went below, a Greek sailor pointed the way and said the others were already in the after bay. He'd forgotten some Cretans were returning with him.

The sight of the two rows of hard metal bunks made him wince as he squeezed along the gangway. On the right-hand side the heads of two reclining figures presented their backs to him. In the upper bunk a couple of spindly arms exercised above a mop of black hair by doing push-ups with a bren gun. In the lower one a larger, brown-haired head scrutinised a magazine held out before it.

He was about to step into the bay when the lad in the top bunk called down to his companion, in Greek.

'Andrea, d'you think this sergeant really will be the malakas the slimy major claimed?'

'The fat bastard's one himself so he should know.'

He slung his kitbag down on the opposite bunk and grinned at them both. 'Hiya,' he said in English.

The brawny Cretan gave him a cursory glance then turned back to his magazine. 'Not as bad as the Lizard, by the look of him. Better give him the benefit for now.'

The youngster nodded. His stroking of a thin shadow of moustache seemed to betray some embarrassment.

'Thanks for that,' Kiwi said in Greek. 'It's a comfort to know I'm less of a malaka than Major Dancy.'

The big man shot up and banged his head on the bunk above. 'Holy shit. How come you speak Greek so good?'

'Guest of your country in '41. For a year.'

The Cretan grinned and swung his feet to the floor. 'A year? So our women taught you Greek and you couldn't drag yourself away from them, eh?'

The image of dragging away from Eleni caught him unawares. 'Not exactly. I hid for a month in a cave with a teacher.'

The smile on the Cretan's open face broadened. 'Ah. A schoolmistress?'

'Sorry, no. School*master*. Since we had nothing else to do, he taught me Greek.'

'Which you then practised on Greek women in Egypt?'

'Only the men.'

The big man recoiled and banged his head again. 'Jesus Christ. Yiorgo, stay up there, in safety, you hear?'

'I meant, in Egypt I was sent on liaison to the Greek supply depot. That's when they made me sergeant.'

'Huh. Those bastards would turn anyone queer.'

'Don't mind him, Mr… Andreas likes a joke,' the lad in the top bunk called, flourishing the bren gun.

He turned away and undid his kitbag, conscious of big eyes following his every move. The boy called down. 'I'm Yiorgo. What do they call you, Mr…?'

He looked round and met a smile now. The image of Eleni thrust itself back in. 'Er… Call me Kiwi.'

'Kiwi? Shit. I was with them at Galatas,' Andreas said. 'Mad bastards. No fear. Almost as crazy as we Cretans… But you should see the women in Galatas.'

The women and girls bringing water swept back. 'I did. They had no fear, either.'

Andreas shot up, missing the bunk edge this time. 'You were in Galatas? In '41?'

'Until the British malakas pulled us out.'

He climbed onto the top bunk. Andreas whistled. 'You weren't in the bayonet charge, too?'

'For what good it did us.'

'Jesus, Mary and the Devil's Arse. Don't mock it. That was the only reason we got away.'

'Got away?'

'They had us pinned down – the Sixth Greek Regiment – south of the village, before you panicked them. And we were out of ammo. A few hundred Cretans made it back to their villages because of that bayonet charge. Remember that.'

Kiwi lay down and stared at the grey metal above his head. Galatas had always left a bitter taste in his mouth.

'And the sound,' the Cretan continued. 'We could pick it up where we were. Even now I can hear… that war cry. The…?'

'Haka.'

'Like the thrill of a hundred women in your veins, Yiorgo.'

Yiorgos grinned across at him and called down. 'One would be fine for me, Andrea.'

The submarine's engines fired up. The lights went out and flickered back on again. The glow remained dim. He held his breath then let it go. Whenever Galatas came back to him it was the betrayal he remembered. Andreas' view of it came as a shock. And reminded him it should only be the Cretans who mattered now.

Yiorgos was talking. 'Watch me, Mr Kiwi. I can strip this gun in the dark.'

The lad settled on his back, closed his eyes and unscrewed the barrel. It fell on the floor with a clang. Yiorgos looked crestfallen. Andreas grabbed the rolling metal and swung it back up into the top bunk.

'A woman you strip in the dark, Yiorgo. Ain't that right, Kiwi?'

'If you say so.'

The Cretan's head popped out from the bunk. 'Eh? You mean you didn't have lots of women in New Zealand, Kiwi?'

'I was too busy…'

'Too busy? Who is this malakas, Yiorgo, who only has liaisons with men? Tell me, Kiwi, are all the women in New Zealand so ugly?'

'That's why he's come here,' Yiorgos laughed.

He remembered the fragment of blue dress in his breast pocket. 'If only, Yiorgo… But I'm not here for… distractions.'

'Distractions?' Andreas snorted. 'Women are life, Kiwi. How could you be too busy for women?'

Kiwi reached across and motioned for the gun from Yiorgos. He lay back, closed his eyes and began to take it apart to drive away the memory of the bodies. 'I had to work to support my mother. And study at night. So I could go to university when my brother had finished there. My father died when I was twelve.'

'A perfect mother's son, Andrea. You see?'

'A monk. And you know what they're like. At least tell us your father died in a feud, Kiwi. Like a true *pallikari*.'

He laid down the last piece, opened his eyes and winked across at Yiorgos. The lad was gazing at him in wonder.

'No such luck, I'm afraid.'

Yiorgos' face turned to panic. 'Don't say that, Mr Kiwi.'

He closed his eyes again and felt for the stock. 'He died of a heart attack. He was quite old. A priest. He thought I was a bit wild.'

'I can't imagine why,' Andreas muttered.

Although uneventful the circuitous route – and Yiorgos' unceasing curiosity about his family – did strain his nerves. The lad couldn't grasp his mother's self-pity.

'If *my* mother, God forbid, Kiwi, was widowed, I would expect her to mourn.'

'For years?'

'For ever.'

He lacked the vocabulary, and the will, to explain.

Andreas' solution was predictable. 'If you'd brought home some beautiful New Zealand goddess, the light would soon have returned to her eyes.'

'No chance, Andrea.'

'Ah, so there are no goddesses in New Zealand? Why doesn't that surprise me?'

Turning the focus to his mission brought little relief.

'Has Dancy sent you two back to raise hell?' he asked one day as he watched them play backgammon. Andreas frowned up at him. 'Is that what he's told you to do?'

'As second in command to Captain Fielding.'

Yiorgos looked surprised. 'To Mr Aleko?'

'Is that what you call him?'

'Everyone must have a Cretan name,' Andreas said. 'The Germans aren't stupid. Saying at a roadblock "Yes, officer, sir, I am a poor man from Kyriakosellia and my name is Mr Kiwi," won't help improve your dismal record with women.'

For once Yiorgos also was frowning. 'You won't do much hell-raising with Mr Aleko, Mr Kiwi. He spends all his time at his HQ at Vafe sending radio reports back to the mighty major.'

This wasn't what he'd hoped to hear.

'Anyway, don't get too carried away,' Andreas added. 'Hell-raising is the last thing most people want.'

'Because of reprisals?'

'Because they're worn out. And starving. The women have even gone off sex. Things are very bad there right now.'

'That's what I want to change, Andrea.'

'Then I'm with you on that, Kiwi. All the way.'

'Fighting, Andrea.'

'You've clearly not met our women.'

He raised his eyebrows at Yiorgos. The lad smiled. 'Did your father the priest teach you how to work miracles, Mr Kiwi?'

'Miracles?' Andreas laughed. 'He should have taught him the facts of life first.'

The memory of his father's Presbyterian views threw a further damper on his mood. 'He did, Andrea. They just weren't your kind of facts.'

However, during their week-long voyage the tension only snapped once. After the *Eleftheria* had spent two nights observing the airfield on

Scarpanto, they surfaced to recharge its batteries in a deep cove off the south-east coast of neighbouring Kassos.

He stood smoking with Andreas on the fore-deck. The Cretan was uncharacteristically quiet. Kiwi indicated the dark shapes of the vertiginous cliffs that fell straight into the sea around them. 'Not a place for chasing women, eh, Andrea?'

Andreas shot him a poisonous look, flung his cigarette over the side and stormed off. Kiwi peered into the darkness. What he'd done, he couldn't imagine. Perhaps he should avoid attempts at jokes about women in future.

Fortunately, he wasn't coming back to Crete to create laughs.

Three

Kiwi couldn't stop laughing. In the dark, even in the noise of the gale, he heard the spluttering of the other two. Yiorgos had started it once they'd dragged their stuff onto the shingle, after the wave had tipped all three face down out of the dinghy and into the shallows.

'Just like a woman kicking you out of bed, Andrea?' Yiotgos had giggled. Andreas' gruff response had made Kiwi laugh. Andreas himself must have seen the funny side because he joined in. Yiorgos' giggles became sobs. At last, a release from the week's cramped restriction of the sub and relief at making land.

Even if it wasn't very dry. The chill wind on his sodden khaki drill uniform brought him back to reality. He motioned them quiet and listened. The sucking roar of the withdrawing surf rang loud in his ears. The wind blotted out everything else.

He began to regret his impatience in insisting they be put ashore. There'd been no torch signals from the coast and Captain Harapokos had warned that the gale prevented him from standing in too close. It had been a matter of diving into the boat some way east of the cove and trusting to luck that they could steer in on the wind.

So much for believing that he took a more measured approach these days. Perhaps it was Crete, already blinding his judgment? But the Captain had been adamant the *Eleftheria* couldn't spare the time for a further attempt. The thought of two more weeks in the sub and then a return to Egypt – and Dancy – swung his decision.

He peered into the blackness and realised he hadn't a clue where they were. Earth, sea and sky were one dark mass. Only the white line of surf gave him any bearing. He started to shiver. He didn't even know if it was the right beach.

'Is this where we were due to land, Andrea?'

'Search me, I just want a dry bed.'

31

He felt a tug on his sleeve and heard Yiorgos chuckle close to. The lad's bright eyes peered into his face.

'Exactly, Mr Kiwi. This is Kaloyeros.'

'How can you be sure?'

'I've been here before. I recognise the smell.'

He was about to tell him not to be frivolous when Yiorgos' face frowned and he held up his hand for quiet.

'Shhh.'

Kiwi reached for his pistol and slid the safety catch. There was nothing beyond the wind. He sank onto one knee. Yiorgos gave two sharp whistles that made him grit his teeth. Had he been landed with a boy who was a liability, even more reckless than himself?

'It's OK, Mr Kiwi. They're here.'

He screwed up his eyes at the pitch black inland and strained to catch any sound. Nothing. He rose to his feet.

'Are you sure, Yiorgo? Friends?'

Yiorgos whistled again. 'Hope so. Shine your torch.'

'Hope so? Yiorgo, this is no place for jokes.'

He shone the torch and saw that the narrow beach gave onto low clusters of rocks and stunted trees, from which a young boy came tearing towards them. Had Yiorgos really been able to hear him?

The boy hugged Yiorgos and then pulled at the sleeves of the lad's British Army uniform and giggled. 'You're a soldier, now, Yiorgo?'

'Only in case the Germans were waiting for us. Mr Kiwi, this is Ari. From Koustoyerako.'

'Good to see you, Ari. But can we get off this damned beach and start moving. Before we freeze to death. And is there somewhere to hide the dinghy?'

His second surprise was to find Andreas had deflated and rolled up the dinghy in the dark, besides stacking their packs ready to go. The only sluggard so far appeared to be himself. Then he realised that Ari was here alone.

'Where are the rest? Kapetan Aleko?'

'Come,' Ari called and scampered into the dark. 'To the cave to change into dry clothes. Cretan clothes. Then I'll tell you all. It's a sorry tale.'

Kiwi watched the fire take hold. Its glow flickered on the cave walls. He breathed in the smoky heat and guessed he wouldn't be the only thing coming back to life as the rough clothes also warmed up. Back in the comfort of Egypt he'd forgotten about lice.

Ari sat beside Andreas across the flames from him and Yiorgos. He caught the flash of white teeth and gleam of piercing eyes through the gloom as he strained to listen.

'The katsikia, they burned Moni and Livada...'

This threw him. He stopped Ari. 'The katsikia? Goats?'

'More self-preservation,' Andreas growled and passed Yiorgos the tin of raki. 'You wouldn't want to be heard shouting "The Germans are coming, would you?"'

'Ah. Sorry. They burned those villages?'

Yiorgos handed him the tin. He tipped it back and his eyes widened as the raw spirit burned his throat and chest. He'd forgotten that, too.

'And shot Uncle Niko.'

Yiorgos' voice screeched in his right ear. 'Shot Niko?'

'Niko?' he asked, annoyed again at his ignorance.

'He led the resistance band here in Selino,' Yiorgos said and snatched the raki tin off him. Tears ran down the lad's frank, open face. 'He was their main strength. But how did they get him, Ari? Surely he wouldn't have tried to take them on?'

'Nikos offered himself.'

Once more he didn't understand and was forced to butt in. 'Offered himself?'

'They seized ten hostages and threatened to take them to Ayia and execute them...'

Yes, he knew Ayia. The prison south of Galatas. The paratroops had seized it on the first day of the Battle.

'... So Nikos went down to Livada to talk to them and ask them to take him instead. And they shot him.'

He saw Yiorgos was shaking his head in bewilderment.

'But why?'

'The women say the traitor Lefteris was with the katsika. He recognised Niko and the German sergeant shot him.'

There was silence around the fire.

'And the hostages?' he heard himself ask.

'They took them to Ayia all the same.'

He breathed out. He laid his hand on Yiorgos' shoulder. So many questions crowded in on him. 'What's the response been? From your band?'

Ari shook his head. 'They sit around in the hideout above our village and do nothing. That's why no one came down to meet you. They complain it's the outsiders who cause all the trouble.'

More incomprehension. And alarm. 'I don't follow, Ari. Do they mean us? Surely we're not…'

'No. Panadakis' band. That's why the katsika burned Moni and Livada. Panadakis had ambushed a supply lorry outside Moni on its way to Souyia and shot the driver.'

He frowned at Andreas across the fire. The briefing he'd had in Cairo had told him none of this. 'Who's Panadakis?'

'From Ammoudara. The plateau of Askyfou.'

His heart missed a beat. He remembered Askyfou. 'He's Cretan? Why's he an outsider?'

'They mean he's a communist.'

'A communist? Here?'

Dancy's warning about communists came back to him. No one had indicated their presence in this area.

'They were over in the west,' Ari said. 'But now the katsika are building up Souyia as a base…'

This, too, was a surprise. Did Fielding have no intelligence network? 'Building up Souyia? In what way?'

'Many more soldiers. A perimeter fence. And patrols in strength to punish any villages that stir.'

'Maybe they heard you were coming, Mr Kiwi,' Yiorgos said, a faint smile back on his face.

Kiwi tried to hold in his anger and misgivings. He brushed aside Yiorgos' banter. 'Maybe. And never mind the "Mr", Yiorgo, I'm not your dad.'

'I'm very pleased to hear that, M… Kiwi,' Yiorgos grinned. 'Especially if you take after your own.'

He grunted and addressed Ari across the fire. 'Does Mr Aleko know of this?'

'Perhaps, he may have heard.'

'Your men haven't told him?'

'We have no radio contact down here. The journey up there is a long one. Nobody has the will to go. But now Yiorgos is back we shall be OK.'

He scowled at Yiorgos for an explanation. Yiorgos bowed his head. 'The pocket Hermes, messenger of the gods, at your service.'

This only worsened his confusion. He turned to Andreas in frustration for some sense. Andreas laughed. 'He can chase over the mountains all day, that one, and never seem to tire. Messages, he's your man. What a waste. If only he applied that gift to chasing women…'

A further unsuspected talent of Yiorgos. But his mind seethed. Why hadn't Fielding come to meet them? Was he another Dancy up there in the northern foothills making sure the paperwork was kept tidy for Cairo?

There was too much to chew on. He'd presumed to find an established set-up here to slot into. Yet the absence of a reception on the beach, the lack of any structure, leadership or morale, the poor intelligence and the presence of a rival resistance group made it difficult to know where to begin. As for the field superior he'd come to serve…

Raising anything, let alone raising hell, seemed like a mighty step. And, from what he'd just heard, the locals would be as pleased to see him as if he'd brought them plague. If it hadn't been for Dancy's reluctance over his returning to Crete, he'd have said the Major had wanted to dump him in the mire.

Although he realised he might not be welcome, he asked Ari to take him to the camp above Koustoyerako, if only to pay his respects before going north to report to his absent and irritating boss.

The first part of the journey up through the trees did revive his spirits. He savoured the warm sweet breath of pine and as they came out onto the boulder–strewn hillside gazed at the broad vista of mountain, sea and sky. He felt his chest swell. He'd forgotten Crete's capacity to expand the soul.

Then the pain began.

He picked his way up the stony path, head down, lungs bursting, the straps of the pack biting his shoulders. His hips and thighs were protesting now at the unaccustomed effort. While Yiorgos seemed to float over the broken ground.

'Too much sitting on your arse in Cairo,' Andreas laughed after he'd been forced to call a halt. 'If you'd chased women more, you wouldn't fail our beautiful Kriti.'

He leant with hands on knees, gasping and looking back the way they'd come. For a moment he saw the blue piece of cloth before the vast blue of the sea and sky swallowed it. A cool breeze on his face and the scent of thyme eased his irritation at Andreas. 'I didn't come back to fail Kriti, Andrea. I may need time to get her measure, that's all.'

Andreas shook his head at him in bafflement. Yiogos moderated the pace after that and again he wondered if he'd underestimated the lad.

His first sight of the hideout swept back the disenchantment. He peered down from the track where they'd halted. 'Is that it, Andrea?'

'What d'you expect, Kiwi, an army of dancing girls?'

The cave looked no bigger than the one they'd sheltered in the previous night. Half a dozen men in traditional headgear were sprawled among the rocks before it, smoking. A couple wore bandoliers across their chests. The dilapidated sheepfold next to them was empty. He could see no sign of guns or defensive positions. 'Not sure what I expected, from a guerrilla band. Probably a few more armed men.'

'The rest will be off with the sheep,' Ari said. The boy looked hurt and made him regret showing his annoyance.

'It's only a place to spend the night in, Kiwi,' Ari went on. 'To avoid being picked up in a dawn raid. I think you mistake how much we could do. Even before we lost Niko.'

Acceptance of that reproof didn't improve his mood.

'Sorry, Ari. Shall we go down?'

'Yiorgos will take you. I must go to the village to tell Mama that I've come back.'

'Of course. And thanks for your help.'

Ari pinched Yiorgos on the arm and darted off laughing. This reminder of their youthfulness depressed him even more. If a twelve year-old was the only one who showed some spirit…?

'Brought us any fucking supplies?'

This was his greeting from Yiannis, the one in charge Ari had pointed out wearing the fringed black headkerchief. The man's eyes flashed resentment from under thick eyebrows. He must have been about thirty but the bushy moustache and dark shadows in his weathered face made him appear much older.

'Not with us. I'll see if we can summon an air drop.'

'Aye, when it fucking suits them.'

Handing round the cigarettes he had, he reproached himself for bringing nothing more. If he'd not let bloody Dancy get under his skin and distract him… Again, he'd neglected the basics. He watched Yiannis resume whittling a stave.

A tapping sound made him turn. A figure in patched baggy trousers and jackboots squatted with his back to them and tossed a steady stream of pebbles into a tin can set several yards beyond. With unerring accuracy. Kiwi gestured to Yiannis. 'Is that his target practice?'

'Costis don't need fucking target practice,' Yiannis muttered without looking up. 'He's the best shot we have. And if he did need practice, we can't fucking waste bullets.'

Another pang of guilt. At forgetting the hardship the Occupation had brought. While he'd been going soft in Egypt. If the Cretans had become careful about firing off weapons, things must be bad.

Yiorgos drew him aside and whispered to him. 'Nikos was Costis' uncle. Ari said that after the shooting they had to tie Costi down to stop him running to Livada and throwing himself on the Germans.'

He studied the lean stooping shoulders, seeing his own abortive leap at the young German guard. 'They really tied him down?'

'The only way,' Andreas said. 'Costis never says much but he's as stubborn as a mule. And he thinks deep. If he does speak, do what he tells you. Fast.'

This implication of his own slowness stung again. And made his reply more caustic than he meant. 'I'll bear in mind your advice, Andrea. But, you know, you haven't given me any about women for two hours?'

Andreas screwed up his face in panic. 'Jesus Christ, Kiwi, don't start thinking about women down here. You so much as look at one, you'll have your throat cut. Didn't you learn anything on your wanderings?'

More implied shortcomings. He knew he was letting his frustration entangle him but couldn't help retaliating.

'Yeah, respect. Which you mocked me for.'

'That was timidity. It's a question of judgment and nerve.'

'Is it? Well, as I judge there's little chance of Major Dancy's hell-raising happening here, we should go.'

'They're in shock, that's all,' Yiorgos said.

The young man's perceptiveness came as another rebuke. And brought him out of his own introspection. He did have material to work with here. These people could teach him a lot if he only had the patience to see it.

When he told Yiannis he was leaving for the north to report to his HQ, Yiannis' reaction also caught him off guard. 'Gonna take the fucking radio with you?'

'You have a radio?'

'Doesn't fucking work. We should've dumped it long ago.'

'Why didn't you?'

'Nikos was told the big boss in Cairo would send us nothing more if we lost it.' He tossed his head towards the cave. 'So it sits in there like a fucking curse.'

'Can I take a look?'

'What for?'

'I might be able to mend it.'

'Huh. So the Germans get a fix on where we are?'

'Could they do that?'

'Who knows? They don't fucking need to. Radios are just an excuse to turn over a village. Like Livada.'

'If you operated it from higher up in the mountains..?'

'There's no point. The codebook is kept at your HQ. If we sent an uncoded message to Cairo, the fuckers would only intercept it – and any supplies.'

'Then dump it. I'll tell the major the Germans were about to capture it.'

'That's the first fucking useful thing you've said since you came. We don't need a fucking radio repair man.'

With that Yiannis stumped off into the cave. Kiwi raised his eyebrows at Andreas. 'On that encouraging note…'

The defeatism made his skin prickle. Would Fielding be as bad as this? He glanced towards Costis, who'd stopped his target practice and stood up. As Costis turned, he saw a sad-eyed face dominated by a hooked nose. Again too old for its years. The man nodded a sombre greeting.

Sudden cries from above made Costis snap into action. With all the rest. In a moment the apathy was gone. Rifles appeared from nowhere. He whirled to the source of the cries. Ari came careering down the slope towards them in a clatter of stones. The boy slithered to a stop before Yiannis and spluttered out through his breathlessness.

'Yianni, Costi, the katsikia have surrounded the village. They're driving everyone into the square.'

Instead of galvanising, this information seemed to paralyse the men. Dismay spread across their faces. They looked to Yiannis. He waited for Yiannis' reaction and found himself on the end of an accusing stare.

'Any good ideas on how to fucking mend this, New Zealander?'

The question came like a slap. He struggled to think, with the others' eyes probing him. 'How far is the village?'

'Not far. But look at us. What the fuck can we do?'

He rummaged for his binoculars. 'I don't know. Let's go and see.'

The cliff-top overlooking the village square gave a clear view of the open space four hundred metres below. A few women and children cowered in front of the kafenion from the rifles of two Germans. He focused the glasses on the jeep parked opposite them and shivered to see the gunner on it assembling a tripod. For a heavy machine gun. He glimpsed several other grey uniforms further off, ordering people out of their houses.

His chest tightened. The herding of the elderly villagers into the square was taking time but time was no help if they couldn't act. And, as Yiannis had implied, the band was outnumbered. In any case shooting from here, he knew, would only be fatal to the villagers.

On the far side of the square someone tumbled over. Laughter echoed up the cliff. It stirred grunts of fury.

'Old Manoli,' Yiannis growled. 'He's blind. The bastards tripped him.'

He watched a soldier drag an old man along and shove him towards the women and children. More laughter wafted up. A ripple of protest came from the crowd. An abrupt command cut it off.

He picked out the stocky figure who stalked into the square. A sergeant. Bare-headed. The sergeant called something to the gunner in the jeep then flourished a stave at the villagers and barked what sounded like abuse.

'He's asking where Panadakis is,' Yiorgos said.

'You can hear that?'

'Shhh, M... He claims their men are with Panadakis.'

'The l-liar, he knows that's n-not true,' Costis said.

'And the radio, he wants the radio...'

'What did I say?' Yiannis hissed. 'Fucking radios.'

'Oh, no, Sofia, don't...' someone behind him moaned.

He scanned the crowd. A woman had stepped forward. With her arms folded in defiance. A well-built woman. Not young. She was shouting something at the sergeant. Behind them he saw the gunner set the barrel on the tripod.

'She says their men are shepherds and off with the sheep, not with a ...'

Yiorgos broke off. The sergeant strode forward and beat at Sofia with the stave. Her fellow villagers shrank back, shrieking. She took the blows without flinching and then grasped the stave and pulled. The sergeant staggered. As he fought to tug it free, he gave a vicious yell.

'Show him, Sofia,' he heard a voice urge to his left.

The sergeant let go of the stave. Off-balance, the woman fell back still holding it and slipped to the ground. Kiwi glimpsed the pistol raised. The shot echoed as he swept the glasses to the woman. She writhed on her back. He swung the glasses away. For a moment there was silence. Then a ragged chorus of wailing rang out below.

Around him he heard sobs and curses.

'We have to do something,' Andreas said.

'Rush them,' someone urged.

He shook his head. 'It'd be suicide.'

'You got a better fucking idea, New Zealander?'

Below, the machine gunner fed in an ammunition belt. Kiwi exchanged glances with Costis and heard again the pebbles in the can. That gave him an idea. A crazy one but all he had. And time was against them. He turned to Ari. The boy was staring in horror at the square. 'Ari, to save your mama...'

The lad gaped at him.

'Run down into the trees and shout "Mama" as loud as you can. But don't show yourself to the katsikia. OK? Then go.'

Ari dashed off. In the square more elderly residents were being driven to join the crowd. Sofia lay still now. He saw an old woman go to help her. She was driven back with threats. He waved the men up. 'Yianni, the rest of you. Down the hill. As fast as you can. But don't fire until you hear a shot. No, not you, Costi.'

'You sure you know what you're doing, New Zeal..?'

'Costis does. Just go.'

'Even if we make it in time...'

'Go!'

They went. He nodded to Costis and stared at the sergeant. He hoped there was time. The German was berating the villagers again. What about, wasn't audible. A female figure with a shawl covering her head appeared to push forward from the rear but the others held her back. He watched the sergeant step to the side and turn to the gunner. He glanced at Costis. 'The last moment, Costi, to give them time, it has to be the last moment...'

Costis nodded, his eyes fixed on the scene.

Just then Ari's cries burst from the trees.

'Mama! Mama! Mama!'

In response a wild shriek broke from another woman who also struggled to break free. She did but crashed straight into a guard. He shoved her back and gestured the others to hold her still. Ari's cries continued to echo. The sergeant shouted something and two of his men stumbled up the slope towards the trees. The squat figure stepped back and raised its arm.

Kiwi held his breath, praying Costis would judge it right. He wasn't sure Yiannis and the others could have made it yet. And if those troops caught the young boy...

A new shout broke into Ari's cries. It was the blind old man. He limped out of the crowd and stopped, his face appearing to search the sky beyond the machine gun. His cry came again, reverberating against the cliff. This time Kiwi did catch the words.

'Kriti – Freedom or death!'

He watched the sergeant's arm drop and swung the glasses onto the machine gunner. Saw him stoop forward to fire. It had to be now for Costis or it was too late.

'Come on, Costi,' he willed. 'Come on...'

In slow motion the gunner's stoop seemed to continue. His arm reached out. There was a pause. A jerk. But only one shot echoed in Kiwi's ear. He blinked. The gunner lay crumpled across his gun. To another echo, the sergeant fell clutching his left leg. Costis swore in annoyance at the miss.

The crowd ran screaming off the square. A crash of gunfire burst from the trees and two more Germans dropped. Costis picked off a third. The remainder milled about then turned tail. A soldier hoisted the sergeant on his shoulder and staggered after them. The engine of a lorry behind the trees burst into the din. Kiwi followed the trail of dust that rose along the road out of the village then laid down the glasses.

'Congratulations, Costi. What a shot. I think you just made the first payment for your uncle.'

Costis nodded. There was no pleasure in the sad eyes.

'N-not the l-last, I hope… You g-go, I'll st-ay here a while. I'd l-like a m-moment…'

When Kiwi reached the square, the villagers had re-emerged, their faces a mixture of shock and relief. Ari's mother hugged him to her. Yiannis' men stripped the German bodies of weapons and gathered discarded rifles. Andreas hauled the dead gunner off the gun and examined the wound. He cupped his hands and shouted up to the cliff. 'Straight down the line, Costi.'

A hand waved up there. Kiwi turned to the black-clothed women bent down over Sofia. 'I'm sorry we were too late for…'

One of them glanced up. Young. Her shawl thrown back onto the black hair. Dark, searching eyes. Eyes full of concern. Something lurched in him and felt himself sway. Everything stopped. He stared. The girl's concern became a puzzled frown and his paralysis snapped. 'Eleni?'

He watched her clamber, in slow time, it seemed, to her feet. She peered at him and his heart lurched again. She gave no sign of recognition. He must be mistaken. How could he ever have thought..? He screwed up his eyes in anger and shame and looked away.

'Are you all right?' he heard her ask.

He stared into the dark eyes. No, he wasn't mistaken. About them or the voice. But… it couldn't be. It wasn't possible. How could it be? His head whirled. He found words but they came out in a gabble. ''41. Asyfou. During the retreat. You gave us water.'

She shook her head at him but her face clouded. He'd stirred some memory. His mind screamed to be put out of its uncertainty. He spluttered on. 'No? A Scot grabbed your sister..? Kiwi..?'

There was a flicker of recollection. A surge of hope swept him. The impossibility of it cut that off.

'But you were dead…'

The incomprehension in her face made him blunder on.

'I found a pile of bodies… By the house… Burnt…'

Her whole body shuddered. He was conscious of the other women now, standing and gaping at him. He heard himself gabble, still in an agony of doubt. 'We were left behind. At Sfakia. The Germans marched us back up the Gorge. Past the house. I went to look…'

Her eyes stared at him, dark still but unseeing. Then she looked down, nodding to herself and spoke very softly.

'In the chaos after your soldiers left one of our lambs had wandered off. I'd gone to search for it…'

He fumbled in his breast pocket and pulled out the fragment of singed blue dress. 'This was by the pile…'

Her hand shook as she accepted it. She gazed at it then stared at him again, seeing him this time. In agony. 'It had been washed. Maybe Poppy…'

She shivered. He wanted to reach for her but couldn't move. Even now there were things he couldn't square. He struggled to explain his continuing incredulity. 'And once, later, after I escaped – I escaped from the prison camp at Kalamaki – I passed nearby. The house was a guard post. From across the valley I could see four crosses…'

She caught her breath. 'Yes… My grandmother was in the house.'

'My God. I'm sorry…'

She regarded him with a level gaze. 'It's two years now. We carry on and do what we can. But you speak Greek. You haven't been here all this time?'

'No, I came back. Didn't I say I would?'

The attempt at familiarity sounded foolish. With a jolt he realised that the girl he'd carried in his head was now a woman. Her self-possession unnerved him. He floundered on. 'I just didn't expect… What are you doing here?'

This question appeared to unsettle her. She glanced aside and he followed her gaze. The other women were carrying Sofia's body towards the houses. Eleni looked back at him and held out the piece of blue cloth.

Keeping his eyes on hers he replaced it, puzzled by her hesitation. A clatter made him jump. A pile of rifles lay on the ground. Andreas grinned at him. 'No time for distractions, eh, Kiwi?'

Andreas bowed to Eleni with a broad smile. 'Excuse any disrespect from my friend, if he was forward. In New Zealand, where he comes from, all the women are too ugly to look at, so he's out of practice.'

His glance met Eleni's then he looked away. Yiannis emerged from a house under a large bundle.

'No time for flirting, now, Kiwi,' Andreas said. 'We have to move. The Germans will be back.'

'Yeah, right, of course…'

Others staggered from houses carrying heavy loads and he saw they'd understood the situation quicker than he. Again he'd switched off. To hide his blushes, he gathered the rifles Andreas had slung down, while calling back to Eleni: 'Do you need help with your belongings?'

'Aren't your hands full already?' Andreas winked at him. His companion had the machine gun barrel on one shoulder, an ammunition belt over the other.

'I was only visiting here,' Eleni said. 'And…'

A volley of shots drowned her explanation. He dropped the rifles and threw himself on her, pushing her to the ground. No? Surely not already? It couldn't be, could it? Once more he'd neglected his training. No sentries… The shots echoed. He heard screams as the villagers scattered and glimpsed Andreas fumbling the machine gun. He reached out for a rifle.

'Stop!'

He did, on hands and knees. Because the order was in Greek. He looked to Andreas for clarification. Andreas was peering at the wall beyond the jeep. Gunmen appeared from behind it, their rifles levelled and covering the square.

With relief he saw they weren't German, took in red flashes on their arms as he stood up. He gave Eleni his hand and pulled her to her feet. The alarm in her face surprised him. He'd expected her to be of sterner stuff. She let go his grip and he sensed her move away from him. He felt a surge of anger at the advancing guns. 'Who the hell are you?'

A tall, booted figure dressed all in black, with fringed headkerchief and a dark blue cloak thrown over his shoulders regarded him from beside the jeep. The man made no attempt to reply to the question.

His eyes were chill and unmoving. Kiwi felt himself being weighed up. As if a predator was appraising him and about to spring.

He made to repeat his demand. Before he could the eyes swept past him and he saw the head jerk with a curt nod. He went cold. Eleni, looking down, trailed towards the rifles. He wanted to grab for her but instead he heard Andreas' laugh.

'Comrade, what kept you?'

The eyes swept away to Andreas then he felt them bore into him again. For reply the blue-cloaked figure inclined his head at the square. 'Whose reckless idea was this?'

'Mine,' Kiwi said.

'You took a ridiculous risk.'

'We were left with no choice. Perhaps if you'd turned up earlier, like Andreas said…'

The predator's brow furrowed. He seemed unused to contradiction. His voice took on a tone of quiet menace.

'Who are you, with that accent? British?'

'New Zealand.'

'The same thing.'

'And King Kong's a kiwi.'

This did confuse him. Eleni still stood behind the intruder with her head bowed. The sight of her submission provoked Kiwi to defiance. 'If you're going to shoot us, get on with it. Before Jerry does come back. Or return your hostage and clear off.'

To his surprise all this brought was a scornful snort.

'We'll take the machine gun with us as well.'

'Go to hell.'

'You're in no position to refuse.'

'No, but Costis is.'

His nod directed the arrogant gaze to the rifle glinting above the cliff. 'And the machine gunner was a smaller target.'

Fury flushed his opponent's face. A voice from behind curtailed his own satisfaction.

'You owe us the fucking machine gun for Moni.'

He wheeled. Yiannis pointed to the dropped rifles.

'And we'll need these for the recruits you've sent our way from there. Anything we can't fucking carry, you're welcome to.'

At this a red-haired youth stood out from his superior's side and worked his rifle bolt, sneering at Yiannis. 'I spit on your threat but don't insult us.'

'Wait, wait.' Kiwi stepped between them and glowered at the leader. 'Let's not get into schoolboy fights, kids. Aren't we forgetting who the real enemy is?'

'Pavlo,' the chief said to the youth.

The lad glared and stalked back to where Eleni stood. With shock Kiwi watched Eleni place her hand on his arm.

'The real enemy, Neo Zealandi?' The predator broke into his confusion. 'Maybe only time will tell for that.'

The leader turned away and put his hand on Pavlo's shoulder. Kiwi frowned to see that, instead of making her escape, Eleni was talking to the man. He wished she'd hurry back before it was too late.

Andreas grinned at him, shaking his head. 'You know who that is you've just pissed off?'

He shrugged. 'Sounded like my dad. I could almost see him reaching for the strap.'

He frowned again towards Eleni and the intruder. Were they arguing? Why was she taking more risks? Andreas gripped his arm and pulled him away. 'Worse than that. You've just made a friend for life of Petros Panadakis. Leader of the Communists.'

'Communists? Miserable bastards. Never got my vote.'

He twisted free and turned back. Eleni was coming towards him. Panadakis had gone. She stopped and held out her hand. He shook it, puzzled. His heart thumped. She gave a shy smile. 'I didn't thank you for saving us.'

'It's in return for a tin hat of water. I'm just glad to see you alive.'

'I think my debt is greater, Kiwi.'

'Oh, the hostage threat? No worries.'

'Hostage threat?'

'Costis would have made sure they didn't take you.'

'Take me?'

'It was my fault. I shouldn't have let you do it.'

'I'm sorry? Do what?'

'Offer yourself as a hostage.'

'You misunderstand, Kiwi. I meant for saving our lives…'

Something in her face unnerved him. She nodded behind her to where the gunmen had stood. 'These are my people, now…'

He heard Andreas say 'Oh, shit.' He couldn't think. A blankness was swallowing him. Her voice sounded far off.

'I told you, I was visiting here. My godmother lives in the village.'

He didn't want explanations. His growing panic made him rattle on. 'You do know how to give a bloke a shock. I don't know what to say… So you'll be leaving with them? Before we could even…'

He trailed off. His mind refused to focus. She looked down. Andreas broke the silence. 'Kiwi, we have to be going, too.'

He blinked at Andreas. Eleni moved away. Was this about to be another Askyfou? Another goodbye.

'I guess there's no chance of another meeting, then?' he called after her. 'Even if I crawl to Karl Marx?'

She stopped and looked back. 'Karl Marx?'

'Your boss. Joker over there. Panadakis.'

'Petros, you mean.'

'Yeah, Petros, if you must. Can you put in a good word for me? You got any influence with him?'

She stared. Her eyes had gone dark.

'I'm married to him.'

He watched her turn away and hurry off.

Four

Repeated trips from the village salvaging possessions only laid exhaustion onto his emptiness. He told himself he'd come back thinking Eleni was dead so he was no worse off. It didn't ease the aching sense of loss.

During the afternoon he made sure they kept sentries watching the road up from the valley. There was no German response. The villagers had time to bury Sofia. He also made them drag the dead soldiers inside the kafenion to protect the bodies from scavengers in the night. There was no point to provoking more retaliation than would already come.

The sun hung still high in the West when Yiannis called a halt. They'd already removed far more than they could carry with them higher into the mountains. The point was in denying it to the Germans.

He sensed from the arguments going on that some of the older people were reluctant to leave but he was too tired to care. Leaving Andreas to torch the jeep, he staggered off up the hill humping a wooden mule-saddle.

'It suits you, Kiwi,' Yiorgos grinned. 'The fat major in Cairo would be pleased we've put you to good use.'

'I'm glad I provide amusement, Yiorgo. We're not going to have much else to laugh about.'

'No, indeed. But there is often a funny side to things if you can see it.'

'I'm struggling to find the funny side of this.'

'Well, it's given me an idea for your Cretan codename. Donkey. Think how that will fool the Germans.'

He looked askance at Yiorgos, whose bouncy gait appeared unaffected by the bundle of blankets balanced on his head. 'So everyone can assume I'm a fool?'

'That's often the best disguise, Kiwi.'

He didn't need a disguise. How could he have expected that a girl he'd seen for ten minutes would have any feelings for him? He'd built her out of a figment of his imagination. Andreas had been right to scorn his naivete over the facts of life.

He plodded on refusing to let Yiorgos' anecdotes about the leave in Cairo lift his mood, although the lad's comic impression of their own briefing from Dancy almost managed it. When he arrived at the camp his depression swept back.

He stopped as Yiorgos whooped and ran ahead to greet a stranger perched on a rock. One of the shepherds from the flock, presumably. The newcomer didn't appear to be stirring himself to help stow the villagers' gear. This now made the apron in front of the cave resemble a refugee dump. Just like the shambles of the retreat two years before. Had he come full circle in this, too?

At the camp he laid the saddle beside a rock and stretched. An old woman took his hand and jabbered thanks. Other smiling faces nodded gratitude. He felt ashamed of his self-pity. They valued what was important. Life.

Even though he knew it was the Cretan way, when he saw the stranger staring at him his irritation returned. Closer to, the man looked more of a dandy than a shepherd. Apart from the mulberry-coloured sash around his waist and dark-blue mountaineer's breeches tucked into black riding boots, his fair hair, thin moustache and black silk shirt gave him the air of a Cairo waiter. In one of the seedier joints.

The waiter stood up, smiling, and came across, offering his hand. Very full of himself. Just what was needed after a day of madness. When he spoke, Kiwi had another shock.

'Glad you could make it, old chap,' the waiter said. In upper class English. 'Alec Fielding. You must be Watkins.'

He blinked at the smiling face. It was too young. Not much older than Yiorgos, by the look of him. And this was his boss? 'You can call me Kiwi. All the others do.'

'Do they? You'll need a Greek name...'

A smart Alec into the bargain.

'So they tell me. Don't worry, Yiorgos has come up with one that I'm sure will fit. Yiorgo…'

Yiorgos materialised with a bright grin.

'…tell the boss the name you've anointed me with.'

Yiorgos' face fell. 'Oh, no, Mr Kiwi, that was our little joke.'

'It was "donkey",' he said to Fielding. Wrong-footed again. 'You didn't know how right you were, Yiorgo.'

Yiorgos didn't look convinced. The lad shook his head.

'After what you did today Ki.., Mr Kiwi…'

He caught the sideways glance at Fielding as Yiorgos corrected himself and the imposition of formality jarred.

'…It should be Vasili.'

But this time he did laugh. 'King? Come on, Yiorgo. No more jokes.'

Yiorgos looked hurt. 'No, no, Mr Kiwi, that one was not a joke. I'm going to suggest it to Yianni.'

'And don't address me as "Mr",' he called after Yiorgos. When he turned back to Fielding the young man regarded him with a quizzical air. Christ, he was being weighed up again. He let his irritation show.

'Pity you didn't get here earlier. We could have done with a bit of leadership.'

'From what Yiorgos says, you had plenty.'

'He's an impressionable youth.'

'I think very highly of him.'

What did he have to do to ruffle this one's composure?

'I was expecting you to meet us. On the beach.'

'Yes, I must apologise for that. Though I assumed you'd be in good hands. I hadn't heard about Niko.'

'You don't seem to hear about much.'

'It'll change now Yiorgos is back. Got tied up with a lot of incoming signals from Dancy.'

'You wouldn't want to miss those, then. Must have been vital stuff?'

'Load of guff, actually. As always.'

The irreverence took him aback. Was it affectation?

'Is that so?'

'Yes. But this time more interesting than usual.'

The half-smile in Fielding's eyes increased his annoyance. He'd been played with too many times today.

'I wouldn't have wanted you to miss us for anything trivial. But look, I'm done in. Can we continue this later?'

He stomped off. Could he have imagined anyone worse than Dancy except an English public schoolboy? They'd be discussing rugby next.

However, around the fire that evening all he heard was despair. Evacuating the village threatened their survival. If they couldn't re-occupy it – an event they seemed to think unlikely – they faced dispersal or a winter in the high mountains: the snow and absence of food made the latter a dire choice.

The news from Souyia, the Germans' garrison on the coast at the end of the valley, deepened his gloom. Andonis, Costis' elder brother, had been, not with the sheep, but on a scouting mission. His trip to Souyia had hoped to find some weak area at which to strike in retaliation for their uncle's death. It had brought disappointment.

He took in Andonis' restless eyes and sharp features. They suggested a mind of active determination but he saw that what they'd found at Souyia weighed the brother down.

'They're doubling, trebling its size,' Andonis said. 'Putting up barracks huts on the far side. And running a perimeter fence around the whole place.'

'If it's like the one round the prison at Kalamaki, you'll be able to walk through it,' he retorted. 'I did.'

Andonis shook his head at him. 'It's a double line. Barbed wire. They mean to stay.'

'What about the beach?'

'Mined at each end. I saw the skull-and-crossbones warning signs. There's a watchtower at each end of the beach, too.'

'How d'you get in the fucking place?' Yiannis asked.

'There are two entrances, both with guard posts.'

'You didn't risk them?'

'No fear.'

'So you couldn't estimate their strength?' Fielding asked. His superior's excellent Greek only increased his sense of frustration.

'A woman told me they cook for a hundred now. The barrack huts must double that. It'll be a large base.'

'Then all the bigger its fall,' Kiwi said but no one laughed. He felt the rebuke in their silence.

'They obviously mean to put a squeeze on the whole fucking area,' Yiannis muttered. 'As we saw today. Some chance we've got. And you said there's a new commandant?'

'Bortmann. The woman reckons he's a grumbling sod. Old soldier. Wermacht. Getting on. Drinks too much. Hates being stuck on the south coast.'

'So going to take it out on us?'

'She said you have to watch yourself around him.'

'And how did you get to chat up this woman?' Andreas laughed.

'Bortmann's taken over the buildings that face the sea on the road parallel to it for his headquarters. Those they evicted have had to find shelter in the Lissos valley. Outside the perimeter. I came across her there.'

'The guards are used to locals going in and out?' Fielding asked. 'If we wanted to know more?'

Andonis shook his head. 'Only women and children. They're using forced labour on the barracks. Any man would soon find himself joining them. Unless his papers showed he was from round here, in which case…'

He drew his finger across his throat.

'Any Gestapo?' Fielding queried.

'She thought that underneath this Bortmann's office, because he's on the first floor so he can stand on the balcony and look at the sea, there are cells. But I didn't think to ask about Gestapo. Sorry, Mr Aleko.'

Fielding closed a notebook in which he'd been writing

'No, that's useful, Andoni, thanks, you've picked up a good deal. I'll let Cairo know.'

'And what the hell will *they* do with it?' Kiwi said.

For the first time his superior looked disconcerted.

'What would you do?'

'I was sent here to raise hell. Got to start sometime.'

'Against an entrenched garrison?'

'Easier now than when it's up to full size.'

'And provoke reprisals?'

'Against what? That worried me before I came. But what have we to lose here? These people have no homes.'

'Don't forget the hostages,' Andonis said. 'Besides, even with men from Moni and Livada we are a small band.'

Another excuse for inaction. He cursed himself for forgetting the hostages. His annoyance made him plough on.

'I wasn't thinking of a frontal attack.'

'We are still too few to act in safety.'

'There aren't any other local groups?'

'Only Panadakis' communists. You saw how they are.'

'Well-drilled, hard-looking.'

'You don't expect us to trust *them*?'

'We'd only have to work with them. Co-operate.'

'With their women, too, eh, Kiwi?' Andreas whispered. 'You know Communist women are supposed to be frigid? The passion's all in their heads, not in their...'

He pushed Andreas away and continued. 'You wouldn't fight alongside them? Not even for Kriti, for Freedom? What about old Manoli's cry today – Freedom or Death? Doesn't that count now?'

'Of course we want freedom,' Andonis said. 'And we don't fear death. But you English lecture us about freedom and death and all we face is death. Where is our freedom?'

'I'm not En...,' he began but a loud shriek from behind cut him off. A commotion of women's voices filled the night air. Yiannis swore and stamped off.

'Women's freedom, Kiwi,' Andreas laughed. 'To kick up a fuss.'

'It's more than we're doing.'

'You're too sour. What you need is a good woman to...'

'What I need is somebody to get a grip.'

The commotion subsided. Yiannis flopped back down.

'She'd fucking cheer you up, Kiwi. That was old Maria. She wants freedom *and* death. The freedom to go and die in her own home. If we let her go back, she'll fucking get it tomorrow when the Germans return.'

'I'm only trying to say you don't have to give up. Look at Costi. With that firepower and accuracy… And you were outnumbered today. If we'd not acted, you know where these people would be. I'm not talking about miracles.'

'Even though your father was a priest,' Yiorgos piped up.

He shook his head in exasperation. 'Look, I haven't come here to tell you what to do…'

'So what was that you've just been telling us?' Fielding's voice had a quiet scorn. 'Wasn't it what to do? Or is it an example of New Zealand logic?'

He glared round the bowed heads of the group. 'Life won't wait for logic. It's like Galatas. Ask Andrea. When you're on your knees, only a desperate throw will save you. And when you've got no choice, making the choice is easy.'

He clambered up and stalked off. Old Maria cried out in the dark. He felt as drained as he had on the dock at Sfakia.

For a moment when he woke he thought he *was* still there. The distant sound of guns. An explosion. Close to, wailing brought him back to the present. In the dawn light he saw Yiannis shooing away a clutch of old women.

'Huh. Old Maria,' Yiannis growled at him. 'The crone only fucking slipped off home in the night.'

'What's the shooting?'

'Means the malakas are already in the village. And these bitches expect me to mount a rescue.'

'You're not just going to leave her?'

'Isn't it what she wants? To die in her own home.'

'Even so…'

'That *would* be a fucking suicide mission. And don't forget, Kiwi, for us home is the best place to die.'

That felt like a reproof. A shriek snuffed out his guilt. Yiannis whirled away from him in fury. Andonis was running towards them from the cave. 'Eva's gone after her mother.'

Yiannis put his head in his hands. A bewildered-looking young boy and girl trailed after Andonis. Old women emerged from the cave and began to wail again.

'Why don't they all fucking go back?' Yiannis groaned. 'At least then we'd have some peace. This makes no difference. We can't take more fucking risks...'

Some of the other men had now joined Yiannis. Kiwi watched them nod in gloomy agreement. A fitful night had not improved his mood. The prospect of a day's journey with his superior, hearing more reasons for doing nothing, irked him further. 'I'll go,' he said.

'It's not the place for heroics,' Fielding retorted in English.

'Sod off... Sir.'

'You have a wish to die, too, Kiwi?' Yiannis asked.

'No, to know if there's a back way in. Costi?'

'I'll sh-show you.'

'When I mocked you for not chasing women, Kiwi, this isn't what I had in mind,' Andreas said.

'Nor me. The rest of you should start moving the stuff higher up. And watch the Germans don't come searching for this place. If I'm not back by night, forget me, too.'

Fielding looked as if he was about to object to being given orders but desisted. More explosions echoed from the village. He checked his revolver and nodded to Costis to lead the way. Was this the recklessness he kept telling himself he'd grown out of? Or pique from last night?

Sneaking into the village was easy. Any German cordon had been withdrawn, from the sound of the explosions, to carry out demolition work. So Costis' path up the ravine below the church led him in undetected.

He scanned the square. A line of sentries stared up at the cliffs. Bodies were being brought out of the kafenion. An officer supervised troops fetching loot to a lorry.

It all appeared very systematic and they'd started at the far end of the village. He slipped away, up the empty winding alley Costis had told him would lead to Maria's house, hoping the German search hadn't reached this far.

It had. He heard a splintering of wood and then a crash. He peered round the corner. Maria's house should be up the alley off to the left. That's where the noise came from. It wasn't what stopped him.

Ahead, her back pressed into the wall and taking quick glances round the corner of Maria's street, was the black-clad woman who must be her daughter. A scream came from up that street. Laughter. More screams. The woman, Eva, stood out from the wall and set herself to charge.

His hand cupping her mouth, he jerked her back and held her tight. She flailed out. When he turned her and let her recognise him her anger collapsed. He put his finger to his lips and laid her to crouch against the wall. She was shuddering.

He peeped round the corner. Maria, he assumed, sat moaning outside her wrecked door. A soldier angled his rifle down at her. Crashing noises came from inside.

He calculated the chances of reaching her. And getting away. Not good. He could take the guard but the likelihood of the one or ones inside not hearing were slim. And if she refused to come? He pushed the thought aside and glanced at Eva. Her face was a plea. He was going to have to risk it.

He drew his revolver and took another quick peek, to see the stocky figure of the sergeant who'd shot Sofia limping on a crutch down the hill. What had been reckless now looked impossible. When would he start listening to advice?

The newcomer glowered at Maria then at the guard. He barked a question in German. The guard's answer included a gesture at the house. The sergeant shouted at Maria. 'Sie. Gehen sie wey. Parti, parti!'

She ignored him and started to sing. Another soldier appeared in the doorway and glanced down the street.

Kiwi jerked back. Eva stood now and stared at him. He motioned her not to move and risked another look. The sergeant poked Maria with his crutch. 'Wunschen sie kaput? Kaput? Gehen wey. Raus!'

Maria spat and resumed singing. The German went to hit her but lost his balance and had to steady himself on the crutch. The first guard bent to pull her up but the sergeant barked something and gestured at the house.

Kiwi saw the two soldiers stare at each other.

'Ja, Feldwebel Hahn?' one asked.

Hahn gesticulated at them. With horror Kiwi realised what the sergeant intended. The soldiers seized Maria's arms, dragged her to her feet and bundled her inside.

Hahn followed them. The street was empty. For a moment he had a chance. A foolish chance but if he could make it to the door... Eva tugged his sleeve. She gestured that she wanted to see. He shook his head. But the moment had gone.

The three Germans came out. One held up some rags to Hahn and he lit a match under them. Maria's singing grew louder. As the rags flared the soldier slung them through the door. Smoke curled into the gap. Kiwi breathed out. If he shot the sergeant and they made a run for it... It was foolhardy. It was pointless. But he'd dropped himself in it. He set himself. The singing soared.

Eva pulled him back. Indicated her ears. He couldn't catch the words. She motioned to him to come away. 'My mother's defying them to do their worst,' she said. 'She's quite sure she wants to stay.'

He glanced back but she took his arm and drew him off.

'A mantinade from the time of the Turkish wars?' Yiannis spluttered.

Eva looked up from where she knelt hugging her children. 'Yes. You must know it. "I'm here... I don't fear you now/This is the refuge of my peace." I'm sorry, Yianni, I should have known she'd stay. And to you, Mr Kiwi, for risking your life. Thank you.'

He lifted a hand in acknowledgment. The closeness of the call made him shiver. At this rate he'd be *in* hell, not raising it. How Dancy would enjoy that.

He trudged away some distance, slumped down against a rock and stared at the cloudless sky.

'Still, she'll be grateful.'

He glared at Andreas who inclined his head towards Eva.

'Always get a woman in your debt. Never fails.'

'Go away, Andrea, and leave me alone.'

It wasn't only the futility of the escapade and the further reminder of his own recklessness that cast shadows. Like old Maria, his mother had lost the will to go on. Unlike Maria she had merely bemoaned her bad luck. He tried to shake off the memories. In the end he'd run away from there, too. He closed his eyes.

When he opened them Fielding and Andonis stood regarding him. He groaned. Would no one leave him in peace? He squinted up at them, into the sun.

'Yes, I know. It was a stupid, reckless gesture that achieved nothing. I'll keep my mouth shut in future.'

'On the contrary, Kiwi,' Andonis said. 'You saved the mother of two children from the consequences of *her* recklessness. And how else would we have known of the heroic nature of Maria's defiance? What you saw is what creates legends.'

'Only when you're dead. Jesus, Andoni, I thought Kiwis were…' He glared at Fielding, irked by his inadequacy. 'What's the Greek for "obstinate sods"?' Fielding told him. 'Yeah,' he went on, 'but they've got nothing on you Cretans. We don't go as far as preferring dying to fighting back.'

'Nor do we, Kiwi, in general.'

'You'll have to convince me about that.'

'Give us time. We may have some ideas.'

He bowed and walked off. Fielding remained, looking down. Kiwi waited for some cutting remark but none came. The Captain appeared to be studying something on his foot.

'I suppose I owe you an apology. Sir,' Kiwi said. Using English only emphasised his inferiority.

Fielding looked up, in surprise, it seemed. 'For what?'

'Oh, insubordination, acting without orders, treating the natives with undue deference, that sort of thing. Don't worry, nothing in your report will be new to Major Dancy. It'll only confirm his reservations about me.'

'I'm fully aware of that, Sergeant.'

'You are?'

'Though you have, however, left out "troublemaker", "not to be trusted" and "likely to undermine your authority", as far as I recall.'

'Recall?'

'Yes, that was in the report *from* Major Dancy that delayed my coming to meet you. I threw it in the fire last night after you stormed off in a huff.'

'I'd had a tiring day.'

'After the others told me in more detail how you'd saved it from becoming a disastrous one.'

'That was thanks to Costis.'

'And your leadership. *I* owe *you* an apology.'

'For what?'

'Believing what Dancy said about you.'

'I thought you said he got most of it right? Sir.'

Fielding was grinning now. 'Stop calling me "sir". He missed the key point.'

'That I was an ignorant colonial bumpkin?'

'That you're a natural leader.'

'Ah. Well, OCTU…'

'Thinks officers are only found in the Home Counties. Here it's different. That's why we want you to take over.'

'Take over what?'

'Leading this group.'

'Leading this group?'

He was conscious of echoing Fielding's words. He tried to straighten out his confusion. 'Who's the "we"?'

'Yiannis, Andonis, Costis and all the others.'

'But why?'

'They want to start fighting back. And they know, as I do now, that you're the man to lead that.'

Five

Yiannis' weathered face creased with astonishment.

'Where the fuck did they all come from?'

'Not in that one lorry from Souyia.'

Kiwi ran the glasses over the lorry and ruins of Moni. Unlike their own village the Germans hadn't wasted much dynamite on it. Most of the houses were still standing, if as blackened shells. That wasn't what drew a collective gasp from his men as they peered down.

'Unless it fetches a few each day and they stay here,' Andonis suggested.

'No. The lorry will bring up the labourers and their escort. The rest must be a platoon out on exercise.'

He counted more than fifty German infantry, lying in the sun, on sentry duty or supervising the re-building work. Andonis had suspected that's what they were at, establishing strong-points along the road to Hania to secure the lowlands. From an eyrie on the crest of the ridge at the edge of Kostouyerako, he'd observed a lorry heading each day towards Moni. So Kiwi had brought these ten men down across the valley to make sure. But the number of Germans puzzled him. Where had they sprung from?

'They aren't f-from S-souyia,' Costis said. 'We'd have s-seen them. R-reinforcements on their w-way down there?'

'They don't look as if they've marched from Hania.'

'Perhaps from K-kandanos, Kiwi.'

'In which case, there may be more about. We should go.'

This brought groans and mutters of disappointment. He knew the men were keen to try out the new rifles and sub-machine guns from their first successful parachute supply drop. The one bright spot in a week of frustration.

Fighting back had proved easier to urge than to do. Establishing a new camp higher up on the east flank of Ochra had had to be the priority. It wasn't, however, the only cause of Kiwi's frustration.

'You don't want us to fucking pick off some first?'

'No, I don't.'

'I thought we were here to raise hell?' Andreas laughed.

'Do your new boots hurt, Andrea?'

'Not too much, why?'

'If we stir up that wasps' nest, they will by the time you've run all the way home. Unless the lorry cuts us off before we've got…'

A burst of firing stopped him. Although hidden in a thicket of holm oak, he ducked down with the rest. The firing continued. But nothing came their way. He trained the binoculars again on the village. One German lay on the ground. The rest crouched behind a low wall that gave a solid defensive position on the far side of the houses. The attack had come from beyond there. He scanned the scrubland for puffs of smoke from the attackers' guns.

'Oh, shit…'

'What is it, Kiwi?'

'Guess. Not "what" – "who".'

He strained to see more red flashes but Panadakis' men stayed in cover. He handed the glasses to Yiannis. 'What's he doing? He can't have enough men for a frontal attack, can he?'

'It doesn't fucking look like it.'

Yiannis returned the glasses. Kiwi scanned again.

Panadakis' men didn't come near the size of the German force and hadn't taken it by surprise. Panadakis would never over-run it now. And every casualty inflicted would be fatal for the hostages in Ayia. It was the sort of encounter he'd struggled to persuade himself and his own, impatient men to avoid. Didn't Panadakis care?

'It's probably that h-hot-head, Pavlo,' Costis said.

'Pavlo?'

'The red-head. The one who h-had a go at Yianni last w-week. This c-craziness looks like his.'

The image of Eleni's hand on Pavlo's arm thrust itself in. 'Can't Panadakis control him?'

'Pavlo's like you, Kiwi,' Yiannis laughed.

'Thanks. You think I'm as stupid as that?'

His indignation drew more laughter.

'No. I meant he's Panadakis' fucking second-in-command, as you are to Mr Aleko.'

The laughter stopped abruptly. The men had seen what he'd seen. And what Pavlos and his men still hadn't.

'You were right not to get involved, Kiwi,' Andreas said. 'That platoon in the village *is* only an advance guard. There must be half a company coming down the road.'

At a trot, now, he saw. Starting to fan out across the far slopes. Pavlos' men continued firing at the wall. If they didn't flee, in minutes they'd be outflanked and over-run.

'Good riddance, Pavlo,' Yiannis snorted. 'I always said he'd trip up one day. He's no fucking loss to anyone.'

'Yes, he is. The fewer there are of us to fight the Germans, the harder it'll be to win.'

'If you say so, Kiwi. Not much we can do for them, now, though, is there? I'm not fucking selling my life for some Communist.'

'You don't have to. Costi, Andrea and you three, fire at the German column's leading men.'

'At this distance, Kiwi, I'm not sure what I'll hit.'

'Raising the alarm's what it's about. The rest of you, fire on those at the wall. Confuse them about how many sides they're being attacked from.'

He scoured the slopes above his own position. If that was half a company there might be another in platoon strength on the mountain. Unlikely, if the main body was using the road and it wasn't their normal procedure – since they had no fear of ambush from ineffective groups like his – but he'd already had one surprise today.

A curse from Yiannis made him swing the glasses back onto the battle below. Pavlos' men had got the message.

They were slipping away. He saw one man stumble but Costis' fire had halted the Germans' outflanking movement and driven the main body back into cover. If Pavlos' force could make the shelter of the Irini Gorge, the Germans would be reluctant to follow.

The warning to Pavlos had drawn German attention their own

way. It was time to leave. Uphill. Re-crossing the main valley home would now have to be a night job.

'One concentrated burst, lads, and then come away. Costi, Andrea, give them bursts for five minutes then follow us. Yiorgo, you know a way over the top?'

Yiorgos grinned and led the way at a crouching trot through the sparse cover of the wind-bent pines and holm oaks. Although the curvature of the hill hid them from the Germans in the village there was always the chance of a scout's picking them out. Nevertheless they should have a good half hour's start on any pursuers, even if the Germans wanted to take the risk of a further ambush.

Once Andreas and Costis caught them up and the sound of gunfire had died down, he let the men stop and rest. Talk bubbled with the merits of their new weapons and the release of letting them off at the enemy. To himself, he fretted about the intelligence problem, a shortcoming he'd laid at Alec's door. It seemed endemic here.

'Dreaming about her won't help,' Andreas said.

'I'm not dreaming about her.'

'Ha, ha, ha.'

'I'm not. If you must know, I was...'

The shot made them all dive for cover. He peered ahead into the trees, again cursing his inattention, even if for once Eleni wasn't the cause of it. Hadn't he known there'd be another platoon somewhere? He looked at the others. All were unhurt. They, too, scanned the trees. Costis began steadying himself.

Laughter came instead. He felt cold fury. Panadakis stepped from behind a tree, cradling a rifle. Several of his men followed. They stopped and waited.

'Shoot the fucker, Costi,' Yiannis growled.

Kiwi gritted his teeth. 'No, wait.'

He had no choice but approach Panadakis. Again placed in the position of the supplicant. He stood up. The sneer that greeted him fired his own scorn.

'Opening fire too soon, Panadakis,' he called. 'Typical Cretan fault. You need to have patience.'

'If I'd wanted to shoot you, Neo Zealandi,' Panadakis said with deliberation, 'I wouldn't have missed.'

'What was it, then, thanks for saving your wild man?'

'A warning. To not get in our way. The Germans had almost fallen into our trap, before you interfered.'

The two groups glared at each other. Kiwi doubted Panadakis' claim but the man's manner, and the reminder of his treatment of Eleni, unsettled him.

'Some trap. You'd have been late – again.'

'At least we don't sit and luxuriate among our British supplies,' Panadakis snorted, motioning to his men to move off to the left up the hillside.

'Pity, that. Shall I bring you some champagne?'

'Too bourgeois…'

He guessed at the word. Before he could ask if it was rude Petros added 'I'd prefer… chicken.'

He tried to sound unruffled. 'We make do with bread.'

'Even better,' Panadakis said, turning away. 'But there is no need to bring it. We will send to collect flour from you. In return for your interference. Good day.'

Two days later he was still seething at the insult. What aggrieved him most was the knowledge that Eleni must have shared the story of his clumsy dance with her husband.

'Don't hit those nails so hard,' Andreas laughed. 'You'll make the whole thing collapse on me.'

Kiwi dropped the hammer and flung himself down. 'Why does he get under my skin so much, Andrea?'

Andreas laughed and came out of the half-built shelter.

'You know very well, why, Kiwi. Besides, he was a schoolmaster, before. Like them all, he has the gift of tongues.'

That's all he needed to hear. The one who'd taught him Greek hadn't got up his nose. 'How's a schoolmaster get to lead an andarte band?'

'When the Party was proscribed, in '39, he took to the hills. He rules them with an iron hand, it's said.'

'The women, too?'

'Kiwi, there are many good women…'

'I should have let Costi shoot him.'

This only made Andreas laugh more.

'What's so funny?'

'Don't raise your hopes, Kiwi. Didn't you know that a widow must spend two years in mourning before…'

Yiorgos came rushing through the camp, with a broad grin on his face. He began to laugh, too.

'Can we share the joke, Yiorgo?'

'It's the Communists.'

'Are they that funny?'

'They're coming.'

He leapt to his feet and grabbed his rifle. 'Coming? Where? Stop fooling about, Yiorgo.'

'I can't help it. They're here for the bread.'

Andreas burst out laughing again. He glared at them both. Did everyone have to have fun at his expense? 'The damned cheek. Well, they can damn well turn round and clear off back. Come on.'

He strode to the edge of the camp. People had gathered to see the intruders. He prepared to give them a piece of his mind then stopped dead. Eleni stood before him and nodded a curt greeting. Behind her were three other young women wearing headscarves. All had rifles slung over their shoulders.

'Right,' he said, conscious of Andreas grinning at his side. 'You'd better come in. Where's your escort?'

Eleni grimaced and patted the strap on her shoulder.

'Here. With us, women have equality.'

'I must convert,' Andreas said with a bow. 'In our world it's the women who rule.'

Eleni gave Andreas a withering look. Kiwi bade her follow him into the camp. The older occupants stared as they passed.

'They're wearing trousers,' an old woman hissed.

He risked a glance. The defiance of convention added to his confusion. He bid Eleni's women sit.

'We can't stay long,' she said. 'We're only here to take advantage of the offer to share your supplies.'

He tried to hide his surprise. Had Panadakis sent her on purpose to cause him embarrassment? She seemed very composed. Self-contained with a touch of hardness that both thrilled and scared him.

'Won't you have something to eat and drink?'

'Water,' she said and the word swept him back to Askyfou. She indicated the staring camp women, 'Anything more and your masters may eat us.'

The glint of humour in her eye flustered him more.

'Right. Andrea, find some sacks…'

'We have sacks,' the hooded girl beside Eleni said and jumped up. 'Show us where to fill them.'

He realised he was alone with Eleni. 'I'm sorry. We weren't really expecting you…'

'I know.'

'Then why did you take the risk to come?'

'You think I'm the sort to stay at home and play the submissive little woman?'

Christ, even she was laying into him now.

'Attacking that big Scot wasn't very submissive. If it had been me, I'd have run a mile.'

She gave him the sad smile. 'I expect no special favours. If you'd told us to go away, I'd have understood.'

'You weren't asked to demand chicken?'

Her smile vanished. 'I have another message from Petro. He has received orders to work more closely with the British.'

'Can't say he's exactly welcomed me so far.'

'He's been fighting for four years now. Alone. He can be proud of that. And he has always believed that Kriti should become free without foreign intervention.'

'Yet he'll eat our bread?' he said.

She smiled. 'We must survive by whatever means we can.'

A woman's scream stopped his response. He stood up. So did Eleni.

Two of her companions ran towards them, followed by a cowed-looking Andreas.

'Andrea, what the hell have you done?'

'It's Maro,' one of the women said to Eleni.

'She wants to stay here,' Andreas added.

'Stay here? Why?'

Andreas glanced at Eleni then away.

'What's going on? Can someone explain?' Kiwi snapped.

'Her head's been shaved…' Andreas began.

'So?'

Head shaving for lice was hardly unknown.

'It was a punishment, Kiwi,' Eleni said. 'For fraternising with the… opposite sex.'

'You mean Panadakis made…?'

'Petros, if you don't mind. She had been warned. Without discipline, we lose everything.'

'My God. So she wants to stay here?'

'She can't.'

'What if I say she can?'

'Petros would object.'

'I could live with that.'

'You'd risk conflict over a silly girl?'

He knew she was right but blustered on. 'Never going to be blood brothers, are we?'

'I wouldn't forgive you, either.'

Her coldness shook him. He turned to Andreas. 'Andrea, tell her… it's not possible.' He avoided Andreas' frown. 'But tell her…' he looked round at Eleni, 'that if she goes quietly, nothing will be said of this.'

'I have no secrets from Petros,' Eleni said.

The rebuff irked him. He regretted his concession.

'I'm not asking you to have secrets. If she made a mistake… Haven't you ever made a mistake? I do all the time. And I know what it's like not to be forgiven.'

His outburst seemed to shake her. Preparations for their departure were rushed along. At the edge of the camp he offered his hand to

Eleni. She grazed it with her left and then grasped the sling of the rifle on her left shoulder. He glanced at Maro's gun in her own right hand.

'What if she makes a run for it on the way back?'

'I'll shoot her.'

And they were gone.

He set to with the adze so that the pounding of his heart swamped his agitation. Before long he was covered in sweat but his head still swam. Eleni's coldness appalled him. Had Petros made her that hard? Or Communism? Was she really so cold or was it a wartime protective shell? He couldn't square the change from the girl whose image he'd idealised and which haunted him. Would he ever be able to lay that ghost? Or be free of her?

With Andreas around it was unlikely. Nothing deflected the Cretan from his teasing of Kiwi's shortcomings.

'She is married, Andrea,' he tried as a brush-off.

'All the better. With married women, you're on safe ground. After a few months, they've had enough of the husband. So when you give 'em the eye… It's the one big benefit of arranged marriages.'

Caught off-guard he gaped at Andreas. 'Marriages are arranged?'

'Of course. Surely you knew that? All most men ask is a big fat dowry, a nice plump arse and, if you're lucky…'

He jumped in quickly. 'So Eleni and Petros… I thought Communists were against marriage?'

'For her, Kiwi, even I would take the vow. But for you, I'm not sure. She's a man-eater. You just carry on dreaming. Besides, if you start sniffing too close you'll have us at war with them, too.'

He received the message from Alec calling him to a meeting with the Communists at Theriso with mixed feelings. They had to work together or they'd never make any inroads on the Germans' grip of the south west. He was making no progress alone. Yet the prospect of being patronised by Petros depressed him. And the thought of seeing Eleni again disturbed his sleep.

The room in Theriso was dark, smoke-filled and crowded with Petros' men. Yiorgos had guided Kiwi and Andreas up round the rim of the Omalos plateau, through the pass of Stephanoporo and over the mountain of Zourva to reach here. As they entered, the hubbub died.

At the far end he picked out Alec in conversation with Petros and a bearded, heavily-built man in his 50s who exuded an air of massive self-confidence. He saw Petros' eyes scanning the room and his face break into a smile on seeing the visitors. Its absence of scorn unsettled him.

Petros waved them over. 'Neo Zealandi, come and meet our Commandant, General Mandakis.'

He forced a smile himself.

'What's made him so cheery?' he whispered to Andreas. He noted Andreas' grin and Eleni at the same time. Her shy nod seemed to freeze. From his own frown, he feared.

'Eleni, a drink for our guests,' Petros beamed.

'I thought this was neutral ground?' he said, avoiding the glare he knew he deserved from Alec.

'You are our guest in Kriti,' Mandakis said and offered his hand. He took it and looked into the laughing eyes. The General's brand of Communism seemed to include enjoyment of life more than Petros' version.

'I'll drink to that,' he said. 'And an end to the occupation of the damned Germans.'

The drinking took some time before Mandakis called them to the table. Alec faced the General with himself opposite Petros and Andreas facing Pavlos. The spectators crowded close.

'Let me do the talking,' Alec whispered in English as they sat.

Mandakis began with an interminable preamble about the sacred mission of the national struggle and the liberation of their native soil. The heat and heaviness of the atmosphere was oppressive. After a six-hour trek and all the tsikoudia the General's eloquence made Kiwi drowsy. God, he's going to bore us into submission, he thought. He glimpsed Eleni standing in the background and his mind drifted to their last meeting.

A thump on the table shot him awake.

'We won't be insulted, boy,' Andreas was saying to Pavlo. 'Take that back.'

'All I said was *we're* not cowards,' the red-head jeered.

Pavlos and Andreas were on their feet, hands on the table, glaring at each other. Everyone began to shout. Mandakis and Alec attempted restraint, to little effect.

He met Petros' eyes. The scornful gleam of superiority there told him Andreas had been set up. He wasn't ceding the advantage that easily. Without taking his eyes from Petros he reached for his revolver and fired in the air.

The noise cut at once. Dust and splinters drifted down. Still holding Petros' gaze he replaced the gun. 'I'm here to beat the Germans,' he said. 'Not fight among ourselves. Isn't that what we all want?'

The growl among the crowd turned to mutters of assent.

'Well put, Neo Zealandi,' Mandakis said. 'We must find the will and the means to develop co-operation between us for the greater good.'

'I couldn't agree more,' Alec said.

Kiwi's eyes were fixed on Petros. Petros stared back.

'A share of British parachute drops would help.'

'You had a portion of the last one.'

'Only because we came as beggars.'

He glanced at Eleni but she was looking down. 'I didn't notice any begging.'

'Arms would strengthen us...'

'That's what worries them,' Pavlos put in.

He heard Andreas growl. Things might still explode.

'Arms are more difficult,' Alec began.

'You don't trust us?' Petros asked.

'It's not that...'

'Then what is it? Here we are, ready to co-operate with you in any way we can and you won't give us the means to do so. Just like in the Battle, you wouldn't arm the Cretan people. What do we have to do to convince you?'

Petros' air of righteousness needled him. He glanced at Mandakis. The General's benign countenance had to be a mask. This was all bluff. Mandakis' and Petros' true allegiance lay elsewhere. They weren't going to surrender any of their independence to the British.

'There is one way you could persuade me,' he said.

Petros raised his eyebrows. For once, the Communist seemed unsure. 'Go on. We will consider anything.'

'Really? So when a British force lands to liberate Kriti, you'll be there to fight with them, will you?'

The smirk spreading across Petros' face surprised him.

'Is that a "yes"?'

Petros snorted with derision. 'The long-awaited British "Second Front"?'

'What's so funny about that?'

Petros shrugged at Alec. Kiwi swung round to his boss.

'The Second Front opened three days ago,' Alec muttered in English. 'In Sicily…' adding 'Sikelia,' in Greek.

His eyes blurred. He heard Pavlos laugh. Andreas went to rise but Alec pulled him down. So he'd been used. By bloody Dancy. A decoy. No more than a dancing fool.

'Nothing to say, Neo Zealandi?'

He stared at Petros in silent fury. Petros laughed.

'You may grind your teeth, Neo Zealandi, but who is the one lacking trust now?'

The urge to smash that scornful mask boiled. He was twelve again, wordless in front of his father. Through the haze he barely followed Mandakis' conciliatory drone.

'Perhaps, then, we must rely more on ourselves. If the British aren't coming, it is more important than ever that we work together.'

'You're proposing joint operations?' he heard Alec ask.

'What other way is there?'

'But you'd demand a share of the armaments.'

'Need,' Petros said. 'We can't fire air.'

'So who's going to lead these joint operations?' Andreas put in. Petros gave a complacent shrug. 'Whoever has the greatest experience, naturally.'

'Oh, yeah, naturally,' Andreas retorted. 'Say, why don't we go the whole way and join up with you?'

'What a good idea,' Mandakis said. 'For Kriti.'

'It was a joke.'

'Hang on a minute,' Alec began.

His mind snapped awake. 'No, the General's right,' he said. He met Mandakis' gaze. 'For Kriti.'

'Boss!'

'Kiwi!'

He ignored Alec and Andreas and stared at Petros. 'What do you say, Petro? Now that we have something in common.'

'We do?'

'Yeah. The British have abandoned us both.'

Petros looked disconcerted. This couldn't have been in the plan. For the first time he'd struck back.

'Kiwi, Cairo won't sanction...' Alec said, again in English.

'Stuff Cairo. As they've stuffed us.' He turned to Petros. 'Well, Petro? Our camp has plenty of space to share. Then we can get on with the real business. Freeing Kriti from those bastards.'

'These are just words.'

'I'm a man of my word.'

He was beginning to enjoy Petros' discomfort. Mandakis nodded. 'If it can be made to work... Aleko?'

'It'll upset Cairo. They'll block it, if they can. But...' Alec threw his hands in the air. 'As Kiwi says... What the hell. Let's give it a try.'

He reached across to shake hands with Mandakis. A few muted cheers echoed.

'What about the leadership?' Pavlos asked.

Everyone avoided eye contact. Mandakis coughed and looked down. Kiwi had a teasing thought. 'Shouldn't it be shared? Isn't that Communism?'

He smiled to see Petros' face darken and shrugged his shoulders at Alec. He was past caring. To the side he glimpsed Eleni. Her eyes blazed with the grave concern of their first encounter.

That froze his euphoria. Could she, from her knowledge of Petros and the Communists, see something he couldn't? Maybe his invitation had been just another rash act after all.

Six

Kiwi hammered down the final edge of the biscuit tin and stood up. He glared at the sniggering crowd around him.

'Very pretty,' Yiannis said. 'But what the fuck is it?'

'It's a tank,' Yiorgos grinned.

'What, for keeping water in?' Ari asked.

Yiorgos cuffed the boy.

'Ignorant peasants,' Kiwi snorted. 'Just carry on cooking in a hole in the ground, see if I care.'

'Such an oven deserves a woman's hand,' Andreas said.

'Don't you start.'

He filled the basin on the table outside his hut and began to wash. From the Communist side came the sound of drill. He glanced up and saw two of his men laughing.

'Andrea, do something useful. Tell Niko and Taki to stop provoking the Communists. I don't want more fights.'

The process of merger still grated. Despite the invisible dividing line separating the two zones, each side was tempted, as now, to sneer at the other's peculiarities and boast of their own superiority. That Eleni and Petros were holding a teaching session gave him a stab of inadequacy. Their mornings were always well-organised.

Andreas returned with a grin on his face. 'Shall I ask her to come and read you a story?'

'Sod off.'

'What you want to do is send Petro off on a night raid and then go over and…'

'I don't have authority over Petro.'

'Ah, so you have had the idea?'

'No! How can I get it into your sex-mad brain that I didn't have a…' He wanted to say "ulterior motive" but his anger fizzled out into

74

'secret plan in joining with them?'

'You do enjoy seeing her so close, though?'

'No, actually, I don't.'

'Ah, because you prefer to dream, Kiwi. You can't handle reality. You know what is the ideal woman?'

'I'm sure you're going to tell me.'

'The one in your arms.'

'Thanks. Now clear off and check the sentries.'

Proximity had confused his feelings, although the link between the girl of his dream and the woman in full bloom was now evident. Her teaching, her control and readiness to work softened that hardness of her last visit. But she was the other side of a dividing line.

Not the line between the camps but marriage. Her marriage must have been arranged. And Petros never made any public show of affection. It was still an immovable fact. Not to mention, of course, he told himself as he went inside the hut, the small matter of her never having shown the slightest interest in him.

He re-read Alec's letter. That didn't cheer him, either. Though Dancy's outrage – and Alec's bland responses – had made him laugh, the implied threat from Dancy of an end to supply drops was worrying. They needed to do something soon to convince Cairo that the alliance made sense. Except that Cairo seemed only to want non-co-operation and quiescence.

Alec's other news was more disturbing. Cairo had intercepted German radio traffic from South West Crete. The building up of Souyia was as a base for 'cleansing' the whole area. Burnt villages were to be resettled with 'loyal' Greeks or Cretans from the north. Other settlements that proved recalcitrant would be 'punished.' Males over eighteen had to report for forced labour. Deportation to Germany was thought likely. And an SS Major Jacobi had been sent to implement this policy.

It all added to his irritation at the lack of action.

He translated the main points of the letter and walked to the dividing line. He held the paper up to Petros. And winced when Petros nodded Eleni to collect it.

'When he's read it, we need to discuss our response. At the table at lunchtime, tell him. Sorry, no, *ask*, him.'

He turned away before she could reply.

The long row of tables straddled the boundary. Little talk was exchanged across it. The men of each side were served by their own women. He tried to avoid his eyes following Eleni. If he failed, Andreas dug him with his elbow. He was aware of Petros' gaze on him.

'We should raid Souyia,' Petros said.

'It's an armed camp.'

'I meant by night.'

Andreas coughed in his ear. He shoved him away. 'To what purpose?'

'You have the letter. To let them know we're here.'

'I'd prefer them not to know. Yet.'

'So what do you propose to do? Nothing?'

Yiannis growled. Kiwi tried to stay calm. 'Hit and run. Until we're stronger.'

'We saw your running. When have you hit?'

The laughter from Petros' men struck a nerve.

'Moni, when you were too late… again.'

Eleni fumbled some plates on the table. Pavlos stood up and stalked off. Someone laughed. Petros rose, too. 'We're going to reconnoitre Souyia.'

'And I thought Communism was all talk and no action.'

'While you'll be staying here?'

Kiwi held up the tsikoudia bottle. 'Developing plans for co-operation.'

He remained with the bottle as the table emptied. At the far end Eleni wiped it. He pretended not to watch her.

'This won't work unless you try to make it,' she said.

He looked up in surprise. She was scraping a spillage.

'Did you tell Petros that?'

'He knows what must be done.'

'And orders everyone to do it. You think we haven't been waiting for any opportunity to hit Souyia? This is supposed to be a shared command.'

'Hasty decisions sometimes have to be taken.'

'Does that apply to your marriage?'

She scrubbed at a stubborn mark. 'The marriage was arranged before the War. When I was fifteen. There was no haste involved.'

'He wasn't after your dowry?'

She straightened up and her eyes flared. 'Petros is not a person who believes in that sort of thing.'

'Isn't fifteen a bit young?'

'It's our way, here. He was the village teacher. My parents thought him a good match.'

'Back home he'd have been arrested. What about you?'

'Your parents always arrange the marriage.'

'And what if it doesn't suit you?'

'You make the best if it.'

'You sound like my mother. She liked to suffer in silence. Most of the time.'

Eleni stopped and glared at him. 'You think there are choices for a woman whose family are dead?'

'It wasn't out of the frying pan into the fire?'

'Petros is a good man.'

'I'll take your word for it.'

'I regret nothing. We were forced apart twice – when the Party was banned, then by war. And then my family…'

'Yeah, sorry.' He pushed the bottle away. 'Excuse my rudeness. Your ways are none of my business. I'm from a different world.'

'True. But you came back to ours? To Kriti. Why?'

His eyes met hers. Did she really want to know? 'I came back because of you.'

She looked puzzled. 'But…? When you thought..?'

'For the past two years you've been in my head. Your voice. Your smile. That look of concern in your eyes. You never leave me.'

She shook her head. He held up the scrap of blue dress.

'Nor does this.'

'Stop. You mustn't…'

He shrugged and replaced the cloth in his pocket. 'No, you're right. It was all a mistake.'

'Yes. You must forget it.'

'I have… I came back to seek revenge on the Germans for what they had done to you.'

She seemed relieved at this. 'There are plenty more victims to avenge.'

'Indeed. And the freedom of Kriti to win.'

'So to return was not a mistake?'

'Far from it. Or the dream I carried of you.'

'Ah. You know you must banish your dream from here.'

'I will. It isn't necessary any more.'

'Good. I'm pleased to hear that.'

He looked her in the eye. 'Yes. Now I see the reality in front of me, I have no need of dreams.'

Her face clouded. She shook her head then hurried away. He stared at the table and closed his eyes. Shit.

Someone was shaking him. He shrugged them off.

'Kiwi… sheep in the low pasture have escaped. The katsikia have found them. They're taking them to Souyia.'

He peered with a bleary mind at Yiorgos. 'Where's Yianni? Andrea? The others?'

'Yiannis took Andoni and the rest to the heights to watch how the Communists approach Souyia.'

'Shit. Is Costis still here?'

He was. And Andreas, too. They would have to do.

'Yiorgo, we need a place for ambush.'

And before the sheep thieves ran into Petros' men. He didn't need more scorn. They would need guile, though, he realised as he surveyed his paltry force.

Eleni approached with two other armed women. He shook his head at her but she stared through him. 'Joint operations. That was the agreement.'

'I can't be answerable to Petro if anything…'

'I answer for myself.'

'Kiwi, we must go,' Yiorgos said.

'OK,' he sighed, indicating to Eleni the women's rifles. 'I hope they know how to use those things.'

She tapped the stock. 'This part's for knocking sense into bone-headed men.'

The last part of the scramble down to the track above the sea was hard-going but the women kept up. Where the thieves' route wound round a shallow valley Yiorgos found a place with enough tree cover for an ambush.

At least it was going to be a small-scale affair. Four harassed German soldiers struggled to herd the few dozen sheep that had fallen into their hands. Behind them a jeep carrying an NCO bumped over rocky ground it wasn't designed for. The Cretans' major problem would be how to catch the sheep.

However, Ari had brought a dog. It made him laugh for the first time since the alarm. 'You've done this sort of thing before?'

'It's always happening, Mr Kiwi. They think it's a wild dog, we get the sheep back – and no reprisals.'

Yes, reprisals. Then he saw who was in the jeep. Costis had seen, too. This changed things. He sighed, nodded to Costis and bid Ari prepare to let go the dog.

Sergeant Hahn risked standing up in the vehicle to berate his hapless shepherds. It lurched and threw him down. At that moment the dog swooped at the head of the flock, barking, milling them and then driving them past the desperate troops and back they way they'd come. Dust and curses swirled around the jeep. Hahn clambered up.

The soldiers' panic-stricken faces made clear what Hahn's shouting meant. They threw down their rifles and began to run after the sheep. Costis' shot stopped them.

Hahn turned, as if also puzzled by what it was, then pitched over the side into the dust. The soldiers hurled themselves into the scrub beside the track. Their rifles lay scattered out of their reach.

'Shall we finish 'em off?' Andreas grinned.

'No.'

'No?'

'They're unarmed.'

'That was never a protection for us,' Eleni said.

Her eyes had the coldness again. He gestured Yiorgos, Ari and several other men after the sheep. 'Catch them and take them back. Andrea, Costi, you others, cover me.'

'Kiwi, it's no time for heroics.'

'No, guns and boots. Come on.'

He waved a white handkerchief and stepped out onto the track. He hoped none of the Germans had pistols.

'Kamerad,' he called. 'No kaput if...'

He mimed removing belts and boots. 'If no kamerad...' He gestured to his covering force to fire high. A volley swept the trees. There was a pause then shouts of 'Kamerad' and Germans came out with their hands raised. Most were kids, shaking. They threw down belts and boots. He pointed along the track. They gave distrustful glances and bolted.

One of the women took aim. Eleni knocked her rifle down and snapped at her with a vehemence that took him aback.

'Joint action. No dissent,' she said to him.

He patted Costis' arm. Costis shrugged. 'It w-was n-no recompense. N-niko was w-worth ten of him.'

With Hahn's body in it, the stripped jeep was rolled over a cliff into the sea. Loaded with their booty the rescuers staggered back up the slopes. After their earlier exchanges he kept his distance from Eleni. He felt no sense of triumph. Andreas laughed and indicated the heavily-laden women to him. 'Kiwi, you know the advantage of a donkey over a woman?'

'I'm not sure I want to.'

'They're both equally stubborn and both can carry a good load, but only a donkey knows when to shut up.'

They trudged on in silence for a while. Shots in the far distance towards Souyia made them stop.

'Sounds noisy for a reconnaissance,' he heard Andreas say to Eleni.

'They know how to look out for themselves.'

'That's what I always say about Communists.'

'Do you have to make everything a joke?'

'Life is for enjoying, that's the differen...'

Their friction was playing on his nerves. 'Andrea, take Costi and check on the sheepfold.'

'Understood, Kiwi. Discretion is my middle name. And if his rude manners offend you, Eleni…'

'I'll know who taught him them.'

'Ouch. And don't forget what I told you, Kiwi.'

Andreas set off with a cheery wave. Eleni grimaced.

'What don't you have to forget? Some joke about women? Or Communists? Or both?'

It didn't seem wise to mention man-eaters. 'No joking in Petro's brand of Communism, is there?'

'The freedom of Kriti comes first.'

'Of course. But will he cheer up after that?'

'I'm not here to discuss my husband.'

'No, sorry. Again.'

This did bring a smile. They set off, too.

'How young those Germans were,' she said after a while.

'We're a… how would you say, an unimportant place?'

'A backwater? Thanks. Should we be offended?'

'They need the tough ones elsewhere. Like Russia.'

'I'd still have shot them.'

It was a matter-of-fact comment. He glanced at her.

'Why not? You have cause.'

'Yes, but I'd have been wrong.'

'You would?'

'We have to make a better world, when we can.'

'Is that the Party line?' he said and regretted it. But she smiled again and then surprised him further. 'I'm not fixed on the Party line.'

'Can't you be shot for saying that?'

'I told you, Kriti comes first.'

'Does Petros share your view?'

'Before the Party was banned there was more moderation. Then the Germans came. And after I found my family…'

'You *found* them?'

'Of course. I saw what you saw.'

It had never occurred to him before. 'Jesus. How?'

'From the mountain I heard shots. I had the lamb by then. I saw the smoke. I wanted to rush down and see but something told me not to. I sat and held the lamb until they left. Then I went down…'

He could see it now. He listened in silence.

'They were dead but the bodies were still smouldering. Before I could do anything the Germans came back.'

'Came back?'

'Others maybe.'

'They didn't see you?'

'No, I had time to hide. In the chimney. They caught the lamb. And killed that, too. Then stayed till dusk. Singing. Laughing. I wanted to scream at them to stop but I couldn't. I couldn't move…'

'You don't have to tell me…'

'It's all right. The stones of the house were still hot. Sticky… with soot. You understand? And wet. But worst of all were the petrol fumes. So heavy. I could hardly breathe.'

The nausea from the paraffin swept back at him.

'Then… they left. I must have sat there through the whole night. In the dark. Knowing that only a few metres away… In the morning I couldn't bear to look. I just ran. Ran until I dropped. Some shepherds found me way up near Kalli Lakki. They made me drink milk. Put me to bed. Only then did I start to cry.'

They'd stopped below a rock. The others trudged on ahead. He laid his hand on her arm. She glanced up at him with a wan smile. Tears coursed down her cheeks.

'Sorry.' She paused. 'No one asked before.'

He stared at her. She looked away.

'Better move,' she said, wiping her face, 'Or we'll be late.'

The ground became more broken and walking required care. He went on for some time with his own thoughts. Nothing in Crete was ever flat – or simple. They entered the trees above the camp. A breath of smoke on the wind brought back her courage and the shameful memories of his own loss.

'I was twelve when my dad died,' he said. 'But all *I* did was shout and scream.'

'You were young.'

'No, I was mad with him.'

'Mad with him? Why?'

'For leaving. Without giving me the chance to make things right. Now I'd never have the chance.'

'I don't understand. Make what right?'

'Two weeks before he died he'd accused me… of writing something on the wall of the graveyard. Names.'

'And had you?'

'Yeah. But I denied it. He didn't believe me. Never did. If I hadn't done it, he still wouldn't have believed me. So I got the strap and another lecture about how much of a disappointment I was to him. He didn't speak to me for days after that. Then he was dead. I wanted to go and hit his body. Beat him into coming back…'

'You didn't?'

'Only because my big brother locked me in the coal shed, in the dark.'

'That's awful. For how long?'

'Till I calmed down. Hours, I expect. I was covered in soot, too.'

'Did you blame yourself? For his death.'

'No. They said he'd had a bad heart for years. But I was a… you know, a horrible little… What would you call them?'

'Brat?' she smiled.

'Yeah. A little devil. Then I grew up into a big one.'

'Is your brother a brat, too?'

'Hardly. He's a priest. Same as my dad.'

'A priest? So you're the odd one out?'

He was glad to see her smile but affected a frown.

'It's no fun being called an "oddy".' He used the English word.

'An "oddy"? What's that? Not another strange creature, like your kiwi?'

'Quite different. And worse.'

'Oh, dear. Then it must be bad. Did your brother call you that as a punishment?'

'No. It was a girl. When I was fifteen. I suppose she was lucky they didn't force her to marry me.'

She raised her eyebrows but in amusement.

'Muriel Spink, her name was. The sound of her voice still makes me shiver.'

He murdered the whine of an adolescent girl. "You're an oddy, Dudley Watkins. Oddy, oddy, oddy…'

Eleni laughed again and shook her head. 'How terrible. Is an "oddy" worse than a brat?'

Her laughter gave her a lightness he'd not seen. 'It's not funny. I was a shy boy. Still am. Girls don't realise how sensitive we brats are underneath. "Oddy, oddy." Ugh.'

She laughed even more. And walked into Petros.

Kiwi felt the air chill. And a surge of resentment. Petros stood with folded arms, glaring at Eleni. Had he been waiting for them? There was soft menace in her husband's accusation. 'You left the camp.'

'Germans were stealing the sheep,' she said.

Petros' eyes swung onto him. They were slits. 'My people only accept orders from me.'

Eleni butted in before he could answer. 'I made Kiwi take me, Petro. You weren't here.'

Petros stared at him then gave her a curt nod of dismissal. Kiwi couldn't see her face. She strode past her husband into the camp. Petros' face remained blank as it regarded him. 'We must remain vigilant at all times.'

'I'll remind the sheep of that.'

The man's sharp gaze bored into him. Still in the glow from Eleni, he ignored it. And realised for the first time how insecure Petros was behind that shell.

'You have no wife in New Zealand?' Petros asked.

'Never found the right opportunity.'

'Our ways in Kriti are more… formal.'

It occurred to him that flippancy wouldn't help Eleni and he forced himself to apologise. 'Yeah. Don't mind me. I'm always rushing in and giving offence. Sorry.'

When they reached the fork at the edge of the camp Petros turned away without speaking. Suffused with both pleasure and guilt from talking to Eleni, Kiwi felt the need to offer recompense. 'Come and look at the guns. Take your share.'

Petros seemed to hesitate then nodded. They entered the camp and walked side by side to the pile of captured weapons and equipment. Petros laid a hand on his arm.

'We don't allow women on raids in case they're captured.'

With a pang he accepted the justice of the rebuke. 'I didn't think of that. I'll know next time. Anyway, how did you get on? We heard firing from Souyia.'

Petros squinted along the barrel of a rifle. 'Yes. We were seen.'

The matter-of-fact tone rekindled his irritation. 'You let yourselves be seen? Jesus.'

'We were taken by surprise.'

'Shit.'

Petros flinched. 'There was a working party outside the wire. We stumbled on them. A labourer ran towards us.'

'You should have run, too.'

'Like you would have done?'

'I wouldn't have got into a fight over that.'

'We had no choice.'

'Why not?'

'The guards shot him. We had to return fire.'

'Then what? Did they drive you off?'

'No. They forced the labourers back inside and raised the alarm. But we were gone by then.'

'That's a relief. And the man they shot?'

'We brought him away but he'd been too badly hurt.'

There was a pause. Kiwi sighed. 'You satisfied now? Should give them something to come after us for.'

'They already are coming.'

'Why?' He couldn't keep the anger from his voice. 'You didn't leave them a trail to follow?'

'Don't take me for a fool, Neo Zealandi.'

'Then what? I thought I was the reckless one.'

'We may have saved your life.'

'Thanks. I can't wait to know how.'

Petros seemed undeterred by his sarcasm. 'Before he died the labourer said to watch out. A force is being sent in two days time to probe the mountains above Koustoyerako. We're in its path.'

He stared at Petros. Why had the man held back the news? Was it in retaliation for Eleni? Or a compulsion to keep the upper hand? He indicated the camp.

'We'll have to shift all this higher up.'

Petros raised his eyebrows. 'You'd run again? What's wrong with meeting them below?'

'It's too open. They'll either...' He mimed "outflank". 'Or retreat and come back in greater force.'

'You've just had the nerve to criticise my withdrawal. Yet you'll allow them to drive us out?'

He refused to let Petros' scorn deflect him or be drawn into more folly like Moni. He stared the other down. 'No.'

'That's not the way it looks.'

'This time we're going to hit.'

'Indeed? Without confronting them? How?'

'By leading them on. Higher up towards Achlada. Where we'll meet them on our terms.'

Petros showed his surprise. Kiwi waited for the objection, more contempt. The reply was unexpected. 'Good. Yes, good, Neo Zealandi. It makes sense. We must ensure that together we can make it succeed.'

Petros turned and stumped off. Here was another marvel. For once, Eleni's husband had agreed with him.

Seven

Kiwi picked up the German column in the binoculars at the foot of the deep, V-shaped valley. He scanned for scouts but he couldn't see any. The ruse had worked.

Petros came from deploying their men as they'd agreed, in the trees just below the head of the pass. Kiwi handed him the glasses. 'They're not expecting opposition. They must believe we simply fled.'

Giving the camp the air of a hasty departure hadn't been difficult. Much evidence of women and children had been left, the same type of effects that were scattered on the trail up towards Achlada. To this site for the ambush.

'Not much more than platoon-strength,' Petros said, handing back the glasses. 'They under-estimate us.'

'Good. Let's hope they're not right.'

'My own men have always proved themselves so far.'

'As long as we don't open fire too soon.'

Restraining his excitement was difficult. This was what he'd come back for. His policy of holding off until they were ready seemed to have lulled the Germans into complacency. Yet if he wasted this opportunity… Galatas crossed his mind.

'There is one other thing,' he said. 'In the heat of action, both of us can't be giving orders.'

'So?'

'I've told my men your word is final.'

'You're too kind.'

'It's the only way. And you are the teacher.'

Before Petros could retort, Yiorgos bounded in with a broad grin, followed by a panting and dishevelled Alec. Alec shook Petros' hand and stared at the clumps of men scattered among the tress. 'Bugger me.' He used English. 'What is all this?'

'Our first major joint operation. That's what I sent Yiorgos to tell you. I wasn't pressing you to take part.'

'That's not why I've come.'

'From the scowl on your face it's not to bring good wishes, either.'

'I need to speak to you, Kiwi. Alone.'

'Is there a problem,' Petros asked, 'that you don't wish me to hear?'

'Sorry, Petro,' he shrugged as Alec drew him aside. 'I think I've been a naughty boy again.'

He could feel Petros' scathing look following them.

'OK, so what have I done?' he asked Alec.

'Cairo aren't happy about this collaboration.'

'That is a surprise. I thought they'd be delirious.'

'Dancy says London want it stopped.'

'They've chosen a good moment to tell us.'

'I had hoped to warn you in time.'

'We're about to do what I was sent here for. I suppose Dancy would prefer us to stop fighting.'

'It's not a preference, it's an order.'

'We can't do this alone.'

'I'm sorry, Kiwi. It's a blanket instruction. Anything that could help the long-term Communist cause is on hold.'

'This is about Crete. And the next few hours…'

'Dancy specifically named you on the order.'

'Tell him he can come and sort out the Commies later.'

'Kiwi, I'm all for taking the piss, but…'

'Then do so. Send Dancy one of your obscene notes. Tell him the code means I've got the message. How's he going to know any different?'

'It may be safer to keep quiet.'

'In that case clear off now with Yiorgos. What you don't see won't incriminate you. We can always claim the message didn't make it in time. Or blame the code.'

'You're taking a big risk.'

'Yes, with the enemy. To free Crete. You think some paper-pusher in Cairo's a bigger one?'

He stalked back to Petros. 'New British order. Before every attack I have to apply in writing. Ten days in advance.'

'You take pleasure in breaking rules, Neo Zealandi?'

'I take pleasure in getting things done. Come on.'

The Germans halted on the first of the series of folds up which the valley floor rose. Kiwi watched an officer in an eye patch briefing a small group of men. If that was Jacobi, he could see no SS insignia.

This group pushed on ahead of the main body. The officer wasn't a fool. He'd reduced the chances of being caught in an ambush. If his advance guard spread out across the hillside, he might eliminate it altogether. They'd be bound to stumble on the hidden Cretans well before the main body could be encircled.

He held his breath. Once their presence was known they could pick off a few Germans. They could have done that by using Petros' original tactic of meeting the enemy below the village. And stayed undisturbed for longer in the camp. He feared a return to former disputes.

However, the Germans were keeping to the track. Even though its broken surface made progress difficult, they must have decided it was easier than ploughing through the spiky maquis of the slopes.

'Change of plan, Petro,' he said. 'We have to let this advance guard up and over the ridge without hindrance. To draw the rest of them fully into the net.'

'Yes, I had assumed that, too, Neo Zealandi.'

'Send Pavlo and ten men to wait for them over the top. And tell everyone to hold their fire until I say.'

Petros' face was stone. 'Until you say?'

'Sorry, until you give the order. I'll pass it to my men.'

As he scurried round briefing the waiting fighters he saw they were all as wound-up as he was. So long as no one tried to emulate Pavlos' attack on Moni. It wouldn't take much for someone to loose off a premature shot and blow it all. Had Petros picked up the implication in his changed order that Pavlos might prove too rash?

The Germans came on. The gap between their two bodies of troops widened. The Cretans had pulled back higher to lessen the likelihood of detection but it would only take a flash of sun on metal or a sharp-eyed soldier to undo them. However, the steepness of the ascent and the scree-strewn path made the Germans toil with heads down. They passed the silent Cretans without any sign of alarm. Behind, the officer led his main force upwards.

Kiwi watched the advance party crouch as they reached the crest of the ridge. Ahead they would see the empty plain. Then they were over. One turned back and waved to the following group. Kiwi breathed out.

The main body trudged on up. It seemed hard going. They might have done plenty of marching but the high mountains found out even the fittest. The head of the column came level with him and Petros. He saw the black eye-patch on the officer. That definitely wasn't an SS major.

Shots rang out from above the ridge.

'The damn fool,' he shouted at Petros and stepped out from the trees. 'Now!' he screamed and fired a burst from the bren. Volleys from both slopes deafened him.

The officer and several others fell but some of these troops weren't kids and they put up a steady retaliatory fire. They also had an eye for cover in the boulder-strewn slopes and withdrew in groups down the hill. He glimpsed the officer being dragged away.

'If only you'd brought the machine gun,' Petros said.

'If only we had the ammunition for it.'

They wouldn't have needed it if Pavlos hadn't fired too soon. It sounded as if he was heavily engaged up above. Kiwi's own men were also showing themselves too much in their eagerness to close in for the kill, one which, now, was unlikely to be complete.

'Hold it,' he shouted. 'Costi, take ten men and see them on their way. Pick off any you can but don't run risks.'

'Take some of mine, too. Tasso, pick ten and,' Petros glared at him, 'follow the orders of Costis.'

Kiwi glowered after the pursuit. From beyond the ridge there still came a flurry of gunfire. And from the isolated shots close by, he realised that the Cretans were finishing off the wounded. He cursed himself for not warning them against that.

'Let any walking wounded go,' he called out.

He received several scowls for his trouble.

'Only finish off those too bad to move.'

Yiannis had his knife to the throat of a blood-flecked German. This one *was* a kid. Whimpering for mercy.

'Put the knife away, Yianni,' he said. 'Unless he's beyond help.'

'They're all fucking beyond help.'

'Even so… Is he wounded?'

'Only with the blood of others while he cringed in the bushes. The fucker doesn't deserve to live.'

He remembered the young soldier at Asyfou. 'No, but ones like him are more use to us alive. Keep your knife for an important job.'

Yiannis forced the lad to remove his boots and kicked him on his way down the track. 'With luck he'll run into Costi. I could have saved us some fucking bullets.'

'At least Costi will only need one.'

'Fuck off.'

He counted twenty-one dead Germans.

'And another two hundred up there with Pavlo by the sound of it,' Andreas snorted. 'What's he doing?'

'We better go and see.'

'Disappointed, Kiwi?'

'I'd hoped for the lot but you know how it works. And we could have had more, if I wasn't so soft.'

When he told Andreas about Yiannis and the kid, he expected a joke but all that came was a dull shrug. He showed his puzzlement. 'I should have let him do it? Cold-blooded murder?'

'Yiannis would be hot enough.'

'What's that supposed to mean?'

'You weren't to know.'

'Know what?'

'After the Battle. When the death squads went down the valley from Platania, in Kirtomades all his relatives were shot.'

Up above he found a stand-off. Pavlos' men had allowed the advance guard to pass but had been seen. The Germans were in cover among rocks and Pavlos lacked the numbers to dislodge them. He had one dead and two with slight wounds.

'Sorry, Petro,' Pavlos said. 'We should have taken more care...'

'Can't be helped,' Kiwi told him. 'The main body had slowed up too much on the climb.'

Petros seemed surprised by this. His own tone sounded conciliatory. 'What now, Neo Zealandi? Shall we rush them?'

'No, if you get men up there...' He indicated the scree slopes above the pass. '...you can push them out. They'll have to flee across the plateau and be in the open.'

Petros directed several men to scramble up the scree. Sure enough, their fire panicked the exposed Germans. This time, however, Pavlos' men were too slow and the Germans managed to scamper clear across the wide rocky plain. Kiwi gritted his teeth but said nothing. There was no escape for the fugitives. They were being forced higher into the mountains. Nevertheless it could be a lengthy pursuit, until their ammunition – or the Cretans' – ran out.

He left Petros to it and scanned the lower sections of the valley. The firing from below was sporadic. Costis must be stalking his targets. Being hunted like that would further dent German morale.

Around him the stripping of the bodies and gathering of weapons went on. Andreas had the dead dragged to one of the fissures in the rocky slope and pitched in. He shuddered at the thought of the depthless dark and then laughed at himself for his squeamishness.

Practicalities were more important now. They would have to re-locate the camp higher up, which meant that in a few months' time winter would pose a bigger strain. They'd need to disperse a number of the women and children among relatives in distant villages.

That brought back Eleni. Memories of two days earlier had been pushed aside in the hurry to dismantle the camp and set up the ambush. Since Petros' curt nod had sent her into the camp he'd hardly seen her. She'd not looked at him and he wondered if she regretted letting her guard down over the confidences she'd revealed.

He couldn't forget her laughter. That *was* a different woman. The girl he'd first met. He screwed up his face. She *was* still a girl. How old, barely twenty? Yet with Petros she'd become hardened, the joy squeezed out of her. All that potential deadened by the demands of war and politics. He felt a sadness for her. And a longing for more laughter.

He made himself stop. It was foolish, dangerous, futile. The task ahead was formidable. Today they'd barely started. He saw again the waves of Mountain troops coming at them up Red Hill before the line broke in front of Galatas. Compared to that this had been a jaunt. And, from what Alec had said, if they pressed on it would be in defiance of orders. In collusion with those his political masters regarded as the next enemy. He couldn't imagine Dancy reacting to that with equanimity.

He was glad to see Andreas come grinning onto the crest. 'What's made you so cheerful, Andrea? Didn't leave some women behind, did they?'

'No, it's the sight of you standing there like some love-lorn ram looking for his lost ewe.'

'Thanks, I'm touched by your comparison.'

'You must stop always thinking about women.'

'Me?'

'Since we joined with the Communists you can't take your mind off her.'

'Rubbish. I was thinking about something else.'

'How to get rid of the husband? Want me to tip him into one of these pits? More permanent than a night raid.'

'Don't talk nonsense.'

'It's been done before.'

'You're not serious? You haven't…?'

'Me? No, of course not. What do you take me for? You think I'd wish to be saddled permanently with a widow? But one hears things. For you, what's the choice? That, or becoming a monk like your father.'

'He wasn't a monk.'

'Being a monk's in the mind, believe me.'

He didn't want to know. The sound of shooting reverberated from the plateau.

'Is it really? Better go and see how Petro is getting on. I thought he'd have finished them off by now.'

Petros hadn't. At the far side the plain dipped into a shallow bowl a few hundred yards across and surrounded by stunted trees. In the centre of this sheltered spot stood two round stone mitatos. The sight stirred a memory. In his twelve-months on the run these cheese-making huts had often given a safe refuge.

Petros' men lay around the rim of the bowl and peppered the stonework of one of the huts. To little effect, it appeared. One dead German lay on the slope, another close to the door. The rest must be inside. Petros gestured to him in frustration. 'Your plan pushed them out all right, Neo Zealandi.'

'They won't be moving from there.'

'No, but how long will we be stuck here before they starve to death or give up?'

'They won't give up,' Pavlos said. 'They know what will happen.'

He glared at Pavlos but tried to stay calm. 'They're only in the one hut?'

'The other's blocked up,' Petros said. 'And before you say, we have used it as cover to get close. But the only windows are those slits at the front. Too narrow for a grenade and almost impossible to get a shot through.'

'Costis might manage it.'

'He's not here, is he?'

'You tried the door?'

'Walking up to it and knocking, you mean?'

'No one's tested its strength?'

'Those mitato doors are thick and solid. And the window slits mean they can shoot at anyone forcing it.'

'You're not going to rush them, then?'

'I've told you before not to take me for a fool.'

The sight of Eleni walking off with her head down flipped back. If this disagreement continued, they'd be at each other's throats again. He jumped up. 'I'm going for a look.'

'You don't trust my judgment?'

'It's not that. Fresh pair of eyes.'

He reloaded his revolver, avoiding Petros' eyes. 'I worked for a building company in New Zealand before the War. There's often a weak point.'

He ran at a crouch round the rim. A bullet kicked up dust nearby. So they were still alert. In their place he'd stay put and hope a larger force from Souyia would come to rescue them. It wasn't that fantastical a hope. As Pavlos had observed, if they surrendered, they'd fear their fate.

He worked his way closer using the empty hut as cover. He waved up to Petros and hoped Andreas' presence would ensure they didn't shoot *him*. That would be a way of disposing of a love rival. He told himself he wasn't a love rival and to stop thinking like Andreas. To avoid distractions. All that did was recall Eleni.

He peered at the thick, uneven stone blocks of the mitato and felt a twinge of shame at his lie. Some expert on construction. As a clerk in the firm's offices. But he could see the cheese-hut was solidly-made. And a way to climb on top.

He stamped on the broad slabs of the flat roof. They didn't give. Several men might shift the ventilation slab but the gap was too narrow even for the point of a rifle barrel.

Lying on his stomach he peered over the front edge. The door was hidden by the overhang. The window slits weren't. He saw the pistol barrel just in time and jerked back as the shot rang.

Shouts from the rim of the bowl were telling him to come away. Several figures gestured, too. He gave a wave of acknowledgment and jumped down.

From the left-hand front corner he could see the window slit beyond the door. He fired at it and saw stone fragments split off.

'Surrender! Kamerad! Kamerad!' he shouted.

A bullet spat on the stone by his head in reply. Their shooting was better than his. Again he heard the cries from the rim. He took out a grenade. He held it up for the Cretans to see. 'Covering fire! A burst!' He moved back.

They understood and bullets splattered on the stonework. When it stopped he darted to the door, laid the grenade and scurried back into cover. A shot followed him.

The grenade blew. Pistol out, he dodged to the door through the smoke and kicked at it. It didn't budge. He glimpsed the gun barrel in the right-hand slit. As he ducked he slipped. From both sides bullets kicked up splinters of stone around him.

Something punched his left shoulder. The impact threw him away from the door. His arm went numb and his legs felt leaden. All he could do was roll away and flatten himself behind the body of the dead German.

A hail of shots followed him. The German body jerked. Then a fusillade of fire broke behind him from up on the rim. He heard a scream from the hut and their shooting subsided. A call nearer was Yiannis.

'Don't move, Kiwi, we're coming.'

He tried to shout 'No' but nothing came. He couldn't move either, or see much – just bare ground a few feet to his side. He cursed his stupidity. He'd only confirmed what Petros had known and caught a stone splinter for his recklessness. Who was the fool now? The thought of Petros' justified disdain made him grit his teeth.

The firing from the hut stopped. Instead he caught a steady beat of bullets on the stonework. The rhythm of pebbles in a tin. Costis had arrived.

A stab shot through his back. He tried to scream but Yiannis' grip on his neck choked off the sound. His back flamed as he was bumped face down across the stony ground. Then he was in the shelter of the second hut. Through the convulsions he heard the fusillade of Cretan fire resume. He tried to roll over onto his back but the splinter jabbed.

'Lie still, Kiwi,' Yiannis said.

'I'll be all right. Just get this piece of damn stone out of my shoulder so we can finish the job.'

Their grunting breaths stopped. Andonis' voice muttered, in annoyance, it seemed. 'Piece of stone? This is no piece of stone, Kiwi. It's a bullet. And it's still in there. You'll need a doctor to finish this job.'

He groaned, in anger. He *had* made a fool of himself. For the same old reason. Trying to show he knew best. He closed his eyes. That brought back Eleni's concerned face. He forced himself to focus on what was being done to him.

'This will hurt,' Andonis said, shifting him to wind the bandage under his chest. It did, in waves.

He heard Andreas' voice close by, teasing. 'Don't worry, Kiwi, women like a nice wound.'

'This isn't a nice wound,' Andonis retorted then the bandage was jerked tight. The pain made him cry out.

'Sorry,' Andonis said, 'got to stop the bleeding.'

He sensed Andonis stand up and became aware of others.

'Why can you never do as you're told, Neo Zealandi? Any more crazy ideas?'

Helplessness and shame doused his irritation. 'No, you were right, Petro. Apologies. Again.'

Petros' acknowledgment sounded grudging. Just like his dad's. Before he could shrink further into himself he remembered the ventilation slab. 'Fire.'

'What d'you think we've been doing?' Pavlos said.

Andreas' voice no longer mocked. 'Jesus Christ, he's delirious.'

He went to twist to see more but a spasm hit. That familiar childhood feeling of trying to explain away another misdemeanour deflated him. He grunted at them, his words coming in spasms. 'No... Light fire... against the door. If you... block the ventilation slit... on the roof...'

Something thumped his shoulder and the judder stopped him. His back started to numb once more. Petros' voice came and sounded more measured. 'Perhaps not so crazy, Neo Zealandi. We'll see.'

Things blurred. The bustle of activity receded. He became conscious of Andreas' boots. His friend squatted on his haunches regarding him with a grin. That did goad him out of his torpor.

'What's up, Andrea? And no, it didn't happen because I was distracted by thinking about women.'

'About *women*, Kiwi? Why would I ever think it was more than one?'

'Sod off.'

'However, you will need a nurse now.'

'I'd prefer peace and quiet.'

'It's the perfect cover. The husband never suspects a thing…'

'Andrea, if I recover from this…'

'When, Kiwi, it'll break her heart if… Ah.'

'What's happening?'

'Your brilliant plan is working. Don't try to look. A white flag has appeared from the window… The door is opening. Someone's coming out.'

'Just don't let Pavlos shoot them.'

So the job was done, was it? But look what he'd landed himself with. You bloody fool, was all that his mind kept saying. You bloody fool.

His breathing came in shallow gasps. His eyelids felt too heavy to stay open. Oh, God, I'm going, he told himself.

All for showing off. He wanted to call out to Andreas to pull him back but nothing came. What a waste, he thought. What a bloody waste.

Eight

It was dark. He wasn't sure where he was. Lying, face down, on a ledge of rock, it felt like. Shadows and light flickered on a rough wall. He could smell damp and wood smoke and sensed a roof above him. From somewhere nearby came voices. He strained to hear. Andreas?

'He must have a doctor.'

'With Germans everywhere? You won't get a doctor through. And it risks leading them here.'

That was Petros. Getting his priorities right, as usual. Who were they discussing. A prisoner?

'We h-have to t-try,' he heard Costis butt in. 'Every m-movement f-forces the bullet f-further down his back.'

'He was fucking lucky it was a ricochet,' Yiannis said. 'A direct shot would have fucking killed him.'

It wasn't a prisoner! Why were they panicking? He heard Andreas again. In far too grave a tone for Andreas.

'Nevertheless, without a doctor, he'll die.'

This was nonsense. He swung his left leg off the ledge.

'Stop fussin…'

A blade sliced down his back. The pain swept at him in waves. Angry shouts resounded in his head. Then he was being eased back onto the ledge with a gentleness that surprised him. He closed his eyes. The waves settled, to a dull irritation. 'OK, OK, you know best.'

'Actually we don't, Kiwi,' Andreas' voice said. 'The wound is more serious than we thought.'

'Yes, I heard, but…'

'The bullet…'

'Will have to come out. So just get on with it.'

'There are practical difficulties…'

Petros this time. Typical. Always objections.

'What difficulties? You've got a knife, haven't you?'

'But no doctor. And…'

'Who needs a doctor? You're used to cutting up sheep. Where's the difference?'

That silenced them. Then he heard Yiannis. 'Usually the fucking sheep is dead, Kiwi.'

'You want me to wait?'

There was a scream from across the cave.

'Is that someone practising?'

'This is no joke, Neo Zealandi.'

Now he was being told off, as well, was he? They sounded as if they'd moved away from him. He levered his head up gingerly to see them and make them do as he said.

'Get a move on, then. Who's the best with a knife?'

He made out shadowy figures and caught mutters. Then the panic in Yiannis' voice. 'No, no, fuck off. I'm only a fucking butcher.'

'Fine,' he called out. 'That's kiwi for surgeon.'

'It's madness, Neo Zealandi. Even for a doctor the job, out here, would be dangerous.'

These objections were fraying his nerves. 'Don't fret, Petro. What's the worst he can do?'

'Kiwi, no. Fuck it. If I should kill you, I'd…'

'Get a medal, from Major Dancy in Cairo.'

Another cry from over by the prisoners cut off any response. He heard Andreas laugh. 'It's New Zealand humour, Petro. Dulls the pain.'

'If you say so, but it doesn't help. Send for a doctor, if you must, but the nearest loyal one is in Kamaria.'

'There's no fucking time, is there?' Yiannis said. 'I'll do it. With this.'

He glimpsed the long blade and ornate handle. The knife Yiannis had been about to use on the German captive. He swallowed. Maybe he should have kept quiet. Petros' voice broke in, querulous still, now addressing Yiannis, he assumed. 'Have you done this before?'

'Only in a fight,' Andreas said.

'Then I won't be held responsible if anything does go wrong.'

Oh, Jesus, Petro, he thought. Don't let Dancy have you up on a charge on my account. Shall I give you a chitty to say…? But spasms racked him as he was carried and set on a wider slab of stone. Andonis barked orders for water, cloths and more light. He watched Yiannis thrust the knife into the fire.

'I suppose it's too late to change my mind?' he said more to avoid thinking. The anger that aroused in Petros came as a shock.

'Shut up, Neo Zealandi. Shut up!'

Petros stalked off. Andreas pressed a piece of cloth into his right hand. 'Saved it from your tunic,' he whispered. 'Don't worry, the husband's not looking.'

For the first time he felt a shiver of fear. He tried to make his mind go blank. A piece of wood appeared in his eyeline. In Andreas' fingers.

'Bite on this. No nurse to hold your hand, I'm afraid, but you can always imagine…'

When he opened his mouth to retort the wooden gag was jammed in. He bit into it. Olive wood.

'Can you trace its course?' he heard Andonis ask.

Yiannis' reply sounded too hesitant for reassurance.

'It's gone deep. I think the fucking kidneys are somewhere here. If I make an incision…'

A paroxysm lifted him. His teeth ground into the gag.

'Hold still, Kiwi, or you never know what he'll chop off,' Andreas said.

Hands tightened their grip on his arms and the pain came again in waves. He caught a further whisper from Andreas. 'No mistakes, Yianni, please. Without him we're lost.'

'Lost. A lost soul,' his father had said. 'That's what you'll become if you don't change your ways…'

The twelve year-old boy leaned against the doorpost and stared at the gaunt, dead face set on the pillow, as severe now as it had been in life. The white sheet drawn to its chin only emphasised the greyness of the corpse. The accusation echoed in his head. Above the bed the embroidered 'Bless this House' added a further barb to his father's condemnation.

His mother knelt with her forehead against the side of the mattress. She straightened and looked at him. Her face looked wet. Before she could speak he turned and was running down the hall...

... was swinging the kitbag onto his shoulder as he turned away and strode down the path. At the white wicket gate his mother's voice from the door cut into the pounding of his head. 'You know your father hated war. If he was here, he'd have tried to stop you going, you know that, don't you?'

Of course he knew. Why did she have to keep going on? He unlatched the garden gate. He wanted to run but the voice pulled him back. 'Your brother's grown too soft, or he'd have put a stop to this foolishness...'

He was being marched towards the door of the coal shed. The handle was ingrained with black dust. Not the dark. Anything but that. He was sorry... In future he would behave... He fought to wrench himself free... Yes, next time would be different. He'd show...

But how could there be a next time? He'd ruined everything, hadn't he? Something was forcing him down towards the dark.

From somewhere his mother's self-pitying cry echoed.

'What am I supposed to do now? Don't expect sympathy if you get shot. Your father always said you'd end up in hell...'

Everything went black.

If this was hell, shouldn't it be hot? The rough rock against his cheek smelt familiar. His whole body ached. The dark seemed impenetrable.

He tried closing his eyes and re-opening them but it made no difference. He heard a groan. Were there other damned souls here? Then a snore. He remembered a ledge. He still lay face down. Easing out his right arm he touched damp stone close to. The darkness lightened.

His mind felt clogged. Images from home groped around in it. His back was cold and numb. That couldn't be from the strap? Hadn't he heard talk of an operation? Had it taken place? And how long had he been in this position? Minutes? Hours? If so, why hadn't the buggers covered him up? He could catch his death like this.

He began to drift away again. Low voices floated from somewhere close. He couldn't tell whose. Why were they whispering? Was it because of him? He lay still and strained to hear. One voice was Pavlos'.

'Make your move now. While he's... If you're the undisputed leader...'

Talking to whom? But the other only went 'Shh.' Pavlos didn't seem to take the hint. 'I still say sharing their camp was a mistake.'

'A means to an end. You have to take the long view.'

Petros. Spouting politics as usual. Shouldn't they be sorting out what happened next? He went to protest but Pavlos did first. 'We can't trust the British...'

'We only need to trust their supplies. And their radio. Use any means available, you know that.'

'While People's Democracy in the South West remains on hold?'

'Everything is on hold as long as the Germans remain here. I told you, a means to an end. The day will come.'

They must have moved away because their voices faded. He tried to concentrate on what they'd said but he couldn't find the will. He wondered whether he'd dreamed that, too. His body felt heavy again.

Something roused him. Sounds of panic. Pale light gleamed above his head. He heard men grabbing rifles and boots scraping on the rock. The sound faded.

Waiting for the pain to strike, he dragged his head round to see. There was only a dull twinge.

One or two shapes came back and flopped down by the fire. After a while he caught gruff greetings and made out three figures struggling in, bent under packs. He hoped they'd brought blankets. With a start he realised that the newcomers were women.

'There are Germans everywhere,' one said.

Something jabbed his back. That was Eleni. What was she doing here? He held his breath to listen.

'The whole garrison is out on the rampage. You must have hit them hard. They shoot at any movement.'

'You shouldn't have come,' Petros' voice said.

The censure in the man's tone grated. Eleni sounded as if she'd ignored the complaint. 'We've brought you ammunition and food. You need to move higher.'

'And the people?'

'Already on their way. Have you had casualties?'

He didn't hear Petros' muttered reply. He did the note of panic in Eleni's gasp. 'Kiwi?'

Again he missed the answer but not her stifled cry.

'Where is he?'

He closed his eyes and lay still. Her footsteps approached. Petros' fretful tone followed her. 'It was his own fault. He wouldn't listen, as usual.'

She stood over him without speaking. He was conscious that only the bandage covered his naked back. Your own bloody fault, Petro, he thought. If you'd not been so busy spouting politics, I'd be covered up.

Petros' voice came again, this time sounding more conciliatory. 'We've sent for a doctor.'

The reference puzzled him. He had a vague recollection of discussion about a doctor. Hadn't there been some problem? He was about to ask but Eleni spoke. 'How long's he been like this?'

Shouldn't you be asking me, he complained, before Petros' response stunned him. 'Twenty-four hours.'

Through his shock he heard Eleni catch her breath. Gratitude surged for her concern. But what the hell was going on? Why hadn't they woken him?

She moved away. In his right hand he felt the piece of blue cloth. And was staring at the bodies of her family.

His eyes shot open. Petros, arms folded, faced Eleni. As at the camp after the sheep rescue, after she'd related the story of finding those bodies... He called out quickly, 'Any chance of a drink for a kiwi?'

Pandemonium. The amount of cheering shocked him. He saw grins. Andreas held out a bowl of water. For a moment again he was back at Askyfou. He winced as he tried to lap from the bowl. 'You think I might be allowed to sit up? All this crawling is giving me neck-ache.'

He was eased upright. The pain in his back remained dull. He let Andreas steady his right arm and hold the bowl to his lips. He regarded the anxious faces as he drank. Eleni stared at him, with a strange look of fury. He wondered what he'd done wrong now. And noticed how Petros' eyes didn't leave her.

The tension made him feign light-heartedness. 'So where's this bullet, Yianni?'

Yiannis balanced it between fore-finger and thumb.

'Came to rest centimetres from a fucking artery.'

'My dad always said the devil takes care of his own. Getting shot in the back will take some living down.'

'At least you're alive.'

He peered across at Eleni. The accusation in her face made him glance at Petros and he saw the husband's eyebrows raise. He couldn't work out the reason for her attitude. It did cut his flippancy. 'Yeah, well, not through too much commonsense.'

He changed the subject. 'Did I hear somebody mention food? At this rate I'm going to starve to death.'

Eleni stumped away and went to rummage in one of the packs. Her reaction still had his head in a whirl. He watched Petros' gaze continue to follow her. Andreas' voice intervened in his ear. 'What did I tell you about a nice wound? Pity she couldn't hide it from the husband.'

'She didn't sound too pleased to me.'

'Ha, ha, Kiwi. You really are an innocent where women are concerned. Let me tell you…'

'Go to hell.'

'That's where we've been for the last day. But I'm glad to see you're your own miserable self again…'

'Andrea…' he began but it felt like too much trouble to argue. His shoulder ached now, though the fog in his head worried him more. What was Andreas trying to say? It didn't seem credible. He lay back and closed his eyes.

He was being shaken. Bloody Andreas. He resisted.

'I told you, leave me alone.'

'Kiwi,' Andreas whispered. 'Sit up?'

'I don't want any more lectures about women…'

'No. It's Yiorgos. He's brought news. You need to hear it. Petros says you're not to be disturbed.'

Some recollection forced him awake. 'I'm OK. Tell him to bring Yiorgo here.'

With Andreas' support he struggled to sit.

'Kiwi's up,' Andreas called. 'Don't keep Yiorgo down there.'

He studied Yiorgos' gaze as the lad approached. Yiorgos' eyes showed the same horror, he remembered, that they had at the news of Niko's execution. To lighten the mood, he indicated the swathe of bandage across his chest.

'It was covering my mouth, Yiorgo, to shut me up, but it slipped.'

'I'm thankful to find you alive, Kiwi,' Yiorgos said with a grave face. 'Very thankful.'

'You might look it, then. What's up? Not seen a wounded donkey before?'

'Many times. And always the result of their own stubbornness.'

'You could try to show some sympathy.'

Yiorgos' face remained serious. 'Unfortunately, sympathy is in short supply.'

'What do you mean? Why are you here?'

'Mr Aleko has had news from Cairo…'

A sense of foreboding kept him flippant. 'That'll be bad, so let's forget it.'

'We should hear him, Neo Zealandi,' Petros said.

He made to retort but his back jagged. Yiorgos went on: 'Mr Aleko's is not the worst.'

'There's something worse than Dancy? That is worrying.'

His attempt at facetiousness fell flat. He changed his tone. 'Come on, Yiorgo, tell us.'

Yiorgos glanced at the assembled crowd. 'I had to avoid crossing Omalos. The routes into it are blocked. There are spotter planes and a big troop movement. Even the entrances to Agia Irini were guarded. It was necessary to circle to the West. They're everywhere.'

'So?' Pavlos put in. 'We're leaving, as soon as…'

A jerk of the head indicated who the problem was. That brought an uncharacteristic sneer from Yiorgos. 'I wasn't thinking of you. I kept coming across the evidence of the Germans' passage.'

Kiwi's heart jumped. 'Reprisals, you mean?'

'Not systematic. Just anything in their path.'

His eyes met Eleni's. He wrenched them away. Into Petros'. The husband's face was a mask.

'Go on, Yiorgo,' he said.

'The first was above Prines. You know the farmstead of Uncle Kotsi? I heard firing and hid in the trees. I could see a cordon closing round the house. They were shooting it up. I edged along to be able to see the front. The house seemed empty so I hoped Uncle Kotsi was away. Then a white cloth appeared at the door.'

Faces turned towards where their German prisoners lay. He guessed what was coming. Yiorgos went on. 'Uncle Kotsi came out slowly. Stood with his hands up.'

Yiorgos paused and himself glanced across to the prisoners. 'There was a burst of fire and he fell back into the doorway. His dog appeared and began to whimper beside the body. They shot that, too. They smashed anything that would break. Then they threw grenades in. When the house was ablaze they went off, laughing.'

There was silence. A prisoner coughed.

'Nothing in their path escaped. In Tsiskiana the houses were burning but I think the people had fled in time.'

Yiorgos looked hard at him but didn't seem to see him.

'It was the same up this way. Where the path comes down from the village I came across the body of a man beneath that of his donkey. Who, it was impossible to tell. And I had to hurry on.'

'The fucking bastards,' Yiannis said.

'So they were not taking prisoners?'

Kiwi ignored the heavy emphasis in Petros' question. Something Yiorgos had said was nagging at him. 'Your message from Aleko. You said it was less bad, Yiorgo?'

'No, only that what I saw here was far worse.'

'So this one's bad enough? Tell us, then.'

Yiorgos exhaled slowly and looked him in the eye.

'There is to be an offensive in the Greek islands…'

Something stabbed his back. 'But not this one?'

'Leros. The eastern Aegean. Kriti is being sidelined.'

'Shit… Shit… Shit…'

The grinding of his teeth set off more spasms in his back. Angry groans and curses echoed his own.

'It may be worse than that, Mr Aleko thinks.'

'Worse? What's Dancy going to do, ditch us altogether?'

'Order men from here to Leros.'

The groans turned to cries of protest. Before he could speak Petros shouted: 'Quiet!'

The silence bristled.

'None of my men is going anywhere,' Petros went on. 'Not to serve some capitalist adventure. And if the British try to make us go, we will be at war with them.'

'Major Dancy might like that.'

'Your 'humour' is again out of place, Neo Zealandi.'

'You think it was a joke?'

'I don't care. Just go and leave us your supplies.'

'Sorry, no can do.'

Petros' face tautened into a sneer. 'You'll refuse to leave us anything?'

'Sure.'

'What is this? More British treachery?'

He let himself savour the mounting indignation. 'You know I'm a New Zealander.'

'Your treachery is the same.'

His wound jarred. The insult served him right. He met Petros' glare. 'What can I leave you…? When we also will refuse to go.'

The cheers, he noted with some relief, were not only from his own men. He felt the need to heal the breach.

'You're right, Petro. The task is here. And from what Yiorgos has seen, it's just become more urgent.' He clenched his jaw against the pain. 'Our aim must be to drive them out of South West Kriti. After all, their attention will be elsewhere, too.'

'You make it sound easy, Neo Zealandi.'

'We've shown that we're a match for them. So long as we fight on our terms.'

'And then?' Pavlos asked.

'We'll have created a base here for the liberation of more of Kriti. If we succeed, maybe the British will then see reason and change their tune.'

This brought an ironic cheer.

'There is just one problem, Neo Zealandi.'

He might have expected there would be. 'Yeah. What's that?'

'You.'

He tried to laugh. And winced again. His back was making itself felt. 'No need to be personal, Petro.'

'The state of your wound. Thanks to your wildness, our ability to move, let alone to exploit our advantage, is reduced to dust.'

He was relieved that that was all. Even if it was true.

'I'm fit enough. I won't hold us back,' he retorted. 'I can move now, if you want. So let's get started.'

Everyone scattered. Watching their preparations he felt the justice in Petros' complaint. If he'd not tried to finish it himself, they could be in a position now to capitalise on their success. Hadn't *he* allowed it to become personal? Trying to make a point to Petros?

He shoved these thoughts aside. The physical task of moving would be sufficient problem for him. His claim about his fitness had been another over-hasty boast. Was that, too, one that would also soon find him out?

For the first time he regarded the prisoners. Five in all. One badly wounded and two with slight wounds. He wondered which had shot him. In the bustle no one was paying them any attention. A suspicion dawned. 'Aren't you going to rope them together?' he asked Petros.

'No need.'

'We are taking them with us?'

'Didn't you hear Yiorgo, Neo Zealandi? The Germans are killing everyone in sight.'

The coldness appalled him. He stared at Petros. 'I don't kill prisoners.'

The other met his gaze with a supercilious shrug. 'And we only those who deserve it.'

'They surrendered.'

'They should have known better.'

If Petros wasn't going to back down, nor would he. 'I was a prisoner of war myself, once.'

'Doesn't that clinch my argument?'

'Very funny, Petro.'

'I also do not make jokes, Neo Zealandi.'

'I had noticed.'

He called to Andreas. 'Rope these together, with the fit ones to carry the wounded man.'

Then to Petros: 'They won't escape.'

'They'll slow us down.'

'Not more than I will. You want to shoot me, too?'

Petros turned away. 'You're taking a great risk,' he called over his shoulder. 'If there's any alarm or...'

'... Need to do it, I'll do it myself.'

'On your head be the consequences.'

'Don't worry about that. And don't forget, if you want democracy, where I come from it includes decency, too.'

Petros swung round and gave him a searching look then snorted and stalked to the cave door. Eleni moved aside to let her husband pass. She must have been listening to them. Her face showed the same frown of concern from the first farewell in Askyfou.

He shuffled to the rear of the cave and sat on the ledge. This wasn't how it was supposed to be: Petros alienated, Eleni caught between them, the British posing as big a threat as the enemy.

There was also, the throbbing from his back reminded him, his own rashness. Because of that, hadn't he, as Petros alleged, already reduced their hopes to dust?

Nine

Kiwi did cause their progress to be slow. The still-hot autumn sun, beating from a cloudless sky, reminded him of an earlier ordeal. Even on Andreas' shoulder he struggled. Trying to hurry, he stumbled.

'Watch what you're doing, Kiwi,' he heard Yiannis growl. 'You'll burst my fucking stitches.'

'Burst your stitches?' Andreas laughed. 'You know what he used on you, Kiwi? Parachute twine.'

'Doesn't that mean I can fly?'

'You can try anything. Except jokes.'

It became obvious to him that this large group, moving at such a sluggish pace, was vulnerable to sighting by a spotter plane, the more so as they went higher and the tree cover thinned out. Petros made his displeasure clear.

'I don't want to say "I told you so"…'

'But you told me so?'

He suggested that Yiannis and Costis form a rearguard, while Andonis should lead a group off east to distract any pursuit. To his relief Petros made no objection, proposing besides that Pavlos took men to scout ahead for trouble.

'We'll look after the prisoners,' Pavlos said.

'No.'

'We're better able to take care of them.'

That was what he feared. 'They'll slow you. Leave all us wounded donkeys together.'

He also sent Yiorgos back to Alec with instructions to tell Dancy they *were* obeying orders. And to ask for more supplies for the families through the winter. He had no great hope the deception would work.

In late morning a Storch spotter plane appeared. They heard the droning and were in cover before it flew over. After several passes the plane rose higher and headed east. They waited in silence and after a few minutes caught the sound of gunfire. He grinned at Andreas. Andonis was making his presence known.

As they prepared to move on, he noticed Petros and Eleni arguing. He punched Andreas' arm to pre-empt a ribald comment. The action made him wince.

Eleni led one of the other women towards him. With a jolt, he realised it was Maro, her hair now grown out again. She appeared reluctant. He flinched from the prospect of another personnel dispute. And was surprised.

'Petros thinks you should hear Maro,' Eleni said. 'About developments in Souyia.'

Was that what the argument had been about? He could imagine who had really thought he should hear.

'She succeeded in getting inside,' Eleni added. 'Let her tell you as you walk along.'

'Always glad of female company,' Andreas said.

Eleni stalked off. Kiwi glared at Andreas but Andreas held out his hands to deny the blame. He turned to Maro. Even now Eleni had gone she looked hesitant. No wonder, though, was it? After he'd sent her back to Petros when she asked to defect.

'Don't mind Andrea, Maro,' he said. 'Tell us about Souyia. How did you manage to get inside?'

The question seemed further to disconcert her. 'An invitation. But you want to hear how it is?'

'Go on.'

'They have two hundred men, perhaps more. There is a disagreement about what they should do.'

'Who told you this?'

'A German soldier. He says they all know it.'

'How?'

'The new Major, Tsacobi...' Her Greek pronunciation of the "J" threw him for a moment. '... and the old boss...'

'Bortmann?'

'Yes. They argue in public about it.'

112

It was reassuring to hear he and Petros weren't alone in their disagreements. But he felt disappointed. 'Jacobi will get his way. That's why he's come,' he said. 'What's so special about all this?'

'The soldiers don't like it. Tsacobi is SS. Many of the soldiers were wounded in Russia. As they retreated they saw how the activities of the SS meant they could receive no mercy if they were captured. They fear the same here.'

He glanced at their prisoners trudging ahead. His guess was that crushing Cretan morale would still be the SS priority. Even this wasn't top grade intelligence.

'Did you see this SS man ... Jacobi?'

'No. They say to keep away from him. He seizes people. There is a torture cell in his headquarters.'

'Then the sooner we put a stop to him the better. Did you learn anything else?'

'Only something silly.'

'Even so, tell me.'

'He is a lover of music. He plays it late into the night. It is special music. He will not allow the soldiers to sing and make their loud noise near him.'

'It's not to cover the sound of torture?'

'I don't know. I don't think so. Soobert.'

'Schubert? Ah.'

'You know him, too, Kiwi?' Andreas laughed.

'Only the name. My dad had some of his gramophone records. You know what those are?'

'You take me for a peasant, Kiwi? Not love songs, then, if they were in your father's collection?'

'Dunno. Though if my dad liked him, Schubert probably was a miserable sod.'

'Is that all?' Maro asked. 'I know no more.'

'Yes, thanks, Maro. Well done.' He tried to sound grateful, though the information didn't amount to much. 'It was brave of you to volunteer to get inside Souyia.'

Eleni was coming back. Maro gave him a pained look.

113

'I didn't volunteer. I was instructed to go. To make myself friendly to a German soldier who might talk.'

'Jesus Christ,' he heard Andreas say.

Maro rushed off, brushing past Eleni. He stared at the newcomer but she turned away and followed Maro. 'Use any means available' flashed into his mind. So Petros had practised what he preached, had he? The gulf between them seemed to gape wider than ever.

By the afternoon they'd climbed above the tree line and rested on a bare, fissured slope in the shade of huge boulders. Or, most of them did. From what he knew could only have been spite, the German prisoners, still roped together, were ordered to lie some way apart, in the sun. Though their one guard had found himself some shade.

Everyone looked done in. Except Petros. His restless gaze swept across the wide expanse of mountain below them. And came to rest from time to time on the sleeping Eleni. Was her presence starting to undermine her husband's self-assurance, too? Maro's experience suggested not. The subject further dampened Kiwi's mood.

'Believe me, Kiwi, if it wasn't for the husband, you'd be in there,' Andreas whispered.

'I'm trying to sleep.'

'Sweet dreams.'

He dozed fitfully. Once, Andreas' snoring woke him. He glanced towards Petros. He, too, had now settled. Beside Eleni. Dispirited, Kiwi drifted off again.

The boy ran up to the garden gate to see the spare, grey-haired figure leaning against the porch of the house. His father stared in his direction then went inside without speaking. The door shut. He turned away and kicked out at the stones on the path.

People were shooting at him. It was Galatas but the firing came from behind. He sensed Maro shooting. He didn't want to be shot in the back. His father was sneering and muttering 'Shot in the back? I might have known.' He rolled away and found himself hugging a dead German.

114

'Your father always said you'd end up in hell,' his mother whined. He writhed to escape from her accusations. Someone with a gun was overhauling him. He couldn't turn to see who. There was a scream. His? He was running too slowly and felt the gun being aimed at him again.

Another cry. Too sharp though it was receding. He rolled over onto his right side. A stab of pain told him to stop but his eyes were open now. And understanding.

He jabbed Andreas with his elbow and his back screamed, too. 'Andrea! Guard! The prisoners.'

He watched the guard stumble in slow motion from his shade to be blinded by the light then stagger in confusion peering for the prisoners, as yet unable to catch on.

Men grumbled awake, bleary-eyed from the heaviness of midday sleep. Eleni was alert at once. Petros, too. Kiwi's glance took in the guard lumbering up the slope. He shouted at Andreas. 'Help me up, Andrea. Come on!'

As he was dragged into the light his shoulder jagged. He closed his eyes against the pain and glare and tried to see. The guard was raising his rifle. Following the aim he saw figures scrambling along the rocky slope. They hadn't gone more than a hundred yards. For an escape bid it was crazy and futile. He heard the safety catch click and called out. 'Don't shoot, man, the noise will…'

The crash of the shot reverberated off the granite. Andreas stumbled and let him slip. He dropped to one knee. The prisoner on the far right, who appeared to be propping up another, straightened and flung out his right arm.

Kiwi thought his eyes were playing tricks. The end man seemed to jerk forward and both he and his burden fell from sight. Then, in a sudden rush, the other three were gone, too.

'Quickly,' Petros shouted. 'After them. They're making a run for it.'

No, they're not, he knew. That wasn't a jump. He pushed away Andreas' hand. 'Leave me. Go and look.'

Andreas hurried off. Kiwi pushed himself up, catching his breath. The pursuers had halted in line abreast and were looking down. They seemed to be where the prisoners had disappeared.

Hands steadied him. Eleni and a woman he didn't know. Surprise jolted a stab of pain. And a jibe. 'What's the penalty for sleeping on guard duty? You have to go to Souyia and try the torture cell?'

'Everything has to be paid for.'

The rebuke for his pettiness made him plough on. 'Some of us prefer more conventional punishments.'

'The hair cropping was the punishment. Souyia was restitution.'

'"Restitution"? Oh, right. Going to be pretty harsh, this new world, if you lot take it over, isn't it?'

'People must learn the hard way if they won't listen.'

He tried to turn the reproach into a joke. 'The strap never made me into a saint.'

'Didn't it? Perhaps for difficult cases like you only a dark coal shed is the answer.'

He twisted to see if she was joking but the jab in his back stopped him. He doubted it. Another reminder of their different worlds.

When they reached the line of halted pursuers Andreas took him from the women. Two men moved aside to allow them through. He stared over the edge.

The mountain fell away before him in a series of broad, granite ledges. Empty. The next level, several feet below, was the shape of a saucer. In its centre gaped a dark hole. The mouth of a pit.

He scanned the slopes again. Nothing. He listened to the silence. Someone pointed. His eyes followed to the near lip of the drop. There, snagged by a shard of flint, lay a shred of grey cloth.

Like his fragment of blue dress. He must have swayed because Andreas tightened his grip and drew him backwards.

'The poor bastards,' Andreas murmured.

'It was for the best. They would only have given us away,' Petros said, face the expressionless mask again.

'Let's hope the gunshot didn't.'

Petros glared at him. 'I will deal with that.'

He cursed his quick tongue. What "restitution" would he cause this time? He softened his tone. 'Don't be too hard on him. We all make mistakes.'

'And look where they've brought us.'

Before he could retort Sifis held up a hand.

'Shh. Listen!'

There was still silence. Someone exhaled.

'There,' Sifis said.

It *was* a cry. From the pit. Then a longer one came. The wailing of a wounded animal. He shrugged at Petros. 'Not quite for the best.'

Running feet made them turn. His back jarred. For a moment he feared this distraction, too, had caught them off guard. But it was Yiannis, Costis and the rearguard.

'What the fuck's going on?' Yiannis asked. 'We thought you'd been fucking ambushed.'

He gestured to the edge. Yiannis looked and grunted. Costis also peered down then turned back to him. 'The P-pit of T-tafkos.'

'You know it?'

'We know to k-keep well clear of it. A stray s-step and you s-slide in. Many a g-goat has ended up d-down there.'

A sudden vision of Eleni and the lost lamb swept at him. He glanced round for her. Then frowned at Costis.

'Did you ever get them out? The goats.'

'How? It's t-twenty, thirty m-metres deep.'

'And rumoured to contain fucking ghosts.'

'The ghost population is due to increase,' Petros said.

A shout echoed from below. Kiwi regarded the lip. 'Not for some time, though, by the sound of it.'

'Then we should move on, Neo Zealandi.'

'And leave them to die? Slowly?'

'You were the one who denied them a quick death.'

'And I'll never hear the last of it. We have to put them out of their misery. If they're found…'

'Who'll find them up here?'

'If they have m-matches to m-make smoke...' Costis said. 'It h-has been d-done elsewhere.'

'Sling in grenades,' Tasso, one of Petros' men proposed. 'That'll show 'em.'

'Someone used the last one on the door of the mitato,' Petros said.

He ignored the taunt and tried to listen to the wailing from below. A harsh shout cut it off but then it resumed. Petros' complaint was just. It decided him. 'Fetch the parachute cord, Andrea.'

'You don't expect someone to go down, Neo Zealandi?'

'No.'

'Then, what...?'

'As you so helpfully keep pointing out, this is all my fault. So what's also down to me is the... "restitution".'

Eleni's involuntary start cheered him. Petros' glare was contemptuous. 'Yes, but you're too weak.'

'Then I'll go,' Andreas said.

'No,' Petros commanded and turned to Sifis. 'Fetch me the rope. I have no fear of ghosts.'

'Petro, don't be a fool,' Eleni cried.

Petros whirled on her. 'Keep out of this. Go on, Sifi, I said fetch the rope.'

Kiwi bit his lip. What had he done but complicate things again? They couldn't risk a delay in the open. And this time he'd brought public humiliation on Eleni, too.

He sat on the ledge. Below, lying on his stomach, Costis peered into the pit as the rope was paid down. With his right hand Costis elaborated on his instructions to the men straining to take the now-vanished Petros' weight.

'H-hold it. Then slowly. S-slowly! T-take the strain.'

He was conscious of Eleni standing near him on the ledge but his eyes never left the pit. Petros had only just gone from sight. Thirty metres? How long should it take? The knotted parachute cord would hold one man or more easily enough. It was the thought of the pitch dark that made him shiver.

A man on the rope lost his footing and for a moment the line began to slide. Costis cried out in panic but Yiannis dug in his heel and the line steadied. Once more they fed out the cord. He glanced at Eleni. She bit on her fingers. He gritted his teeth.

Then caught another cry. From below. Petros. 'Hold me! It's slipping!'

His gorge heaved. But the cord wasn't slipping. He tensed as the men dug their heels in and strained. The rope stretched taut. It wasn't giving. They were holding. What was Petros...? The men lay in a heap. He stared at the slack parachute cord dribbling into the hole.

'Petro!'

Eleni lunged for the edge. Her companions grabbed her and dragged her back. She thrashed to be free but they forced her down and pinned her to the ground. He turned away but her sobbing cut into him, merging with the jolts of pain.

Costis' calls roused him and he focussed on the pit.

'P-petro. Petro. C-can you hear me?'

The men hovered around it, keeping their distance. Andreas held up the end of the cord to him. 'It's not frayed. A clean break. The knot must have slipped. That's what he meant.'

He forced himself to ignore Eleni's groans. 'How far down was he? Costi, could you tell? Can you see him?'

'I c-can't see three m-metres. How f-far? I don't know. Halfway? If he was n-near the b-bottom he'd be sh-shouting and cursing by now, w-wouldn't he?'

Ten, fifteen metres. Thirty, forty feet? Survivable? Possibly. At least one, no, more than one, of the Germans had survived the full distance. But the silence was ominous. Even the earlier wailing and shouts had stopped. Costis shrugged his shoulders at him. He looked for Andreas. 'Come and help me down.'

'There's no need to make sure,' Andreas whispered as he eased him onto the saucer. 'Even a Communist couldn't talk his way out of there.'

He glanced back at Eleni. She stood still now, the women each grasping an arm. Her eyes were following him.

'Your sensitivity's touching, Andrea. Go and fetch the spare lengths of cord.'

'What?'

'You heard. And make sure this time someone checks the knots. Preferably a fisherman.'

'Kiwi, you're not…? Your back…'

'Feels better already.'

'This is madness.'

A chorus of protests agreed with Andreas.

'Anyone else volunteering?'

He noted guilty sideways glances. No one spoke.

'Good.'

'But, Kiwi, if both of you are lost in that fucking hole…' Yiannis said. 'Just don't let Pavlo take over.'

He wondered how far this bravado would last in the dark. Or was it only guilt? He knew Yiannis was right. There was less justification in this than even the attack on the mitato. But it had to be done. He half-hoped Andreas would offer again. Yiannis continued to rant. 'I knew from the start you were a fucking lunatic.'

'Why'd you think Major Dancy wanted to get rid of me?'

'Stop fucking making a joke of it. Did I go through that operation just so you could throw your life away on a fucking lousy Communist?'

'I take it that means I can't borrow your knife?'

Yiannis stumped away, snatched the rope from Andreas and begin to uncoil it. Kiwi let out a deep breath. The mouth of the pit yawned black. This was the sort of penitence that would have delighted his dad. He cut off the thought. That's all he needed.

Eleni stood beside him, her eyes also on the pit. A vein in her neck fluttered. Maro held her arm. 'It will be dark down there,' she said.

'Thanks for reminding me. I was trying not to think about it.'

'You don't have to go.'

The waver in her voice made him choke. 'Yes I do.'

She nodded and moved away. Yiannis held up a knot and tugged at it for his approval. He shrugged in reply. A hot-headed bayonet charge in a crowd was one thing. Lunacy alone in the dark quite another.

Costis glanced up from the pit and shook his head at him. Maybe it would be a quick check and he'd be back out? The idea appealed but then appalled him. He glared around.

'Come on, then. Let's get to it.'

He tried to remember the pre-embarkation abseil training on South Island. It was too long ago. Its irrelevance to field gunnery had made them regard it as a joke. And they hadn't had to practise in the dark. He hoped his wound would stand up to the strain. He wasn't confident it would.

He leaned back over the gap. Thoughts skittered about his head. At least this time no one was pushing him into the dark. If he passed out and fell would he land on Petros? In that case would Dancy commend him for reducing the Communist threat? He made himself stop. Concentration was everything. If he messed this up, all *would* be lost.

'If you don't come back, Kiwi...' Andreas called.

'Thanks for the optimism.'

'Leave some women in Hell for me.'

His last sight as he lowered himself into the pit was the frown on Eleni's face.

He strained to keep his legs straight against the side. Every step brought a stab. He heard Costis' calls, angry when they gave him too much slack and he fought to avoid a slip. The dark became total. The sound of his boots crunching on the rock and his rasping breath boomed in his ears. And still didn't numb the shooting pains.

His back felt as if it was splitting. Maybe the stitches were. Yiannis would give him stick for that. He lost all sense of time and where he was. He was in the coal shed. He was falling. He was being squeezed by the walls. He could feel a cold sweat on his face and his shoulders. 'Stop!' he called up.

He held there, legs out stiff, gasping for breath.

'K-kiwi,' Costis' voice drifted down. 'You all right?'

'Yeah, great,' he called back. 'Now, lower.'

They let go too fast and he swung, kicking at the wall for purchase, the pain pounding his back. So much for a rest. He forced himself again to focus. To count the steps. How many was a metre? He mustn't try to think how far he had to go. What if Costis' estimate of the depth was much too low?

A stink engulfed him. Dead animal. He retched and almost lost his footing. But it brought hope. He lowered himself further. With one boot on the wall he reached back with the other. It caught something. He swung down and stumbled then was sitting on something soft.

A body. He scrambled up, too fast and swooned at the tearing in his back. He lunged against a wall. The miasma kept his mouth clamped shut. Costis' voice carried down. He gave two tugs on the rope and shouted up. 'Down!'

The sound echoed round and deafened him. He retched again in the fetid air and felt for his torch. No sound came above his own gasping and the pounding in his head.

He shone the torch. He'd landed on three bodies, German, tied together, crumpled across each other. The ground was littered deep with bones and skins. Another German lay to the side and seemed to be breathing. Then his torch beam found Petros.

The Cretan was lying face down with no obvious sign of life. So the fall hadn't been broken by the Germans? He went to step past the pile of dead to check. His torch shone beyond Petros. He froze.

A German sat propped against the pit wall and stared at him, eyes unmoving. To have made it there this man must have survived the drop. Was he the one who had shouted? Then the cadaver blinked and a pained smile flickered across its face. 'Willkommen in Hell, Kreta,' the German said in a hoarse whisper.

Kiwi stared at him, paralysed. The wounded man added in a mixture of German and Greek, 'So now, Kreta, we shall all be kaput hier together, ja?'

He swept the light away and stumbled backwards, blundering over bones and onto the bodies, gasping and spluttering. The pain stabbed and flared in his back. He needed deep breaths to steady himself but he couldn't take them in. The urge to scream welled up in his throat.

The throbbing in his back clogged his head. He forced himself to concentrate. Petros. He was here for Petros. His first task had to be to check if…

But he ran the beam along the floor again to the German. And saw why the accuser hadn't made any move. Both his legs were smashed. He risked a further look at the man's face. The eyes were closed now but the chest quivered. The breathing sounded uneven. He told himself to get a grip.

He shone the torch on Petros and peered down. Petros' left foot twisted out at a grotesque angle. So much for a soft landing. Kneeling, he put down the torch and felt on Petros' neck for a pulse. He could find nothing.

'Come on. Petro, breathe. Or speak, then. Even if it's only some Communist crap. Anything.'

There was still no response. Wheezing and coughing, he heaved the body over onto its side. Petros gave a jerk. And screamed. Deafened, Kiwi watched the eyes open and the face contorting. The echoing din drove him to screw up his eyes. He gripped Petros' shoulder until the noise faded to a whimper. From above he caught anxious cries but could make no reply.

Petros' eyes were closed again. Had that only been a death cry? He gasped in foul air and shook the body.

'Stay awake, Petro. You hear? Stay awake.'

Petros opened his eyes and stared at him. The assault on his senses made it hard to clear his thoughts. With a broken foot Petros wasn't going to get out of there fast. And he wasn't sure that was the man's only injury. Given what he'd seen of the Germans, it seemed unlikely to be. He gritted his teeth over the nausea and peered at the casualty. 'Petro, listen to me. Your ankle's bust. Tell me if there's pain elsewhere. Can you move?'

In reply Petros shoved and pulled himself to half-sit, half-lie, screeching with each movement. Kiwi made to help but was shrugged off. He wasn't sure what Petros was trying to prove. He cursed the Communist's obduracy then remembered how he himself had got them here. A sharp rattle of breath startled him but it came from in the dark. He saw in the gloom that Petros was glaring at him.

'Why you, Neo Zealandi?'

'Like you said, it was my fault.'

'Yes. But thank you…'

'Don't sound too grateful. There is the small matter of getting out of here.'

He clambered to his feet and eyed Petros' ankle in the light of the torch. There was no chance of putting weight on it. He saw that the German next to the pile now lay still then searched for the end of the rope. He gave two tugs and gained some slack. Petros' voice jolted him.

'If you finished me off, who would know?'

'Lying never was my strong point.'

He fashioned a loop with a slip knot. If he didn't get Petros out, it occurred to him, many would believe that he *had* finished him off.

'You think I didn't notice?' Petros said.

He almost asked 'Notice what?' but caught on in time. This was no place for death-bed confrontations.

'Can you save the chat for the top? If you keep rambling, I'll begin to think you landed on your head.'

Petros didn't take the hint. 'I told you, your ways are not ours…'

That's all he needed now, another bloody lecture. He tried to concentrate on making sure the knot would slide. Petros' next words stunned him. 'You understand? With us, a woman who strays chooses death.'

At first he didn't grasp it. Then thought he'd misheard. He gabbled to block out the horror. 'Yeah, right, Petro. Fine. But I need you to try to stand on your good foot. Get you over to this rope. Think you can manage that? I only ask because if you can't, it won't be a question of *choosing* death…'

The effort of manoeuvring the injured man to the rope and tightening it round his chest brought him respite from thought. He gave two tugs on the cord and steadied Petros' waist as the lift began. At the same time he saw the torch flicker on the floor. The reminder of total darkness made him shudder. Down here, now, he couldn't face that.

The cord began to raise Petros. And evoked screams. It was obvious at once that it wouldn't work. Petros lacked the strength to guide himself. Each time they pulled, the smashed ankle banged on the side. There was only one way in which the rescue could be done. If at all…

'Stop!' he yelled. 'Lower him!'

After several attempts he made Costis understand and they lowered the burden. Petros was close to collapse. If the injured man did pass out their last hope might go with it. He urged Petros to help him. 'Just try to lean against the rock, Petro, until I can fix the rope round us both. Stay awake. You hear?'

Then he remembered. And cursed. The original purpose of Petros' descent. Had he the time? The torch's glow was fading. If it went before he could manipulate the rope around both of them… And would Petros manage to stand unaided? He snatched up the light, tugged out his knife and directed the beam across the pit.

He took a deep breath. 'Sorry, Fritz, but the time has come.'

He recalled his assertion that if it needed doing, he'd do it. Another careless boast. If he got out of this, there were going to be no more wild claims. If he got out… Huh. In mid-stride the faint glow picked out the staring eyes. He stopped. Caught his breath. And peered closer.

His sob was of both relief and despair. Jesus. So this nightmare had all been for nothing, had it? If they'd only thought to wait… The torch flickered. He took a step forward, bent to the dead body and pressed its eyelids closed.

He had Petros slumped across his right shoulder when the light went. The injured man breathed in shallow sighs but sounded barely conscious. He set the cord to keep it low down his back. In the blackness, he talked to reassure himself. 'Dancy told me not to get too close to the Communists, Petro. I see he had a point. Especially as, if this thing breaks, it'll be me who hits the ground first.'

He readied his feet to push against the pit walls and gave two tugs on the rope. Petros' weight squeezed his breath so that he had to fight even to wheeze. His back screamed. If coming down had seemed to take ages, the ascent was going to feel like eternity.

Unless the cord wouldn't take the weight of two men, he reflected. In which case eternity would come sooner. That had a certain attraction.

How long it did take he didn't know. Or where the agony began and ended. From the start he could do no more than try to keep the two of them from swinging heavily against the sides. The men above took the whole weight.

After an age, it seemed, he became aware of a greying of the dark. Then he was in daylight and hands were grabbing him and lugging him and his load on their sides up over the rough lip. Onto his bad shoulder. He thought he was inside a scream.

He came to lying on his front, the right side of his face against oily sheepskin. He couldn't lift his head. Or move at all. His whole body felt numb. For a while he luxuriated in the absence of pain and gazed at the shadows deepening on the mountain that fell away beyond him. This was a place where you could rest for ever. A chuckle broke the spell. Yiannis knelt beside him. Grinning.

'What's so damned funny?' he protested. 'Never seen a lunatic before?'

'Not a fucking lunatic like you, Kiwi, no. But you should see those stitches. Not a break anywhere.'

There was a cry from somewhere near. He twisted and his own pain shot back. He could see nothing. Until Andreas came into his eyeline. 'Don't worry, Kiwi. Only Costis setting a splint on Petros' foot. Not Sifis telling him about the wife. Trust you to miss an opportunity down there. Will you never learn?'

'Clear off. All of you.'

Anger only deepened the waves of pain that drilled into the back of his head. He shuddered under them and cursed the pricking of his oblivion. When the pain did ease the relief made him want to cry. He felt emptied out. He began to drift off. Until a cough shook him awake again.

'Sod off, I told you. I don't want any more of your unfunny jokes, Andrea. Especially about women. You hear?'

A hand touched his shoulder. A light touch. He opened his eyes. Eleni's brown trousers. He squinted up into her face. It was anguished, streaked with tears. The sight of it wrenched him. He couldn't speak.

'Thank you, Kiwi,' she said. 'For my husband.'

She patted his shoulder again, straightened and moved away. The look on her face stayed with him. He strained to hold it, even though, like her scream when the rope broke, it tore at his soul. Behind it, Petros' threat – 'With us, a woman who strays chooses death' – pulsed in his head.

And woke another horror. Jacobi, the new SS man, would, from Maro's report, need no excuse to escalate reprisals. While he'd just put both their own leaders out of action. If only he'd listened… His neck throbbed. In future it had to be different. But would he now get the chance?

Ten

The next two weeks passed in a blur. For the first few days he kept the group moving but it soon became clear that the Germans wouldn't pursue them into the high mountains. Gathering the separated groups together at Achlada, he set them to re-build the camp up there.

Till then he'd suffered no reaction, either to the wound, which responded well to the clean air, or to the extra stresses he'd undergone. The main inconvenience was Yiannis' insistence on showing the stitches to every new person they met.

'Look at those fuckers, doc,' Yiannis boasted to the doctor they'd brought to treat Petros' ankle. 'What d'you think? Not bad for a novice, eh?'

'No, indeed,' the doctor said, peering at them. 'I've seen worse stitching on a sheepskin coat.'

He winked at Kiwi. 'I hope he charged you extra for those. I wouldn't want to see my business undercut.'

'Your business is safe. Only my peace and quiet is at risk.'

In general he had little appetite for humour. Word filtered up of reprisals, even though in many villages the people had been alert and took to the hills when German punishment squads were spied approaching. Still, the old, the bedridden or stubborn, paid the price. Guilt, and inability to retaliate, gnawed at him.

Although Costis and Pavlos fought several skirmishes with the Germans, these were defensive operations, to deter enemy forces from venturing into the mountains. He also regretted having allowed Ari, against his better judgment, to infiltrate Souyia to obtain intelligence. The boy's continued absence weighed on him.

Eleni's constant proximity, since on the march the two casualties moved at the same pace, added to the strain. Especially when he saw how her care of Petros received scant reward.

'Eleni, where are you?' for the third time in an hour set his teeth on edge. Couldn't the man see how exhausted she looked? He made Andreas pause to let the others go on out of earshot.

'Bet you'd be a more appreciative patient, Kiwi,' Andreas grinned.

'I'd be more appreciative if you shut up.'

'It's only your guilty conscience protesting.'

'My guilty conscience has got other things to think about.'

'Jesus Christ, Kiwi, this constant blaming yourself for what you call our troubles can be really boring. Can't you be more positive for a change?'

Petros' threat about women who strayed still reverberated in his head. 'It's not that easy.'

'Of course it is. I'll say your wound needs a woman's eye.'

'No.'

'You'd feel better in no time.'

In fact, he fell apart. Once they reached the camp and the stress lifted, a reaction hit him. His strength failed and he lay in bed for a week. In some ways it was a relief because his mind shut down, too, and dulled the sharpness of his self-reproach. Eleni looked in on him from time to time, never entering his tent, however, and leaving him the impression of always looking over her shoulder.

His own weakness did appear to spur Petros' recovery. With the ankle set Petros was able to move round the camp on a pair of crutches, driving the building work and scorning Eleni's appeals to take care.

When he was visited by Petros, Kiwi sensed the old arrogance, as if the Communist believed a speedier recovery demonstrated his superiority. The thanks were repeated but, even without any reference to the exchange in the pit, there was also a guardedness. He could feel the husband's resentment not far below the surface.

He suspected the response of Petros' own men to his rescue of their leader may have incited this. Several expressed their amazement, others gratitude. Their greetings to him took on a warmth. Even Pavlos, when he returned and had the exploit described to him, showed grudging respect.

One day he was well. Physically at least. It was the same day Yiorgos arrived with a message from Alec.

Andonis had sited this new camp deep in the trees. Part consisted of tents dropped from the air and part wooden huts. Although the two halves remained distinct the central, open space no longer had the invisible divide down the middle. By some unspoken agreement the table had been turned to straddle the line and men intermingled.

Kiwi sat in the sun beside the table and watched the work of the camp. The return of his strength had sharpened his restlessness to resume action. So when Yiorgos trotted in with his face all smiles, the lad's cheerfulness at first raised his hopes.

'Kiwi,' Yiorgos beamed, surveying him, 'What have you been doing to make you recover so fast?'

Andreas' cough made him reply quickly. 'Don't you know donkeys are tough, Yiorgo?'

Yiorgos' face dropped, reminding him how the joke to Alec about donkeys had fallen flat. Andreas did butt in.

'Donkey! You should hear about his latest burden.'

And launched into the story. He had to squirm and protest as Yiorgos listened with widening eyes. Until Petros' arrival cut the excitement.

'What British betrayals this time, Yiorgo?'

'Ah, yes. Mr Aleko sends two messages.'

'There's good news and there's bad news?' Kiwi said.

'No, Kiwi,' Yiorgos frowned. 'What made you think..?'

'It's a joke we have. Never mind. So it's all bad?'

'It's reported that the British have occupied Leros. And the Italians have surrendered everywhere…'

'Then it isn't all bad?'

'Wait, Kiwi. Mr Aleko says that in the east of Kriti it was hoped they would come over to us. And that there would be a British landing.' Yiorgos gave Petros an uneasy glance. 'But…'

'Didn't I tell you?' Petros interrupted. The man's carping began to grate again.

'Just tell us what happened, Yiorgo.'

'The Kapetan Bandouvas attacked the Germans at Vianno and left a hundred dead.'

He felt a sudden fear. 'But the Germans made them pay?'

'Many villages down there have been laid waste. It's believed hundreds have died in the reprisals.'

There was a hush. His stomach muscles tensed. 'And Bandouvas?'

'Major Dancy has ordered him to leave the island.'

As he'd guessed. He tried to sound calm. 'That *is* bad news, Yiorgo.'

'There is worse.'

'Worse? How?'

'On Leros the British are under heavy attack. Major Dancy has ordered all British-led units from Kriti there at once.'

There was shocked silence. Then mutters. 'Don't worry, lads, I'm not British,' Kiwi said.

There were few smiles. Yiorgos frowned. 'It's no joke, Kiwi. He insists.'

'And I insist we ignore it.'

'That won't be easy.'

'I've done it already.'

Yiorgos shook his head. 'Major Dancy has also directed that for any groups which refuse, parachute drops will be called off.'

The muttering became anger. Petros snorted. 'More fine words, Neo Zealandi? Perhaps you'd better obey for once, or we'll all be left to starve.'

He sensed the gloating beneath Petros' rebuke. Their departure would leave the resistance in the Communists' hands. Yet if he did refuse to go...? "So now, Kreta, we shall all be kaput hier, ja?" swept by him. Hadn't Dancy, whether driven by circumstances or not, set the perfect trap? He put on a smile for Yiorgos. 'In that case, ask Aleko to tell him we're on our way.'

'Kiwi?' Andreas yelped.

He heard the shocked growls of others at the table.

'Are you sure, Kiwi? Tell him that?'

'Course I'm sure, Yiorgo. We'll be there... Just as soon as we clear the Germans in Souyia who are blocking our route. And for that we'll need more parachute drops.'

Their relieved laughter didn't buoy him up. It *was* bad news. This bluff might buy some time but that was all. He had the feeling of the pit walls closing around him and shivered. If he didn't re-start an offensive soon, the lack of supplies would defeat them of itself. And he wasn't yet fit for action.

Later that day he began exercising. The Cretans viewed with amusement his 'antics', as they called them and gathered round to savour the entertainment, counting aloud the number of press-ups and affecting derision when he collapsed and gave up. He bore it with grim equanimity.

He lay back full length, gasping for breath. Who was he trying to fool? There was no way he could stabilise this part of Crete before the British pulled the plug. He was their puppet. They'd go on using Crete for their own ends.

Hadn't his own efforts only made things worse? Perhaps he should obey Dancy's order, after all? That would remove the risk he posed for everyone else. Yet the prospect filled him with despair. He was sounding like his mother.

'Not fucked my stitches, have you?'

He frowned up from his gloom at Yiannis. 'Your stitches are fine. It's just everything else I've "fucked up". You were right, I am a... lunatic.'

'That was a compliment.'

'A compliment? Where I come from...'

'You're not fucking where you come from, are you?'

'True. But if it hadn't been for my recklessness...'

'What are you talking about?'

'At the mitato. Getting myself wounded. If I hadn't, the prisoners wouldn't have escaped, Petros wouldn't have fallen, I wouldn't have had to go down and... What?'

Yiannis was laughing. 'Getting shot, being reckless, as you fucking call it, you know why you're the only one who criticises you?'

'No.'

'Because you behaved just like one of us, you fucking idiot. Like a Cretan.'

'Is that supposed to cheer me up?'

'Please yourself. But blaming yourself for everything, that is definitely not Cretan.'

'No, you're right, there. That's Presbyterian.'

'It's what?'

'From New Zealand.'

'Then fucking leave it there. And look after my fucking stitches.'

Petros had also began to exercise. But whereas Kiwi concentrated on building up the strength of his damaged shoulder, Petros seemed intent on compensating for his injured foot. While Kiwi moved on to pull-ups on a tree branch, Petros began running on the crutches. Slipping and falling one day only made him more persistent.

Kiwi sighed, closed his eyes and resumed the pull-ups. A voice broke up his introspection.

'What are you trying to do, Kiwi?'

He glanced down to see annoyance on Eleni's face. The surprise made him drop from the branch. His back jibbed.

'Get myself fit, what's wrong with that?'

'The challenge you're setting Petro.'

'I'm not setting anyone a challenge.'

'He's pushing himself too hard, as you saw. His foot isn't healed yet. Another bad fall and...'

Blaming himself for his own failings was one thing. Her blaming him for Petros' stupidity stung. 'Then talk some sense into him. How's it my doing?'

He should have known better. Her eyes flashed. 'Are you deliberately being obtuse?'

'"Obtuse?" I don't know that word.'

'Don't pretend to be stupid with me!'

Her fury cut off any further temptation to flippancy.

'Look, I'm not trying to be... whatever you said. If I knew what I've done wrong, I'd put it right.'

'You can't. It's too late.'

'Too late?'

He was conscious that one or two people had stopped to stare at them. He hoped they didn't include Petros. His confusion must have been evident because he saw Eleni's anger dissolve. She threw him an anguished look. 'You saved his life.'

'I don't follow?'

'It's put him in your debt.'

'Has it? That wasn't my intention.'

'It's the way it is. Don't you see?'

He saw she was close to tears. He heard Petros' claim "Our ways are not your ways" but she still made no sense.

'If I've offended him…'

'Not offended, no. What you did is what few men are ever given to do. But…'

Her voice faltered. The agony in her face tore at him.

'… after it, you can no longer be equal. All the men know that. You are the leader now in all but name. And he knows he must keep up with you as closely as he can if he is not to lose face. That's what's tormenting him.'

He stared at her. He wanted to reach out and hold her to him but looked down instead. The sound of his breathing pounded in his ears. 'Shit. Sorry.'

'I thought you should be aware.'

He looked up. She strode away, head erect.

Leaving him more confused. And irritated. He'd even compromised the leadership issue, as well, now, had he? What did she expect him to do? Go easy so that Petros didn't feel threatened? That would guarantee failure.

He heard Petros' voice again in the dark: "You think I didn't notice?" And felt a wave of pity for Eleni. He understood then something she either didn't or didn't want to face. Petros' fears weren't about the leadership. They weren't even really about Eleni. Nothing Kiwi did or didn't do, short of leaving, would give Petros peace. And even that would only last until the next, imagined, fear.

He reached for the branch and his back jagged. Yiannis' admonition made him stop. No, he wasn't leaving. None of them were. Damn Dancy. Damn the British. If he had to continue to behave like a lunatic Cretan to secure their future, he would. And if that upset Petros, tough.

Later that day, to his relief and delight, Ari returned from Souyia. His report stunned them all. 'The plan, of Major Tsacobi, is for the systematic destruction of every village in the south west.'

'Yes, we know that,' Petros said. 'So what?'

Kiwi made to support Ari but saw the boy was unmoved.

'There's a big map on the wall of the boss's office…'

'You got into Bortmann's office? How?'

'Let the boy continue, Neo Zealandi,' Petros muttered.

He gritted his teeth but said nothing. Ari grinned.

'I will explain, Kiwi. This map, it has numbers for the villages. From it you can tell where they will start. Have started. Because three are already marked as destroyed.'

For a moment no one spoke. He could feel the tightness in his chest. 'Can you remember which is next?' he asked.

'I memorised the next five names,' Ari said. 'I would have more but the Major Tsacobi came back.'

'He didn't catch you?'

The shock on his face must have shown because Ari gave a shy smile. 'No, I was working there. Perhaps I should explain.' The lad's face became serious. 'The day I arrived a boy was blown up in the minefield outside the village. He was gathering wild greens to cook.'

The chorus of horrified oaths made Ari pause. 'He helped the old German soldier who did their paint work. Carried his tins. I wormed my way into the job. The next day we were summoned to Major Bortmann's office…'

The lad paused again at a gasp from the crowd.

'It seems that when the officer reported back to Bortmann on the ambush, Bortmann hurled a glass of red wine at the wall. The mess had to be cleared and the wall re-painted. I collected up the broken glass.'

'This officer,' Kiwi asked. 'It wasn't Jacobi?'

'No. The old soldier said the operation was Bortmann's idea. Tsacobi was against it. It was revenge for the sergeant who shot Sofia and whom Costis killed. Bortmann had been with him in Russia so ordered the attack in a fit of rage.'

'And now the fucker's in more of a rage,' Yiannis laughed.

The others joined in. Kiwi bade them hush. This was too important for jokes. 'Bortmann was in the room while you worked?'

'For most of the time he was on the balcony: the room is on the first floor and overlooks the sea. The old soldier, Hans, had also known Bortmann from the First War so Bortmann let us get on with the work.'

'And you understood all this, did you? Petros sniffed.

'Hans speaks Greek. After the First War he spent several years at Troia with the German Archaeological Service.'

'And then Jacobi arrived?' Kiwi asked.

'He would have thrown us out but the Major said it was his office. Hans told me later that Bortmann had turned Tsacobi's own words against him, saying that as Tsacobi's aim was "purification" and "cleansing" he must be pleased that that was starting with Bortmann's office. Hans thought all this very funny. I don't really understand, I just memorised the big words.'

'This is trivial,' Petros said.

'I'm only reporting what I heard...'

'Yes, you've done very well,' Kiwi encouraged, hiding his own disappointment. 'Anything more?'

'They also talked about music.'

'This is what you get, sending a boy,' Pavlos began.

'He volunteered. Allow him to finish. Go on, Ari.'

'I understand this next part even less,' Ari said. 'Let me get it straight.'

The lad screwed up his face in concentration. 'It was about... Soobert. Tsacobi praised the... perfection of Soobert and told Bortmann he didn't know the meaning of the word. Bortmann protested that the ambush was bad luck but Tsacobi laughed at this. He said that Soobert had achieved perfection only by an act of will.'

The mutters of incomprehension around the table echoed his own thoughts.

'Did this boasting lead anywhere?' Petros jeered.

'At the end Tsacobi said to Bortmann...' Ari searched his memory again. '"So, to achieve perfection, you must be more systematic. For every one of ours they kill, now execute twenty."'

The cries were of fury and anguish. They decided Kiwi.

He waited until the evening meal was over. It meant upsetting Petros but there was no way of being diplomatic.

'Jacobi's instruction gives us a choice,' he announced to the dozing group. 'Either we hold off and avoid inciting the Germans...'

'Maybe you're beginning to see sense, Neo Zealandi.'

He ignored the interruption. '... Or we can hit them so hard they have no chance to carry out his plan.'

Petros indicated his injured foot. 'While we're like this?'

'Nevertheless, if we leave them unchallenged...'

'There'll be fewer executions.'

'... We'll lose the initiative. And leave Jacobi free to pursue his scorched-earth policy. Of "purification".'

A female scream cut him off. Men rose and grabbed for rifles. A huddle of women surged towards them across the camp. Behind, one of the camp sentries held out his hands in a gesture of helplessness. As Kiwi peered at the women, one he didn't recognise threw herself to the ground at Petros' feet.

Her grey hair was dishevelled and her own, bare feet bleeding. As she knelt up he saw flecks of saliva around her mouth. With her right hand she grasped Petros' knee.

'Today the Germans came at dawn. To Maralia.'

The crowd shuddered. Maralia was the first village whose name Ari had memorised. He watched Petros detach the woman's hand and met Eleni's eyes as she eased the woman to sit on a chair.

The woman, in her sixties, her eyes burning as with fever, struggled to compose herself and went on.

'They gathered us in the square, beneath the plane tree. Only two men were at home. My husband, who had injured his leg...' She glanced at Petros' foot. 'And the village idiot, Takis. Their officer told us through the interpreter, the traitor Lefteris, that we had given support to the andarte band of Panadakis. Takis laughed and shouted that he'd fetch Panadakis to crucify them.'

'He is the village idiot, you say?' Petros asked.

'Was. The officer told him in that case he'd be the one to be crucified. Then had him nailed to the barn door.'

A collective gasp made her pause. Kiwi closed his eyes. So this was how Jacobi's search for perfection had begun?

'You haven't come here to blame me for that?' Petros said.

He glared at Petros. The widow continued. 'No, I come to beg for help. My husband – he couldn't walk, he leaned on me – protested that the boy was mad, he didn't know what he said. Didn't know where you were. "So you tell me where Panadakis is," the officer ordered. Of course, my husband knew nothing and if he had would not have told. I felt him shrug and the next moment he was dead in my arms.'

'Dead?'

'The officer had shot him.'

He felt the silence. The walls of the pit pressing in on him. Somebody moaned. He heard Yiannis curse.

'I'm sorry for your loss,' Petros said, without sounding it. 'But if he's dead, what help can I give?'

'My husband's body hangs from the plane tree. The officer says it will only be cut down when we reveal the whereabouts of your camp. If we remove it before then he will hang more of us, he said. He left a guard beside it. What are we to do?'

He could hear his own breathing, short and tight. He watched Petros shrug his shoulders. 'How can I answer for you, kyria? Since you've found us now, the choice is yours. Will you put a dead man before the national struggle for freedom?'

The woman shrieked and beat on Petros' knees. 'We refused to betray you. Now my husband hangs unburied, his soul in torment.'

Eleni eased the widow back onto the chair.

'Then perhaps you should summon a priest,' Petro said. 'I suppose you're sure you weren't followed here?'

Kiwi felt the bile rise in his mouth. Eleni's face darkened, too. He addressed the woman. 'Kyria?'

She peered at him, but without seeing him, he thought.

'Tomorrow, take me there.'

He heard the snort from Petros. 'Shouldn't we discuss this, Neo Zealandi?'

'The time for talk is past.'

'What do you hope to achieve with this… gesture?'

'It's not a gesture. You know we can't afford to refuse such a request.'

'And if you walk into a trap?'

'Your caution will have been justified. But we can't let Jacobi have the initiative. If he can do this with impunity, he'll never stop.'

The old woman muttered her thanks. Eleni went to help her up. He turned away.

'Kiwi…'

He swung back. Eleni's eyes blazed. 'Tomorrow,' she said, her arm round the woman's shoulders, 'I'm coming with you.'

Petros struggled upright on his crutches. 'I forbid this…'

Eleni flung a scathing glare at her husband. 'You'd have this woman return alone? I have to go. And if you don't know why…'

In a daze Kiwi watched her lead the old woman away. He avoided Petros' gaze. Andreas nudged him. 'Well, well,' he whispered. 'Who'd have..?'

'Kyria,' he called quickly. 'The village idiot..?'

The woman stopped and looked back. 'They cut him down before they left. With a machine gun.'

They reached Maralia in the early afternoon. The small village straddled a rocky spine between two shallow ravines. It appeared inaccessible to wheeled transport. From where he stood Kiwi could see no sign of troops or vehicles. A sentry was posted in the square, the old woman claimed.

Her resilience humbled him. He'd tried to travel fast with a few men but the woman, Despina, and Eleni had kept up. As had Pavlos and Sifis, for Petros had insisted on an escort for his wife.

They probed their way across the ravine and viewed the square. The villagers were indoors, out of the still-hot Autumn sun. One sentry sat dozing on a chair propped against a house opposite the tree. Far enough away from the smell, he guessed. Despina gasped at the sight of the hanging corpse and Eleni had to drag her back.

The guard's position posed a problem. Reaching him undetected in daylight looked impossible. Shooting risked raising a wider alarm. Presumably there was a relief somewhere in the village.

'Let me distract him,' Eleni said, 'while Yiannis takes him from behind.'

He shook his head, keeping his gaze on the square.

'Why not, Kiwi? This is a woman's war, too, you know.'

'That's not the point.'

'Then what is? My husband's view?'

Christ. Till then he'd only been thinking of the risk.

'Sh-she's r-right, K-kiwi,' Costis cut in. 'And I c-can c-cover her.'

He gaped from one to the other then turned to Pavlos but the red head only shrugged. 'All right... Yianni, go. Sifi, with him, cover his back.'

The two scrambled away. He turned back to Eleni. She held up her hand. 'No lectures, please. A woman is as capable as a man.'

Breathing hard, he watched her saunter into the square. With fury he realised the sentry was asleep. Reaching him might have been possible after all. He cursed his own weakness in not standing up to Eleni.

She gave a loud cough. The sentry woke and jumped to his feet then seemed to relax. Was she smiling at him? With a pang he realised he hadn't asked how she intended to achieve her 'distraction'.

She was pointing to the hanged man. For a moment he feared she was going to shout but she only gesticulated. With vehemence. The sentry raised his rifle and waved her away. She didn't move. The guard strode forward and shoved at her with the rifle. She grabbed it. Kiwi had an image of Sofia in Koustoyerako. This was going wrong.

Then Yiannis' left hand cupped the man's mouth as he drove upwards with his knife. Eleni let go of the gun, staggering to regain her balance. Costis lowered his own rifle.

As Yiannis eased the body down an old woman in black slipped from the shade with such speed that Kiwi almost shot her. Eleni forestalled him again: not only grabbing the woman but prizing from her the location of the other German guard. Kiwi waited, chastened by having doubted her, for Yiannis to re-emerge from that house.

At this the women of the village poured into the square and crowded round Despina. Leaving two men to patrol the approaches, Kiwi drew Andreas closer to the corpse.

'Jesus Christ,' Andreas muttered. 'What do we do with it now?'

The body was already swollen and the flies had long since found it. He flinched from the smell. And looked round to see Eleni staring at the dead man in horror. He walked across to her. Her eyes remained fixed beyond him.

'Was this wise?' he asked.

'I came for her.'

'You know what I mean.'

The appalled eyes swept round at him. 'Don't worry. I see them every day. It doesn't take a piece of cloth to remind me.'

He glanced away to where the women still chattered at Despina. Then took refuge in giving orders. 'Andrea, find a ladder. Yianni, Costi, dispose of the guards, all traces. Eleni… tell these women to gather their things. Quickly. They'll have to come with us.'

He was relieved to see that this time she agreed.

'Don't have to touch the cursed thing, do I?' Andreas said on emerging with a ladder.

'Think of it as a route up to a lady's bedroom.'

'Ha, ha, ha.'

'All I want you to do is cut the rope on the bough and lower it down, but slowly.'

'Thanks a lot. Your back too bad for climbing?'

'I'm going to catch it.'

'You're what! I've heard of embracing death, Kiwi, but this is ridiculous…'

He swallowed as Andreas stumped up the ladder. The villagers stopped their preparations and stood in silent groups. Andreas, face averted, began to cut. The flies lifted then settled back. He held his breath and made no response to Andreas' baleful glare.

'Hold him,' he called. 'Now lower.'

Andreas let the body down. The swarm of flies rose again. He heard Andreas retch. Stepping behind it, he steadied the corpse and gagged as the putrid stench drove up his nose. Dried blood coated the man's back. He longed to shut his eyes. The waxen face swung towards him. His stomach heaved. He thanked God *its* eyes were closed.

When the feet touched the ground he reached for the rope above the noose, strained to hold the body upright then swept it in one movement into his arms.

Its weight unbalanced him and its sponginess made him choke. He twisted to gasp in a breath. Through a haze he glimpsed Despina's face. With faltering steps, fearful that the thing would slip from his grasp, he walked towards her.

He proffered the body, knelt and placed it full length on the ground. Stepping back, he snatched shallow breaths away from the smell. Andreas puffed his cheeks out at him. The stink still blocked out all thought.

The widow stumbled to the body. She dropped on both knees then threw herself across it and began to wail. The other women shuffled nearer, moaning in low voices. He realised that Eleni was staring, not at Despina but at him. Rigid. As if she'd seen a ghost. He saw the tears course down her face and felt himself shudder.

'The knife, kyrie?'

He blinked. The widow was kneeling again, beside the body. She grasped the severed end of the noose, pointing to Andreas. When he stepped forward and bent down with his knife she held up her hand as a bar. 'No, let me do it.'

Transfixed, Kiwi followed her laboured sawing motion on the noose. She flung it aside and looked round. Her gaze found him. She held up the knife and inclined her head.

'Thank you for my husband, kyrie.'

Eleni gave a sharp cry. Despina glanced at her. 'I was a true wife when he lived. And now, too, I remain… faithful unto death.'

With both hands she drove the knife into her chest. A smile flickered then she slumped forward across the body. He couldn't move.

Eleni dropped and tried to lift her. She seemed unable to. The struggle registered on his brain but meant nothing. Eleni collapsed in sobs over the two bodies. Several villagers burst into high-pitched wailing.

His stupor snapped. He eased Eleni off the bodies and to her feet. He heard himself bark orders. 'Bury them, Costi, Sifi. Yianni, get these women to move. Andrea, tie the rope back.'

He drew Eleni away and walked her up and down, his arm around her shoulder, conscious of the stench from the body still on him and Pavlos' eyes following them. She appeared oblivious to it all. She sobbed and her body shook. He talked as much to calm himself as to steady her. 'Shh. It's all right... I'm sorry, if I'd known she was going to do that... Shh... She's out of it now... I wonder if she intended that all along..? You know, you Cretan women amaze me... You have some strange customs, don't you?'

Eleni stopped and turned a fierce gaze on him. He recoiled from its intensity. 'I didn't mean... I'm sure she's at peace now.'

She shook her head, indicating the tears and her ravaged face, soundless. He waited, numbed, then her words came gushing in sobs. 'You fool, you stupid fool, Kiwi. Don't you understand? Can't you see?'

He stared at her, his mind a muddle. Then she blurted:

'These tears are not just for her.'

She swung away. He stared at her slim shoulders, their fragility shaken by her sobs. A dim sense dawned of what she meant but its enormity swamped him.

A shrill cry cut his reverie. Costis was pulling the two bodies across the square in a blanket. Together in death. An old woman cried out a lament as she followed.

Eleni continued to sob. He made no attempt to touch her. He wasn't sure he could. He felt on the edge of the pit again. Dizzy. About to topple in. His eyes followed Andreas looping the empty rope over the bough.

The sight brought him back to himself. An empty rope. The sign to Jacobi that his search for perfection had been stalled. What would follow, he could guess. It was no matter now. Jacobi didn't need excuses.

He glanced at Eleni. She seemed calmer. The intensity of her gaze on him as he'd carried the body still seared his brain. He shook his head to clear it and scanned the preparations for departure.

More than one boundary had been crossed here.

Eleven

He sent Andreas and Sifis off to Agriles and Rodavani, the next two villages on Ari's list, to warn the people of the coming threat. He wished he'd had Yiorgos with him. Yiorgos would have reached the villages in half the time.

On their return journey Pavlos stuck close to Eleni. Her composure had returned. Kiwi's was ruffled the more he reflected on the taunt he'd left for Jacobi. With their resources it smacked of self-defeating bravado.

Yiannis dismissed his qualms. 'Fuck that. What's new? Hit the bastards wherever and when ever we can.'

'That's not too reckless?'

'Fuck off. I told you, a Cretan can never be too reckless.'

He remembered Yiannis' relatives in Kirtomades.

'Hit and run,' Costis added. 'L-like you proposed at the start. Their c-concentration in l-larger bases like Souyia makes it easier for us to w-watch their movements. And we d-don't need n-numbers to pick off outlying posts.'

Numbers weren't the problem. Men from the burnt villages flocked to them now. It was supply that was becoming critical. Of both food and ammunition. Thanks to Dancy and allies whose only desire was to obstruct.

That reminded him he'd soon have to face Petros.

Before then, some way below the camp, they bumped into the doctor hurrying down. He appeared in a foul mood.

'You think I take the risk of coming all the way out here just to waste my time... and be insulted?'

'Sorry, doctor, if I'd known, I'd have...'

'I didn't come to see you. Your shoulder's made of iron. But you, lady, if you send for me...'

'Send for you? I didn't send. Why? What's happened?'

The doctor echoed Eleni's surprise. 'You didn't know?'

'Know what?'

'Your husband had a fall. They said he was running.'

Her groan sounded more of anger than concern. 'Is it bad?'

'How should I know? He won't let me near.'

'Why not?'

'I could repeat his insults but I won't. You know your husband better than I do, Eleni.'

Eleni looked down. Kiwi noticed Pavlos slip off ahead.

'You think he's aggravated it?' he asked.

'I suspect he's compounded the break.'

'So it needs re-setting?'

'It needs more of a specialist than I am — even if he'd let me. He has to go to a hospital.'

'We can hardly take him to Hania.'

The doctor shrugged and made to go on his way.

'If he doesn't have it seen to, doctor?' Eleni asked.

'He'll not do any running in future. And as for fighting... Just hope there's no infection in the break.'

Kiwi watched Eleni's face harden. He wondered if she expected to receive the blame for her husband's mishap.

But Petros directed his scorn only at him. Eleni he ignored. The husband lay sprawled across two chairs at the table. His mood sounded worse than the doctor had said.

'What are you looking so sullen about, Neo Zealandi? The twenty more hostages who'll die as a result of your mercy mission?'

Kiwi set himself not to rise to the provocation.

'There is no mercy now. It's us or them.'

Petros glared past him at the village women behind.

'And you've brought more mouths to feed. Well done. Especially when your British have stopped supplying us.'

'We don't know that yet...'

'Petros...' Eleni began but she was brushed aside.

'We know there's another betrayal in the wind, don't we? The smell is unmistakeable.'

Kiwi almost smiled at the extent of the stink on his clothes. He wondered what Pavlos had told his boss. The choice of words couldn't be accidental. Petros' next taunt confirmed it. 'But surely you must have some answers to the problem of betrayal, Neo Zealandi?'

He stared hard in reply and affected unconcern. 'Yeah, I've worked it all out. But I'll tell you later. As you can tell, I need a wash.'

He strode off. A sudden fear struck him that Petros would smell that odour on his wife. And this time draw a more valid conclusion.

At the table that night he could feel Petros' eyes probing him. He avoided looking at Eleni and noted how her husband ignored her, too. He also saw how Petros winced with each movement. Yet the doctor had been dismissed. The man seemed to want to make himself suffer. And force his pain on everyone else.

Kiwi ate without appetite, waiting for the attack. Sourness he could cope with. If it became obstructive, there was no way now to avoid a confrontation.

Petros held up a skinny bone. 'So, Neo Zealandi, this is what a British betrayal reduces us to?'

'Have to rely on ourselves more, then, won't we?'

Petros indicated his leg. 'Yes, of course, so easy. Is that your only answer to the problem? Of betrayal.'

'I'm a practical man. We need arms and food.'

'Neither of which we can find.'

'There is a way.'

'Don't tell me, you'll beg the British to forgive you?'

'We'll take from the Germans.'

'Ah. Take. Just like that? When they're not looking? Why didn't I think of that? So, if we want arms, we simply walk into Souyia and help ourselves?'

He clenched his jaw. Costis' ideas on the return from Maralia had crystallised into this plan. 'Attack their outlying posts. With a dual purpose. First, to gain arms. Food supplies where we can. But also to loosen their grip on the more remote areas. Then force them to withdraw down to the coast or the north.'

'And when they have, your source of supply will be gone, as well.'

'We'll be in control of the mountains.'

'To starve in peace? Brilliant, Neo Zealandi.'

'No, to target supply columns in the passes. And by doing that, to draw more Germans out of the safety of Souyia and ambush them, too.'

'While all the time the hostage executions proceed.'

He knew Petros' arguments were valid but ploughed on.

'They'll proceed anyway. This Jacobi needs no excuse. You heard Ari. And if we don't act, we're condemning the people to death just as much as he is.'

Petros jerked away and started from the pain. Eleni grimaced. Pavlos broke the silence. 'He has a point, Petro. As a plan, it could work.'

Petros rounded on his subordinate. Kiwi barely caught the words. 'So you'd betray me, too, would you?'

Pavlos stood his ground. 'I think we should test it. At Omalos.'

'I'm not fit to go anywhere.'

'I can lead.'

'Yes, of course,' Petros laughed. 'What a plan!'

Christ, was the man even jealous of Pavlos now? A vague recollection from Koustoyerako unsettled him but he tried conciliation. 'Your men are yours to deploy, Petro. It doesn't bother me if Pavlos leads. We fight, we share.'

'No.'

'Oh, for God's sake, won't you see sense?'

'Sense? Oh, yes. I wish I could...'

The clatter of Andreas' and Sifis' arrival broke up the debate. Andreas lifted a jug from Eleni's hands and drank. He handed it to Sifis and surveyed the group. 'Sitting on your arses, eh? Well, drink on. There's twenty people in Agriles that won't be joining you. By the time we reached there, it was too late.'

Kiwi shuddered. And caught the triumph in Petros' tone.

'Didn't I predict this, Neo Zealandi?'

Before he could retort Andreas turned on Petros. 'You had warning of this? And did nothing? You louse.'

Andreas kicked away the chair on which Petros' leg lay. The impact threw the injured man off-balance and when his foot hit the ground he screamed and crumpled. Pavlos grabbed for Andreas but Andreas pushed him back. The red head pulled a knife.

'Stop!'

Eleni's fury halted them all. She bundled Pavlos aside then flapped her arms at Andreas, forcing him to retreat.

'Sense? Sense? Have none of you any sense? You're squabbling like children. Sifi, help me lift Petro.'

Kiwi made to assist but thought better of it. 'Petros had no warning, Andrea,' he said. 'He accused *me* of provoking more deaths from our operation in Maralia. Now it sounds like he was right.'

'No, Kiwi, this had happened before that.'

It gave him little comfort. His gaze followed Petros, eyes closed now, being propped on the chair again with the broken foot raised. He noted how the injured man breathed in gasps and could imagine the pain. The sight of Eleni with her hand on her husband's shoulder curbed his compassion. He looked at Andreas for an explanation.

'Early morning, the women said. The usual tactic. And the demand was the same. This time all the reply it got was silence. This seemed to infuriate the officer – from the description it was Jacobi, they knew the SS insignia – and he ordered twenty hostages to be seized. Women as well as men. And boys.'

He closed his eyes. The hanging body bumped against him. Its stench drove up his nose. He blinked it away and ran his gaze around the group. 'I reckon that decides it. Omalos, then, Pavlo? What do you say?'

Pavlos nodded agreement. Petros' snort cut him off. 'And me? You'll desert me, now, eh?'

Eleni's hand pressed on her husband's shoulder. 'No one's deserting you, Petro,' she said. Petros gave a flick of irritation at her touch. She kept her hand there and carried on. 'But, your foot's in a bad way. It's no use arguing. Your foot requires surgery. That's what you must look to.'

Petros glared round them. 'Been discussing this among yourselves, have you?'

Kiwi felt Petros' scornful eyes rest on him.

'Well? Are you going to deliver me to the hospital in Hania yourself, Neo Zealandi? Or ask the Gestapo to send me a donkey?'

He went to snap back when something occurred to him.

'I thought you could send them a postcard. From Cairo.'

'Cairo?'

Eleni started, too. He hurried on. 'For that injury, Cairo's the only safe place. You know it. Alec can call for a sub to take you off.'

Petros pulled himself into a sitting position. 'I won't let you do this to me.'

'Prefer to be a cripple, or worse, would you?'

'I'd prefer not to be duped by a bunch of scheming…'

'Petro, listen to me,' Eleni said.

'Listen to you?' Petros asked with scorn. 'Why?'

'Because I'm coming with you.'

Kiwi stared at her. She met his gaze, unflinching. 'I'm your wife, Petro,' she said from behind her husband's shoulder. 'What else did you expect?'

Before Petros replied or he could clear his head, Yiorgos loped in grinning and then stopped and frowned at the grim faces that greeted him. He held up a letter.

'From Mr Aleko, Kiwi. He wasn't smiling, either, when he gave it me. So you already know what's in it, do you?'

Yiorgos lifted the jug and drank, holding the letter out of Kiwi's reach. Then he danced aside waving it. This broke the tension and some men began to disperse. He saw Petros frowning to hear Eleni. He grabbed for Yiorgos.

'Quit messing about. Why's it in writing?'

'No idea. He told me to confirm to you that they have stopped the parachute drops. Maybe this one's personal.'

'Very likely. Major Dancy expressing his deep regret at ruining all our achievements?'

Yiorgos handed it over and he walked into the trees to open it. What could be worse than the bastard cutting off their lifeline? Yiorgos followed him and made a show of trying to peep as he scanned it. Yes, it was personal. And something else he hadn't foreseen.

But why was he surprised? If he'd ever paused to reflect, he should have anticipated this, too.

'Not good news, Kiwi?'

'Do you ever bring good news, Yiorgo?'

He meant it as a joke but Yiorgos looked disconsolate.

'And do you know what it is to feel rejection, Kiwi?'

'From an early age. That's why I'm so cheerful.'

'But not now, I'd say? So it is bad news?'

'Not unexpected. Just one more irritation.'

'And is it too personal for me to know?'

'If you promise to keep it to yourself.'

'My silence is absolute.'

'Good... I've been recalled.'

'What! Kiwi, no?'

'Shhh. They'll hear you in Souyia.'

'But, Kiwi, recalled?'

'Keep your voice down.'

'To Cairo?'

'Yes, Cairo. Aleko said nothing of this to you?'

'No. Why, Kiwi...? Mr Aleko hasn't been..., too?'

That part *was* unexpected. He felt a pang of guilt. Then rejected it. Damn the bastard Dancy. That's where all the fault lay. Yiorgos was beating on a tree and muttering rapid curses. He pressed the lad's arm. 'Stop it, Yiorgo. Your silence, remember.'

'I know, but if you – and Mr Aleko – go to Egypt, that's a... What will become of us?'

'Stop panicking.'

'It's all very well for you to talk. Some of us remember how bad it was. But you won't be here. You won't have to face them when they've got us cornered.'

'It won't come to that.'

'Huh. Sure of that outcome, are you?'

'Positive.'

'Why?'

'I'm not going.'

He enjoyed the tumbling emotions on Yiorgos' face.

'But, Kiwi, haven't they ordered...?'

'Ask Aleko to send this message to Cairo? In code. OK? Now: "Recall noted. Await sub. Stuff you." Got that? Right, go. Tomorrow night we're for Omalos.'

He gritted his teeth. Time, that had seemed short, was already draining out fast.

He trained the glasses but could see little. The small Byzantine church had obviously been commandeered as the supply depot at Omalos for its secure position – on the outcrop of rock near the edge of the plain. The low building beside it must house the barracks.

He took reassurance from the accuracy of Andonis' intelligence reports. The post at Xiloskala that straddled the andartes' usual route across the head of the Tripiti and Samaria Gorges had also been unoccupied, as predicted. So he was confident that the other garrison, based two miles away at Agios Theodoros to guard the exit from the plateau to the West, could be handled.

He'd found some difficulty in persuading Pavlos that their priority was re-supply, not mere assault. The verbal part of Alec's message had confirmed what he'd expected. With him was again a small force – and a number of women to act as porters. The Greek view of women as beasts of burden he still regarded as bizarre but shied away from raising it with Andreas.

Up past the Linoseli spring, when the moon showed the plateau of Omalos spread out below them, he'd split their party. Andreas and six others headed west to Agios Theodoros to distract the garrison and reduce the likelihood of German reinforcements threatening them here.

Now he waited beside Pavlos on the low ridge that ran down to the post, for the gunfire that would tell them the decoy was set. And which would mask the cutting of the wire perimeter fence around the church. Because the barracks was closer to the store than he'd have liked, the operation demanded caution if they were to avoid a messy fight. At least this outstretched finger of ridge avoided the need for too steep a climb up to the church.

Pavlos handed him back the binoculars. 'Yiannis is in position. I can only see the one guard up on the rock.'

'Let's hope he gives Andrea his full attention.'

A burst of firing in the distance had them on their feet. He waved the men forward towards the target.

The wire cut, they swarmed through and up the hillock without a sound. Yiannis greeted him with a grin as he drew his finger across his throat. He shone his flashlight on the padlock and motioned to Sifis.

The crowbar snapped the lock but it slipped and fell onto the stone path with a clatter. He froze.

A door opened in the barracks. Surely nobody could have heard that? He pressed himself into the doorway. Someone was coughing. When he peered across he saw a hatless private gazing up at the stars, relieving himself. The man finished, did up his pants and sauntered back to the door.

Then turned. 'Gunther?'

'Ja?' he grunted from the shadows.

'Alles gut?'

'Ja.'

He waited, holding his breath, but only heard a laugh and then the door slammed. He breathed out and eased the door open. Its hinges groaned. If the other Germans had also drunk too much he had to move fast. He flashed the light inside on stacked boxes and waved the others in.

'Pavlo, watch the barracks door. Yianni, search out the machine gun ammunition.'

With rapid efficiency they stripped the store of rifles and passed them down a line of men to the women. The heavier ammunition boxes were more of a struggle but two had already been dragged away when one slipped. And slid off the edge of the rock.

The crash reverberated against the mountain walls. He was outside the church and ushering the raiders away as the barracks door opened and light flooded out. He glimpsed the figure in the doorway and heard the call:

'Gunther, wo bist…?'

153

He glanced back. To see Pavlos shooting. The first figure fell. Two others burst from the door. One dropped and he saw the second dart back inside. The door slammed shut.

'Come on, away,' he shouted. 'Carry what you can.'

A burst of fire from the windows drowned his cry. He guessed troops would be pouring from a rear entrance to cut them off. Bundling Yiannis and Sifis before him he scrambled down the rock and out through the wire, before he realised someone was still firing.

'Pavlo!' he called and made to go back. Yiannis jerked his arm and hauled him away. 'The fucker'll come, don't worry. He's got 'em too scared to move for now.'

The fusillade of fire from the barracks did falter.

'Shit, Yianni, we should have blown the store.'

Again he hadn't been thinking fast enough. He blundered along the ridge through the stony scrub. Most, he saw in the gloom, were already in the cover of the gully that led up into the hill. But was Pavlos following?

He peered back. Gun flashes still showed beside the church. What the hell was Pavlos playing at? Then he saw.

The German firing had renewed. Now it faltered. He glimpsed the figure rushing at the barracks door, spattering the walls as he ran. It was madness. There was no need. Their escape had already been covered.

For an instant he was kicking at the door of the mitato again. He saw Pavlos fall. The shooting ceased, the light flashed in the doorway and troops tumbled out. Next moment the air above them whistled and roared. Yiannis dragged him down and pulled him crouching into the gully. Bullets tore at leaves and pinged off the rocks.

'Come on, get the fuck out, Kiwi,' Yiannis hissed. 'There's no chance of going back for him. Just hope the the fucker's dead. Fucking come on, I said.'

The firing eased. He risked another look. There was no sign of pursuit. Nor would there be, he suspected, in the dark. Pavlos had done a good job. He grunted at Yiannis and followed, his thoughts stumbling as much as his feet.

If the crazy fool had come away when he had them pinned down...
He remembered Yiannis' boast: "A Cretan can never be too reckless".
His mind replayed Pavlos' charge to the door. Had it been an attempt
to emulate him?

And was Pavlos dead? He didn't want to think about that. From
what he already knew of Jacobi, falling alive into his hands was the
worst of all possible fates.

The sound of sporadic gunfire in the distance told him that they
were unlikely to be cut off. He just hoped that Andreas hadn't done
anything rash. Not unless the garrison was full of women, he told
himself and then felt chastened, both by his doubts and by his levity.

When they were well clear of the scattered buildings of the village,
he had his party drop onto the flat ground to travel faster up to
Xiloskala. Once there they would be safe from interception and in
another two hours, beyond the Linoseli col, on the descent to the camp.

Where he'd have to confess to Petros about Pavlos. He cursed the
young man's rashness and then told himself not to be a hypocrite. He
tried to persuade himself it wasn't his fault. But it was his responsibility.
He should have made sure he'd pulled the hothead away.

Whatever the truth, he could imagine the recriminations that
awaited him in the camp. If Petros had felt isolated before, how
threatened would he feel now at the loss of his loyal lieutenant?

Twelve

Petros received the news with an unnatural calm. It was mid-morning when the exhausted party trudged into the camp, weighed down as much by their loss as their loads. Petros ran his eyes over the depleted group: Andreas had not caught them up during the night. 'So Pavlos was your only casualty?'

'Unless Andreas lost anyone.'

Petros sat at the table with his foot on a chair. Kiwi watched the injured man reach his right hand up across his body and pat Eleni's, which rested on his left shoulder. Its presence there seemed to have become tolerable now, he noted with a twinge of resentment.

Eleni appeared more upset by the loss than her husband, whose main complaint was about the failure to steal more machine gun ammunition. Pavlos' death brought a shrug. 'It doesn't greatly surprise me, Neo Zealandi.'

He waited for the reproach to follow but Petros surprised him with an unusual equanimity. 'The youth always was too impulsive.'

'Pavlos had already covered our retirement. I should have ordered him away more forcefully...'

'No one can do everything.'

There was no hint of sarcasm. He risked a glance at Eleni. Her gaze remained on her husband's hand. Her face looked ravaged. He wondered if her distress was the reason for Petros' calmness. Surely Petros hadn't felt threatened by Pavlos, too?

'Nevertheless, I can't help feeling...'

'Stop fucking about, Kiwi,' Yiannis cut in. 'Pavlos stormed the guardroom, Petro. Brave, just too foolhardy, even for us. He had spirit but he was after glory.'

'What Yiannis says is right,' Sifis said.

Eleni scrutinised Sifis then she turned to him. 'You saw Pavlo die?'

'I saw him fall.'

'You mean you aren't sure?'

'He was hit at close range.'

He avoided the alarm in her eyes. Her voice rose. 'But no one made certain? How could you leave him?'

'Because the whole place was coming at us and he was in the middle of 'em,' Yiannis said. 'You wanted more suicides? What good would that have been?'

Eleni squeezed Petros' shoulder and looked away.

'Most of us are done in,' Kiwi said. 'Can we get cleaned up before we have any more of this?'

Murmurs of agreement backed him up. A shout of "Andreas" from the top end of the camp stopped them.

Andreas strode into the square, his face creased with anxiety, searching, it seemed. Then the scowl broke.

'Christ, Kiwi, am I glad to see you.'

'You ran into trouble?'

'No... but then, who was it?'

He felt a cold shadow creep across him. 'Who was what?'

Andreas wiped his brow and peered with a frown round the group. 'We pinned them down as you asked. We heard all hell break loose so we gave them some more. Then it went quiet. We were going to pull out to meet you above Tripiti but I reckoned if there'd been any problem we'd have more chance of seeing it from where we were.'

'And did you?'

'About dawn two truckloads of troops and an officer's jeep came charging up from the south and shot off across the plain. We waited a couple more hours.'

'Please get to the point, Andrea,' Eleni said.

Petros started at this interruption. Andreas gave her a tired shrug and collected himself. 'The jeep returned. Again, fast. But a second man lay slumped in the jeep. Wounded, I'd guess.'

There was a collective groan. Kiwi managed to say 'You couldn't see who?'

'No, do you know?'

'Pavlos.'

'Shit. Are you sure?'

'He was hit. Left behind…'

Eleni stared at Andreas, beseeching.

'It could have been one of their officers…' Petros snapped.

'The hospital's in Hania, Petro, remember?' Kiwi said. 'The lorries will be ferrying their own wounded there. This casualty was too important for that.'

'But if he'd been hit as badly as you say..?'

'He was. We were in no doubt. And this confirms it.'

'Confirms it?'

'That's why they're rushing him to Souyia…'

Eleni's cry told him she'd grasped the implication. Petros' voice came with the hard, querulous edge. 'Then someone should go to Souyia.'

'If you're thinking of a rescue, Petro…' he began. It would be a more hopeless task than at the church.

'No. But we have to make certain.'

Petros' uncompromising practicality stunned him.

'I'll go,' Ari piped up.

'No,' he said, feeling wrenched from one extreme to the other. 'Too risky for you a second time.'

'Then I will return.' Maro's eyes defied him to refuse her.

'Are you sure? It's not necessary to …'

'When I left I said I had to visit Sklavopoula, that my godmother was seriously ill. There'll be no problem. I can be in Souyia before nightfall.'

He wanted to tell her to be careful but couldn't bring himself to look her in the face. He merely nodded thanks.

People drifted away. He threw himself down in his tent but his mind wouldn't settle. The blame for Pavlos' capture nagged at him. The despair on Eleni's face at the news wouldn't go away. And brought back the sight of her consoling Pavlos in the square at Koustoyerako. But what cut into him most of all was her earlier declaration to Petros about Cairo: 'Because I'm going with you.'

He cursed himself for suggesting Cairo. But it was the only option. And why was he surprised at Eleni's decision? What else did he expect? Maybe it was the suddenness that had undone him. The imminence of separation. Like at Askyfou they were going to part with too much unspoken.

When he awoke the afternoon sun was into its decline. The camp was asleep. Except for Eleni, he saw from the tent door. He studied her wiping the table. Her back was to him but she appeared distracted. He slipped across behind her.

'You OK?'

She jumped and threw herself into the cleaning. 'You startled me. My mind was elsewhere.'

'Pavlo?'

'No. I daren't think how they'll treat him.'

'You seemed to take the news hard?'

'How else should I take it? When the bad things don't affect us, what will we have become?'

He remembered Petros' reaction but said nothing.

'Now I hope he is dead. He was, is... maddening at times but he had spirit. And no more than a boy, really.'

'While you're an old married woman?' he said through gritted teeth. She frowned. 'I am a married woman, yes.'

He caught the noises of people stirring behind him. The threat of interruption increased his desperation. 'I want to talk to you.'

'Isn't that what we're doing?'

'Somewhere more quiet.'

'You know I can't do that. And why...'

'But you're leaving, for God's sake...'

'Not immediately. There'll be time...'

'No there won't. You know as well as I do. Is it too much to ask a small favour?'

She didn't flinch under his gaze. 'Maro's ills began with a small favour.'

'What's she got to do with it?'

'When I said earlier that my mind was elsewhere, I was thinking about Maro. And her lost reputation.'

'How's that your fault?'

'You think I wasn't involved in her being sent to Souyia? The first time.'

'I thought that was Petro?'

'When she "fell" I despised her for throwing away her reputation. For bringing dishonour on us all. If I hadn't, maybe I could have persuaded Petro not to make her pay...'

'Would he have listened?'

'You're too harsh on him. His principles...'

'Sound more like intolerance to me.'

'Nevertheless...'

'You'll let him treat you like Maro?'

She glared at him. 'I have to go to the spring for water in a little while. I find I can compose my thoughts there.'

She turned away from the table then glanced back.

'Kiwi? One thing.'

'Yeah?'

'I am leaving.'

He heard her coming through the trees and splashed the cold spring water over his head and face. Now it came to it, he wasn't sure what he hoped to achieve.

She balanced an earthen water jug on her shoulder. And spoke before he could. 'It was the only decision I could make. I'm his wife.'

All he could respond with were the words of the widow in Maralia, before she struck the blow. '"Faithful unto death"?'

'There is no other way.'

'The widow wasn't accusing you.'

'This is Kriti, Kiwi. Can you understand?'

'A wife killing herself over her dead husband? Yeah, perhaps. It's the marriage arranged at fifteen that I...'

'Trying to undo the past won't help. If we could, my family

wouldn't be dead. And I'd still be betrothed to Petro. I wouldn't even know you existed.'

'You think being a clerk in Christchurch is existing? After my dad died, we lived in the past. Even going to university wasn't an escape. But I'd settle for that again if your family were alive.'

'They're not. Nor is your father. That's what we have to settle for. That's what I've chosen to settle for. Now I must go back.'

She motioned to him to step aside and lowered the jug to the spring. A shaft of sunlight through the trees caught the down on her arm and wrenched him back to his first sight of her. What he didn't say now would stay unspoken for ever. Just like with his dad. 'I thought nothing could be worse than when I believed you were dead. Being so close has been bad but it's had compensations. The thought of when you're not here...'

'Stop. You created a dream, Kiwi.'

He held the piece of blue cloth out to her. 'Did I? Then perhaps you'd better have this back.'

She made no move to take it, her attention fixed on holding the jug steady under the flow. He folded the cloth and put it back in his pocket. He tried to sound light-hearted. 'If you did stay, when he leaves...'

She wheeled on him, letting the jug overflow. 'That's not why you suggested that he...?'

'No! No... D'you want to hear something funny?'

'No. Especially if it's one of Andreas' jokes.'

'I've been recalled.'

'Recalled? Where to?'

'Cairo.'

He saw the shock register and forced a grin. 'So while Petros is having his operation, I could be showing you the sights of Egypt. The Pyramids...'

'But... when is this?'

'When you leave. They'll be sending a sub.'

'Then... why the talk of... when you've..?'

Her confusion made him stop teasing. 'Because I'm staying.'

She blushed and stared hard at him. 'Staying?'

The turmoil on her face tore at him. 'You didn't really think I'd abandon your people, did you?'

She continued to stare. Then dropped her gaze. 'Of course not. No more than I can abandon my wedding vows.'

She bent to the jug, slopped the excess water from it and stepped away. She hoisted it to her shoulder. 'My thoughts are with you in the struggle. That's all I can promise. I'm sorry.'

'So am I.'

She nodded and hurried off. As she did so an old woman in black scuttled away behind the trees. He hissed "Shit" to himself and closed his eyes.

Eleni's impending departure threw him into a frenzy of activity. He stepped up the attrition. Keeping Souyia under constant surveillance, they targeted small patrols and isolated transports. Where they couldn't grab supplies they spread fear, hoping to provoke Jacobi to commit another force to be ambushed. The drain on ammunition continued.

Still there was no word of Maro or Pavlos.

He had the useless radio – hoarded by Costis and lugged about with the camp even though he'd long ago advised Yiannis to dump it – laid out on a table outside his tent. He and Costis sat on boxes opposite each other peering at its innards. He kept his back to the camp.

'So the British did send us a fucking radio repair man, after all, Kiwi?' Yiannis stood at his shoulder.

'Costis knows more about them than I do.'

'He did well to keep quiet about it, then. What you gonna do? If you get it to work, it'll only let the fuckin' Germans pin-point where it is.'

'Precisely.'

'Oh, I see. Clever, Kiwi. Just don't expect me to hump the fucking thing up to inaccessible caves.'

'Not even for the chance of shooting the search parties?'

'I'll just do the fucking shooting.'

Kiwi laughed. Yiannis wandered off muttering.

'W-would Aleko g-give you a c-codebook, Kiwi?' Costis asked. 'To c-contact C-cairo direct?'

Costis' question puzzled him. He'd told no one but Yiorgos and Eleni of Dancy's coming though the cutting off of the supply drops was common knowledge. 'What good would that do, Costi? Unless we agree to go to Leros, Major Dancy won't listen.'

'B-but someone else might. If you c-continue to s-send news of our f-fight, s-someone m-might respond.'

You don't know the British, Costi, he thought but said nothing. It was an impossiblity. Even without the state of the radio.

'Surely it needs new parts, Costi? It must be completely dead after all the hammering it's had?'

'P-patience, Kiwi. You n-never know.'

Patience? Chance would be a fine thing.

'With your own radio, Neo Zealandi, you'll be able to do as you please. Even more than you do now.'

He turned in surprise to see Petros leaning on the two crutches. For the past few days the pain had kept him in his tent. The injured man seemed to him shrunken, except for the old fire about the eyes. Yet the barbed tone of his observation stifled any pity.

Wondering what tale the old woman had told, he swivelled back to the table and peered at a valve. 'Need more than a radio for that.'

'I'm sure you'll find a way.'

'Not without a codebook – and a willing accomplice in Cairo.'

'In Cairo? You have one in mind?'

'They'd need to be committed to the cause.'

'And know your intentions.'

Petros didn't sound as if he was aware of the recall. Eleni must have withstood a grilling.

'My intentions have always been plain.'

'And a Neo Zealandis would be proud of that?'

'Completely. Be what you seem. We've got no time for the devious, the scheming, the underhand.'

The sneer heightened in Petros' voice. 'Not even the underhand? You amaze me, Neo Zealandi. I thought you were well-practised in that art.'

'Only since joining with you.'

'Where you've schemed to exploit any weakness.'

The insinuation got under his skin. He swung round to retort. And saw Maro hobbling across the camp, her face pained. Surely Jacobi hadn't caught *her*? He stood up and offered her the box to sit on.

People hurried over. She gathered herself and looked from Petros to Kiwi then at the ground. 'Pavlos is dead.'

He heard the common groan. 'Was it... quick?'

Maro shot him an anguished glance. 'No. They worked on him for over a day...'

He shut his eyes. In Cairo it was reckoned the Gestapo could break a man in twenty hours. Yet if Jacobi knew where they were, why had they seen no movement in Souyia? Or had they become too complacent? 'Then he broke?'

'He died.'

Loud sobs cut into his thoughts. He glanced at Eleni. Was there relief in her agony? He felt none himself.

'He died in silence?' Petros asked. 'Loyal to the cause?'

She gave Petros a curt nod. Then looked up. 'All they know is that there is a New Zealander, Kiwi. They believe all their difficulties come from him.'

'They, too?' Petros snorted. 'And where did you hear this fanciful notion? From Pavlo himself?'

'From Tsacobi.'

'Tsacobi?' Petros echoed his own shock.

'No one would say anything, except that they had a terrorist and that Gluckstein, their Gestapo interrogator, would break him. So last night I got Friedrich drunk...'

'Friedrich?' Petros scoffed.

'Hush, Petro. Go on, Maro,' Eleni said.

'Instead of walking beside the beach behind the tamarisk trees I steered him down the street next to their headquarters building, Ari knows which it is. There is an alley that runs between it and the end houses. I was able to lure him down it and sit looking out to sea...'

She paused as if expecting more scorn then went on.

'I don't know what I hoped to hear. There was shouting from the balcony above. Friedrich protested that we should go but I persuaded him to wait until the men up there went in, in case they heard us and he got into trouble. One of the men, older I'd guess, sounded pleased. Very drunk but laughing at the other. The other said little but all of a sudden I heard a loud slap. There were protests from the older man then a door slammed and we heard no more.'

'Very informative, I'm sure,' Petros said. 'But how does this tell us that Pavlos is dead?'

'I wheedled it out of Friedrich. Bortmann, the older man, had been laughing at the other, Tsacobi, because his interrogator had let the victim die without giving up any secrets. In fact, even though Pavlos was very weak, he had taunted them...'

'Jesus,' was all Kiwi could murmur.

He held her her gaze and waited for her to go on. 'He must have told them that the New Zealander would destroy them all because Bortmann threw the remark in Tsacobi's face and that's when Tsacobi slapped him.'

'Destroy them all, Neo Zealandi..?' Petros grimaced at Eleni. '... Pavlos truly had fallen under your spell.'

'Did Friedrich hear anything more?'

Maro shook her head. 'I don't think so. It wasn't easy to persuade him to talk at all, then... he fell asleep. I had to leave. I was afraid he might remember what he'd told me. I don't think I will be able to return there. '

'You did well, Maro.' He patted her arm. 'Thank you for your courage.'

She gave him a wistful smile and limped off. He sat down again. 'Are you hurt?' he called after her.

'The guard at the gate, when I left. He wanted... I had to fight him off and run. I tripped in a gully. I'm OK.'

The crowd dispersed. He saw Eleni draw Maro away.

'Looking pleased with yourself, Neo Zealandi? What it is to be the height of popularity.'

'Oh, don't be so childish, Petro.'

'Childish? My most loyal compatriot has been tortured to death and you smile. Should I rejoice, too?'

'If you set aside your petty fears, yes.'

'Mind what you say, Neo Zealandi.'

'Why? Will you hit me with your crutch? Listen to reason for once. Pavlos knew what he was about. He's stirred up conflict among the Germans and Jacobi's cut up over this tale about me, otherwise why react as he did? Pavlos has achieved what might have taken us months. If we're lucky, Jacobi will commit a sizeable force to coming after us.'

'After you, Neo Zealandi.'

'Yeah, if that's what spurs him on, but we can then…'

'You, you mean…'

'Christ, you're not still upset by…?'

'No, I'm taking my men with me.'

The statement was his own slap in the face.

'You're what?'

'Their solidarity must be maintained. And without Pavlo…'

'Don't worry. I'm not going to convert them.'

'I can't afford to waste any more.'

'Waste? Who have I wasted…? Oh, right… Listen, Pavlos went his own way. Any attempt at rescue would have been futile. We could have lost everyone.'

'So you say.'

'And s-so d-do your own m-men.'

Costis' intervention stopped the conversation. Kiwi snatched up a valve and examined it. His eyes wouldn't focus. He tried to take in Petros' bombshell.

'It all comes down to trust,' Petros said to his back.

'Your men get my vote.'

'You know what I mean.'

'I told you, Pavlos…'

'It's not about Pavlo.'

He exhaled and looked at Costis but all that drew was a raised finger as if the Cretan had remembered something. Costis stood up and hurried off, leaving him to squint at the valve. 'Got your spies on me, have you?' he said. '"Use any means available"? Even an old crone pretending to pick herbs?'

'You may have betrayed Pavlo…'

He set down the valve and stared into his empty tent.

'I've betrayed no one.'

'You think I can't see what you're trying to do?'

'That's only your baseless fear.'

'Baseless? Hah.'

'And for that you'd cripple us by taking your men away when we stand a chance of inflicting a major blow.'

Petros greeted this with a snort. Then sneered: 'Planning something at the spring, were you?'

He turned slowly to face his accuser. 'Oh, yeah. I thought if I could persuade the wife to remain, then, once the husband was out of the way…'

Petros swung his right crutch. Kiwi ducked, slipping off the box and grabbing the end as he fell. Petros staggered and jabbed the crutch down at him. He parried and shoved back. Petros stepped on his bad foot to steady himself. 'Agh. You treacherous bastard…'

Kiwi scrambled on to one knee. With both hands on the crutch he pushed Petros back and stood up. If Petros didn't concede he'd be forced over. The hate in in the man's eyes showed he wouldn't let go.

'Stop this!'

Eleni grasped the centre of the crutch, her eyes flashing from him to Petros. 'What are you two fools doing?'

With a shame-faced shrug he released his end. Eleni swung away from him and lowered the crutch for her husband to regain his balance. Petros stared at the ground. Kiwi panted, cursing himself for letting himself go.

People had rushed out at the row. Eleni clapped her hands and ushered them away. As they cleared he saw Yiorgos standing behind, bemused. And Alec, who grinned at Petros. 'No time for dancing practice now, I'm afraid, boys. The sub's expected tomorrow night. At Kaloyeros. You'll need to set off tonight and then move down to the beach in late afternoon. So, Petro, your troubles are nearly solved…'

Petros grunted and stumped off. Eleni tried to help him but was pushed away. Kiwi wished he'd finished the fight.

When he turned back Yiorgos was sitting on Costis' box, fiddling with a valve, a broad grin on his face. 'What fun you're having, Kiwi. Can I play?'

'Only if you want Costis to shoot you.'

Yiorgos jumped up and loped off. Kiwi looked round at Alec and found more disapproval. It was the last thing he needed. 'You're standing there like a prefect again.'

'Sounds as though this sub's coming just in time.'

'Before I kill Petros, you mean?'

'Things as bad as that, eh?'

'Almost. Would Dancy give me a gong if I did?'

'Don't count on it. But you can ask him yourself.'

'I'm not going to Cairo.'

'You don't have to.'

'They've not rescinded the order?'

'Dancy's coming here.'

'Dancy? Here? What for, the ride?'

'To replace me.'

'To... oh, come on. Dancy, in the mountains? Tell me you and Yiorgos have made this up on the way down.'

'He's also been instructed to ensure you leave.'

This was becoming unreal. 'Bringing an army with him, is he? Let's hope so. An army's exactly what we need.'

'Kiwi, you can't laugh your way out of this one.'

'Who's laughing?'

'Or disobey a direct order.'

'Want to watch me?'

'He's being sent by Brigadier Keble. With the Brigadier's full authority. To make sure you fall into line. Push him too far and he'll have you shot.'

'Yeah? I think he'd really enjoy that.'

'Well, then...'

'Better shoot the bugger first, hadn't I?'

'That's lunatic talk.'

'Yiannis says I'm crazy.'

'Even craziness has its limits.'

His flippancy was draining away. He glowered at Alec.

'Listen, we – the Allies, the British, all of us – let Crete down once before. In '41. I haven't come back to do it again. I'm not betraying these people a second time.'

'I didn't want his arrival to catch you unawares, that's all.'

'Thanks. Kaloyeros, you said? Pretty rough there when we landed. Andrea, Yiorgos and I nearly drowned...'

'Kiwi, don't even think about it.'

'No, too public. But I do know an interesting deep pit up above Achlada...'

And he knew, too, that this was only a desperate attempt to stave off the forebodings of defeat. On all fronts.

Thirteen

The farewell meal had barely avoided becoming a mass brawl. Taunts of cowardice and betrayal were flung at Petros' men. Only a sense of shame seemed to mute their response. Petros himself remained unmoved.

Kiwi kept the news of his own dismissal – and intentions – to himself. That also was from shame. He'd talked boldly to Alec about what he'd do but in Cairo Dancy had soon cut him down to size. Who was to say the same wouldn't happen here? He drank stolidly. And what had been the sum of his achievements on the island? To leave the Cretans worse off than before he came.

He must have fallen into a deep sleep. He swayed on the rope in the pit, with a leaden Petros squeezing the breath out of him. Then he was clutching the hanged man. He choked, fighting to push the thing away. And saw it was his dead father hanging there, the eyes closed in silent condemnation. He ached to cut down the corpse but couldn't stir. From somewhere came cries of 'You're useless. You never think. Why can't you stop to think?'

When he awoke in the dark everywhere was silent. His mouth felt dry and choked with ash and dust.

He kicked at the pebbles at the water's edge and scanned the sea. On top of everything, they'd come down here far too early. He'd have preferred staying hidden on the slopes that ran down into the bay, but the size of the party and the Petros' difficulty with walking had dictated otherwise. He hadn't had the stomach to object.

He glanced to his left. Most of the party lounged in the shade of the rocks below the the low cliffs that formed the eastern headland. Petros appeared to be lying with his head on Eleni's lap. The thought of the husband's taunts if he approached made him look away.

There'd been no sign of Alec. Slipped off to savour Crete's final autumn scents in solitude, he suspected. Someone else departing without a proper farewell.

He peered towards the western headland, to which the beach curved round and levelled. Much lower than its counterpart, it also ran further into the sea. These two prongs might keep the bay safe from prying eyes along the coast. But they limited how much he could see out.

His mind flicked back to Jacobi. Guarding Petros' departure and the arrival of Dancy were only distractions from the disaster he knew was looming. One they were too weak to resist. One that he nevertheless had to confront. But his resolve seemed little more than fatalism now.

Nor did the feeble precautions he'd left behind help: Ari and Yiorgos watching Souyia for any movement, while above the valley Andonis at least with ammunition for the Kostouyerako machine gun. Even so he felt vulnerable here. Higher ground was always safer.

Ignoring Andreas' suggestive whistling beside him, he gazed inland, over the spines of pine-flecked hills that sloped down towards the sea. Up to the bleached granite walls that formed the high ridges above. Bare, elemental Nature. A world stripped of illusion. One that put man's selfish intrigues into sharp perpective. Today more than ever they taunted him with his own insignificance. He might as well never have left New Zealand.

He turned back to watch Yiannis trudging towards the sentry at the western end of the bay. And recalled how unprepared he'd been for his first arrival on this beach. He sighed.

'Letting it get to you?' Andreas grinned.

'I'll be glad when this distraction is over.'

Andreas laughed and nodded towards Petros' group.

'There's still time to join her...'

'Forget it.'

'But, Kiwi, in Egypt adultery is the national sport...'

'That's not what it's all about.'

'Of course it's what it's about. Sometimes I do despair about you. Are these New Zealand morals or just your father's own special brand of self-denial?'

His gaze was on the sentry scampering across the sand towards Yiannis. And Yiannis staring behind the running man. He heard the shouts. 'Germans! Hordes of them.'

'Shit, Andrea!'

His guard had slipped again. But where the hell had they come from? He glanced at Petros' group. There was no easy way out for them up the cliff. They had to come back along the beach.

Grey uniforms emerged onto the sand at its western end. He cursed himself again for being caught out and wondered why Ari and Yiorgos had brought no warning. If he couldn't delay the enemy before they advanced too far, Petros – and Eleni – would be trapped.

The only cover came from undulations in the centre of the beach – barely dunes. It wasn't much but it was all he could see. Yiannis and the sentry had dropped among the rocks just before them. 'Defensive line, with Yianni!' he shouted.

Yiannis' firing had cut the German swagger along the shore. But others were working their way across its fringes among the trees and he saw his flank needed withdrawing if it was to avoid being turned. 'Fall back,' he shouted.

And regretted it. Seeing a withdrawal, the enemy surged forward. He sprayed their advance then scurried and dived behind a ridge of packed sand. With dismay he saw that Petros' party hadn't stirred. Where the hell was Alec, to get a grip? If they didn't move, they were lost. His present tactics had only slowed the closing of the trap.

He paced his bursts to when the attackers became bold and tried to think. They also were reverting to more calculated tactics, covering each other and crawling forward. To his right a Cretan kept up a steady fire from the side of the dune. He glanced across to offer thanks.

And started. 'Eleni! What the hell...?'

For answer she stood up and fired past him.

He turned to see the German lobbing a grenade. The shot knocked the soldier back as he threw but the stick handle revolved in slow motion as it arched upward. Kiwi glimpsed Eleni rolling away. He struggled to his feet and heard her shout. 'Get down, Kiwi!'

A wall of sand blasted him. His ears rang. He sensed figures jumbled in the gritty haze. His mind protested that the Germans shouldn't have crept up on that flank.

Yiannis' cry carried through the din. 'Kiwi!'

His body felt too heavy. He wondered with irritation where he'd been hit this time. He closed his eyes to pull his thoughts together. And remembered Eleni.

His eyes opened with a start. He lay on his back on the sand. With a German officer pointing a pistol at him. Smiling. A satisfied smile. It was too confusing. He had no time for puzzles now.

His eyes skittered around, searching for Eleni. The dune was bare. The battle sounded further off. His ears popped and he saw he was stuck in a dip in the dunes. Out of sight of everyone.

He stared at the German. An SS uniform, but surely too normal-looking a man? He took in a thin-faced Gestapo captain and and helmeted infantryman standing behind. He wished they'd clear off and let him look for Eleni. The SS officer began to speak, still with the smile. And to his further disbelief, in calm and perfect English.

'So you are the New Zealander?'

The man's assurance only fired his resentment. 'No, I'm a poor man called Vasili from Kyriako...'

The bullet kicked up sand beside his head. The officer's face took on a pained expression. 'Don't insult my intelligence. You can't imagine the trouble you've put me to. How fortunate that we meet...'

Kiwi cringed at the sarcasm. Could this really be Jacobi? The SS Officer nodded towards the unseen Cretans.

'... though not, I'm afraid, for the fools who put their trust in you. They're about to pay for their folly.'

'Go to Hell.'

Jacobi's smile widened. Kiwi still couldn't grasp the man's clean-cut features. Or laughing eyes. He felt cheated. If he was to die, why couldn't he have Petros' sneering hate? Jacobi was calling back over his shoulder to the thin-faced Gestapo man. 'Something Bavarian about these colonials, don't you think, Gluckstein? So provincial...'

The Gestapo officer didn't seem in the mood for jokes, either, but grumbled something in German, the only recognisable word being "Souyia".

'Oh, I will. When he's in your capable hands. As long as you're more careful with him than with the last one.'

Kiwi tried to clear his head. The fighting sounded more sporadic. Had the Germans already over-run Petros?

The indulgent voice cut his speculation. 'A slow death is more satisfying, wouldn't you say? Like a fading adagio. Shooting peasants is so… banal. One has to do it. To remind them of the imperfection of the world they persist in clinging to.'

Kiwi gritted his teeth. How could monstrosity sound so refined? He couldn't get his mind round the contradiction between this man and the hanging corpse in Maralia. His bafflement riled him into provocation.

'Adagio? Gonna sing us some Schubert, then?'

The German's smile tightened. The gun gestured. 'Don't sneer at sublimity, New Zealander. Or you may provoke me into treating *you* as a peasant.'

'Me dad'd agree with you there, about peasants. Right miserable bugger, he was. He liked Schubert, too.'

'Indeed? Then he appreciated how high the music soars, did he? What a pity that, by the sound of it, so little was passed on to you.'

'Should have sung while he beat me, should he?'

Jacobi stiffened. 'I did warn you…'

'Major, don't let him make you…' Gluckstein began.

Jacobi half-turned then stopped. What was it going to be next? More sarcasm? Some observation worse than one of Dancy's? Why didn't he just get on with it?

But a red spot flared in the centre of Jacobi's broad brow. His legs began to buckle. A second shot felled the infantryman. Gluckstein ducked away and the next moment Kiwi's arms were grabbed by Yiannis and Andreas and he was swept off in a whirl of sand.

Back in the line he struggled to understand. Andreas hissed at him that Costis' rapid fire had caused a German retreat. That must have brought the confusion in which Jacobi was shot. He still couldn't grasp it. Then he saw the enemy were massing for a further charge.

He glanced around. This defensive line clung to the last cover before the beach ran along to the cliff. They should pull back or risk being split. He spied Petros with a rifle, propped against a rock. Still no sign of Alec. And what had become of Eleni? A wave of terror swept him.

'Eleni? Where's Eleni?'

'Kiwi, there's no time. Look,' Andreas cried.

German troops had infiltrated along the trees. Another outflanking movement. Swarming fast enough to cut his men off from Petros'. Again he'd been too slow. Now his anger kicked in.

Grabbing a bren, he called 'Retire, Andrea!' over his shoulder and darted towards the sea. His sudden movement gave him a start. As the Germans turned on him, he hared for the low, flat rocks on the water-line and tumbled behind them.

Bullets spat off the rocks and the air buzzed with shards and ricochets. Lying flat, panting, he saw that his rush had given his own men time to scramble back some way along the beach. If they could re-group below the cliff and hold on till nightfall, some might then slip away. It was their only chance – provided the weight of the enemy assault didn't overwhelm them first. And they hadn't yet reached the shelter of the cliff. The German advance needed a bigger distraction. He checked the bren.

Eleni rolling aside on the dune flashed before him. He stood up and fired a burst, ducking back as the rocks took another broadside. If he could draw the Germans' attention further to him, the Cretan withdrawal might be completed. Some could be saved. He felt a shiver of regret at ending it like this. But sometimes only reckless disregard would do.

He leapt onto the flat rock, glimpsing the grey-uniformed wave veering towards him. He sensed it hesitate. Faces stared at him in surprise. Time seemed to stop. Without thinking, he hurled the challenge of Galatas.

'Ka mateh! Ka Mateh!'

The war cry's echo came back off the mountains. There was a momentary pause. A bullet whistled past him. He dived backwards and hugged the sand. Stone fragments sprayed him. At once the air erupted in a fusillade of fire. A deafening storm beyond his wildest hopes.

He gasped for breath below the rocks. The rattling roar went on and on. Human cries rose above it. The fury of noise froze his mind. Yet something was trying to register. He couldn't make out what. Then it did. This time, somehow, the rock above him wasn't being hit.

He risked a quick peep. And ducked down in shock. Swathes of bodies lay on the sand. At the fringe of the beach seethed another broken mass. He saw again the pile before Eleni's door. But these heaps were larger and made no sense.

He glanced to his left. Scattered troops staggered or plunged off along the beach. Several stumbled and fell. As he watched, Gluckstein stepped out from the trees and fired a revolver in the air to halt the panic. A trooper paused, swung his rifle from the hip, shot down the Gestapo officer and followed the others on their way.

The chattering roar ceased. His brain still wouldn't work. He peered towards the cliffs. He could pick out individuals at the foot. Costis… Andreas… Yiannis. He breathed out in relief. Sifis… And Petros. Even so, they seemed too few for the scale of carnage wreaked. His eyes scanned the top of the bluff.

Alec raised an arm to him. So that's where he'd been hiding. A few yards away Yiorgos also waved. Grinning, no doubt. Beside Yiorgos he recognised Andonis. How did they come to be there? On the ground, between Yiorgos and Alec, he recognised the shape. And with a start understood. The rattling roar should have told him. His salvation had been the Kostouyerako heavy machine gun.

The recognition swept Eleni back. He stumbled to the hump of dune. Jacobi's dead face stared at him in disbelief. The infantryman lay crumpled. Two other bodies were men. He waded though the sand. There was no sign.

A shout from the cliff reminded him he stood outlined on the rise. He glanced after the fleeing enemy. None showed any interest in returning fire now.

He worked his way along the beach, peering at bodies, hope rising then wrenched back by bewilderment. How could she have vanished? He sought out Petros again. Petros stood now, among the rocks, using a rifle as a crutch. Eleni was not there. His chest tightened. His mind couldn't think.

'You nearly fucking did it this time.'

He blinked at Yiannis beside him shaking his head.

'When I said you were a fucking lunatic,' Yiannis went on, 'I'd seen fucking nothing. That charge was truly mad.'

'Set them up nicely, though, Kiwi. I take it you'd seen us – with the machine gun?'

He peered at Alec's sweat-streaked face. 'Saw you? No... I just hoped to give the others time to pull back...'

'See what I mean, Aleko. Utter fucking lunacy.'

The sound of shots made him turn. To see Cretans probing among the bodies. He started awake. 'What the hell are they...?'

'No prisoners,' Yiannis said.

'But...'

'Yiorgos met a runner from the north. This morning all the hostages from Livada were killed.'

He closed his eyes. That wouldn't register, either. Had Jacobi had the last word in death? His eyes shot open.

'Eleni? Where's Eleni?'

Yiannis frowned at him then towards the cliff. 'She's with... Isn't she?'

'She was next to me. Firing. A grenade blew. Then Jacobi... And you were pulling me away, Yianni. You didn't see...? Or you, Andrea? Did you see Eleni?'

'Only you and two Germans.'

'How could she just disappear? I've looked...'

'They had prisoners.'

He swivelled to confront Andonis. A downcast face. 'As they pulled back the first time,' Andonis continued, 'they picked up three prisoners. I saw them bundled into the trees. Then that officer came out and stopped the flight.'

'Gestapo officer?'

'I couldn't tell. When they came on again...'

His head pounded. He clutched at hopes. 'If it was the Gestapo officer, he was shot as they fled. By one of his own men. The prisoners may still be...'

'N-no, K-k-kiwi...'

Costis had come up behind. He was shaking his head. 'I s-saw that, too. W-we've been to c-check. There are n-none of our p-people t-there. A-l-live or dead.'

He stared past Costis along the now deserted beach. Another gunshot broke his daze. 'And we're shooting prisoners?'

'They won't know that yet,' Alec said.

'Is that supposed to reassure me?'

'Why do you want reassurance, Neo Zealandi? Haven't you achieved your great victory?'

His gorge rose. Shouldn't the man's concern be for Eleni? Petros had turned away to address Andonis. 'Andoni, thanks. But how did you arrive here so fast?'

Could the husband really be unaware of his wife's disappearance? Andonis seemed to share his own surprise.

'It was Ari and Yiorgos, Petro. They spied the Germans assembling and ran to me. By then we had guessed where they were going. We stripped the gun and came here. Almost too late. But Aleko was the one who fired it.'

'Value of listening to your dad, Kiwi,' Alec said. 'My father was a Lewis gunner in the last war. Always going on about how not to shoot too high. But, Petro...'

Alec's brow furrowed, as if he, too, was bemused.

'...we think Eleni...'

'I saw where she went... Is she dead?'

'She's a prisoner, we suspec..,' Alec began.

'You let them capture her? What were you doing? First, Pavlos, now this. What is it with you people?'

The man's rage sounded forced but there was no time to puzzle why. 'Petro, never mind that,' he said.

'Never mind? If she's in their hands, she's dead.'

'Not necessarily.'

'Better if she were.'

He forced the awful thought away. 'Not if we act fast.'

'To do what?'

'Mount a rescue.'

'From Souyia? Are you mad?'

'Does it matter? Let's just do it.'

'It would be a crazy stunt, Kiwi,' Alec put in.

Why was everyone so full of bloody objections? He rounded on them. 'Anyone got another idea?'

'Isn't this a guilty conscience talking, Neo Zealandi?'

He gaped at Petros. What the hell did that matter? Could the man not see that his wife's life hung by a thread? Andreas broke the spell with a laugh. 'Kiwi likes guilt, Petro. And attempting the impossible.'

'After today, anything's possible?' Alec said.

Petros shrugged. An urge to hit him surged. Instead Yiannis slapped Kiwi's arm. 'Oh, fuck, count me in.'

'M-me, t-too, K-kiwi.'

His fury evaporated in the chorus of assent.

'But let's get a move on,' Alec said. 'Don't forget we have an appointment before the night's out.'

Flinging orders came as a relief. 'Right. Gather German grenades. And all the ammunition you can carry. Yiorgo, Andoni, fetch the machine gun. Go.'

Yiorgos hared off. The others made to follow.

'Wait…'

He turned in exasperation. What did the fool want now? Petros leaned forward on his rifle-crutch, face blank.

'… It's suicide. Pavlos and I reconnoitred Souyia, remember? It's a fortress. There's no way in.'

'We'll work one out.'

'Through the wire? The ground is cleared all round the perimeter. Mined. They'll cut you down before you get close – like you did to them here.'

'I wasn't planning on charging in in daylight.'

'Even so, there are searchlights…'

He gritted his teeth. Why all these obstructions? 'Thanks for telling me. It's been noted.'

'You're taking an unnecessary risk.'

Unnecessary? It was the man's wife they were about to save. A dark suspicion crossed his mind. Before he could retort Yiannis butted in. 'Why're you so fucking worried about our safety all of a sudden, Petro?'

'I merely want you to be aware of the danger you're…'

'Liar. You'd fucking love to see us get a beating.'

'That's absurd.'

'I can't see why else you're fucking panicking.'

But Kiwi could. All of a sudden it was clear. 'You don't want us to try, do you?' he said softly.

Petros' face betrayed no emotion. 'She'd understand.'

'Understand?'

'An individual can't come before the general good.'

'She's your wife!'

Petros shifted his weight on the crutch. 'She knows the way the Party…'

'The Party? You bastard…'

He fought an urge to shatter the impassive mask. Yiannis spat on the ground at Petros' feet. 'Fucking communist shit.'

'They'll still cut you down.'

'No, they won't. We'll walk in.' Alec held up a torn German tunic. 'Wearing these.'

He stared at Alec, unable to follow him.

'Obgleich mein Deutsch ist ziemlich rostig.'

'What the hell does that mean?'

'Either "My German is rather rusty" or "Help me mother, I've lost my sakouli." Shall we dress?'

Laughter broke the tension. Kiwi glanced at Petros, still unable to comprehend the husband's vindictiveness. He shook his head at him. 'This is your reward for her loyalty to you, is it? If I wanted *you* dead, at least I'd tell you straight.'

He stalked off, his heart pounding. Yes, it was a crazy risk. But simply abandoning Eleni…? She'd committed herself to the man. He still couldn't credit it. Until Petros' words in the pit swept back to him: 'With us, a woman who strays chooses death.'

He shivered. Even if they could spring her from the Germans, would that really be salvation?

He decided to take only Andreas, Yiannis and Costis, with Ari to guide them inside Souyia. Stealth was their best hope. He left the machine gun behind with Andonis.

Alec insisted that his knowledge of German, rusty or not, made him essential. Hoping it might cause his boss to miss the sub helped him acquiesce. Maro's offer to distract the guards he also accepted, not caring that his desire to atone drove that, too. In addition he chose a couple of Petros' men for cover.

Only two guards appeared to man the entry post on the shore road. From somewhere inside the town came raucous singing. Hopefully they were drowning their sorrows well.

He motioned Alec and Costis forward and watched them stumble in their German uniforms towards the post. Yiannis and Andreas slipped into the ditch and crept along behind them. Costis fell and Alec called out in German what sounded like a plea. The sole word he caught was 'Bitte' before Alec, too, slumped to his knees.

The guards dashed out and hauled him to his feet. With a loud groan Alec sagged, pulling the Germans off-balance. As one, Yiannis and Andreas had their knives in them and were dragging the bodies to the ditch.

Leaving Petros' men in place of the guards, Kiwi led the others forward to the shadow of the end house – used as workshops, Ari said, so empty at night – and sent the boy to reconnoitre. Apart from the carousing the place seemed asleep. Though it felt an age, Ari was soon back.

'The headquarters is on this street, up there on the left, just past the bend. There's a sentry outside. The cells are on the ground floor. If Eleni and the others are here, that's where they'll be.'

'And the singing?'

'From the cantina on the far corner. No threat.'

'Can we get close to the sentry?'

'Not easily.'

'Kiwi,' Maro hissed. 'I can do this. We must take care. They always have a sentry inside as well.'

When she outlined her plan, Andreas was quick to volunteer. Kiwi over-ruled him: Alec's German made him the safer choice. He chafed for them to hurry. 'Just get on with it, before anyone else appears. Lure him as far from the door as you can. And quietly, Alec.'

He drew back as Alec and Maro, arms round each other's shoulders, swayed up the street. The light was dim but he still held his breath. When he heard their altercation he peered round. Not so loud, he muttered to himself.

Maro made to break free from Alec. Kiwi caught the sound of giggling and again shrank from the noise. If the second German guard came out, they'd be done for. He heard Alec laugh and saw Maro pinned against the near wall. The sentry was crossing the street towards them. Maro escaped, ran and clung to the startled sentry. As she turned him, Alec slipped up behind and broke his neck.

Yiannis and Andreas dragged the body down an alley. The others huddled in the shadow of the building. He listened. Only the singing. He nodded to Alec.

Alec took Maro's left arm while he grasped her right and gestured to Alec to open the door.

Alec backed in dragging Maro, who thrashed to free herself. In the harsh glare Kiwi glimpsed the German guard's surprise. He kicked the door to and heard Alec's laugh.

'Verdammt Kretanische luder. Ist eine zelle frei?'

Kiwi let slip her arm. So did Alec. She threw herself on the floor, grabbed the guard's legs and gabbled up at him. The noise seemed to echo. Alec swore and bent to drag her off. Then drove his knife up under the German's ribs. The guard collapsed with a grunt.

Kiwi bade them stop and listen. Nothing. Easing the outside door open he waved the others in. Two cells gave on the corridor. He slid the bar across the spyhole in the first door and peered in. Too dark. He tried the door. Locked. Shit. If a gaoler was elsewhere with the keys, they were stuck. He peered round in despair. Alec held up his hand, turned over the guard and handed him a bunch.

The third key turned the lock. He pushed open the door. It creaked. Only two occupants. The one sitting on the floor looked up in terror. Takis. He put his finger to his lips lest Takis cry out. The second figure lay on the bench asleep. Holding his breath, he bent to see. Male.

'Where's Eleni?' he hissed to Takis.

Takis stared at him wide-eyed and shrugged his shoulders. He flung out of the cell and fumbled the keys in the second door. He realised he was breathing hard. It was all taking too long. The joyful muttering of the freed captives grated on him.

The door swung ajar. He stepped in. Empty.

He threw a silent plea at Ari. The boy nodded upwards.

'The only other room is the big boss's.'

'More guards?'

'Not sure.'

'Then let's get it over with,' Alec said.

'No, wait, leave it to me...'

He wanted to face bad news alone. 'Besides, we've been here too long. Alec, take everyone back.' And added in English, 'If you happen to drown Dancy on the beach...'

'Kiwi...'

'No. I'm not coming. You know why. Now, go.'

Alec met his stare then nodded and shepherded the prisoners and Ari and Maro out. The other three didn't follow. 'Would I desert a woman?' Andreas asked.

'If her dowry was too small...'

Andreas' pained expression surprised him but there was no time to ponder that. 'All right, come on. Costi, round the front and try the balcony. You two, watch out for the stairs creaking.'

On the bare landing the only light showed under the door to the front. The rear two doors were locked. He put his ear to the front one. A man's voice. A heavy drone. Was the speaker alone? It was of no account. He took out his pistol, nodded to the others and reached for the handle.

The voice became a snarl. He flung open the door.

In the far corner a thick-set, uniformed fifty year-old swung round and gaped. Beyond him, on the floor, Eleni sprawled against the wall. Alive. He saw her shirt was torn. The German's surprise became rage. 'Raus! Ich brauche keine hilfe…'

Eleni raised bound hands as the assailant swayed back to her with a beery laugh. 'Eine fuchsin, diese. Ich habe die behandlung…' The man glanced round again. 'Was? Nicht sie sagen…?

Before the German could move Kiwi flung him across the desk in the centre of the room. He glimpsed Andreas seize him, Yiannis slide the door to and Costis slip in from the balcony as he turned to Eleni.

The fury on her face made him recoil. She kicked at him and raised the bound fists in defiance. He held up his hands. She shuffled away along the wall. He couldn't speak. He tried to implore her but nothing came.

'What's this? Lovers' meeting, New Zealand style,' Andreas called.

She stopped and gaped at Andreas, astonishment flooding her face. Her eyes swept back to him. She grimaced, let out a deep groan, closed her eyes and sank back against the wall. He leapt to her. 'Eleni? You all right.'

He dragged her to sit and cradled her in his arms. She opened her eyes and peered at him then at his tunic. 'Not a good joke, Kiwi. Far too convincing.'

Of course, the uniform. How could he have forgotten? Her faint smile disconcerted him more. She held up her wrists. 'Would you mind? This isn't the most fitting pose for a married woman to find herself in.'

He heard Andreas laugh and scrambled to help her up. Yiannis brought a chair then slit her bonds. She rubbed her wrists.

He turned away at the sight of the red wheals and studied the German, now slumped in the desk chair with Andreas' knife to his throat. His eyes swivelled back to Eleni's torn shirt. 'This animal… he didn't…?'

'No. Your timing, as ever, was excellent, Kiwi.'

'You sure you're not hurt?'

'Only my pride at being caught. He drank a lot and sounded as if he was boasting about something. When he started to make advances I spat at him and he turned nasty. That's when you came in.'

He pointed at the German and said "Namen?" He wished he'd allowed Alec to stay. The German sniffed. 'Bortmann. Herr Major Bortmann.'

Yiannis swung round at the name. 'The one who ordered Livada and Moni burnt? Shall I cut his fucking throat?'

Bortmann's eyes widened as Yiannis took out his knife and proceeded to wipe it on a dirty rag.

'We should take him with us,' Andreas laughed, tapping the top of Bortmann's head with his own knife. 'The women from Livada would have a good time with him.'

'W-whatever we d-do, let's g-go,' Costis said, the sadness in his eyes heavy. Kiwi nodded. Some losses never healed.

Yiannis pocketed the rag and examined the blade.

Bortmann darted for the balcony doors. Costis stepped across to block him. Before he could, Yiannis was on his back, driving in the knife. Both crashed down in the doorway.

Kiwi froze. He heard Bortmann grunt, once. The faint echo of singing floated in. He breathed out.

Yiannis pushed himself up off Bortmann and held up his knife in amazement. It had broken off at the hilt.

'That the one you used on me? Looks like I had a lucky escape.'

'And another one tonight, Kiwi,' Andreas said. 'If you miss meeting your Major Dancy, too.'

His mood darkened. He'd forgotten about Dancy. He helped Eleni up and saw her frown. 'Am I too late for leaving on the submarine?'

He avoided meeting her eyes. 'I'm not sure that Petros...'

'He's not dead?'

The horror in her voice crushed him. 'Far from it. But... We have to leave. I'll explain later.'

He offered Eleni his arm to the door but she demurred and went out first. What the hell did he do next? He hadn't thought. Anything that didn't involve the beach.

How would she take that? Or the news of Petros' rejection of her. He saw again the look on Bortmann's face when the door was flung open. That's what her husband had abandoned her to. And to Gluckstein's successor...

A tearing sound startled him. He swung round. Costis was grinning now, rolling up the map he'd ripped off the wall. 'T-they w-won't n-need this any time s-soon.'

Trust Costis to be the one thinking ahead. It brought home to him the enormity of what they'd done.

He shook his head and went out. Success. Could it really be? He wasn't sure how to handle that.

Fourteen

Daylight. He opened his eyes with a start and jerked round. The camp was still asleep. He stared at the old crone huddled in a chair across the way. The one from the wood. She'd not shut her eyes quickly enough when he turned. Was she Eleni's shadow?

He turned back to the table. He must have put his head down and then dropped off. He gazed at the closed flap of his tent. No sound came from inside. The chill of the clear autumn dawn made him shiver. Or was it the thought of Eleni, asleep there on his bed? So close and so far.

As a result of his cowardice. After they'd cleared Souyia he'd said nothing about their destination. When they'd cut inland, up towards Koustoyerako, she'd stopped them. He dreaded the question he knew was coming. 'Why are we going this way?'

'It's the safer route.'

'Not to Kaloyeros.'

'The sub will have gone.'

'Are you sure of that?'

'Fairly sure.'

He was glad that in the dark she couldn't see him clearly. She must have sensed his evasiveness because she didn't let go. 'Then why don't we…? Kiwi, what are you doing? I said I was leaving. You haven't done all this just to…?'

'No! It's… for your own good.'

'My own good? I'll be the judge of that, thank you. I want you to take me to the beach. Do you hear?'

He groped for some excuse, conscious of the others listening. Yiannis' growl came out of the darkness. 'Oh, for fuck's sake, just tell her, Kiwi.'

'Tell me what?'

'It's not easy to… Can it wait?'

'You don't have to protect me from bad news, Kiwi. Remember?'

'Your bastard husband…' Yiannis' voice came again.

'No, Yianni. It's OK…'

'Well, don't take all fucking night over it, then.'

He could see her eyes glinting in the dark now. 'Petros didn't want us to attempt a rescue…'

'Why not?'

The sharpness in her tone shook his resolve. 'He said you'd understand… That it was too risky. That no individual could come before the good of all…'

'I see.'

'We didn't believe the bastard, either,' Yiannis said.

'So you've decided I shouldn't have the chance to hear him for myself, Kiwi? That was noble of you.'

'He was prepared to abandon you to the Germans. To that drunken sot, Bortmann… To the Gestapo.'

'Nevertheless…'

'He wanted you dead!'

'So you say.'

'It w-wasn't j-just K-kiwi.'

He gave silent thanks to Costis. Her heavy breathing was audible in the dark but the distance between them weighed down on him. He waited for her next onslaught.

Instead a crashing in the undergrowth had him reaching for his gun but Yiannis started to laugh.

'Ari, you noisy little bast…'

'Sorry, Yianni. Kiwi, I ran up to the point. From there you can see the bay…'

Kiwi groaned to himself. No doubt Ari meant well but…

'… The sub's gone.'

He tried to keep the relief out of his voice. 'Gone? You certain?'

'A darker shape. Moving out to sea, then disappearing.'

Somebody coughed. He couldn't see Eleni's face.

'We ready to move?' Yiannis called.

'Eleni?'

'Yes, Kiwi. Wherever. And thank you for rescuing me. All of you. I am grateful for that.'

From there she'd said no more until they reached the camp. And then only on finding new occupants in her hut.

'Don't worry. I can sleep on the ground.'

'No, you won't. Use my tent. Just for now.'

She was too exhausted to argue. When he steered her to the entrance, she stumbled inside and flopped on the bed. She was asleep before he draped the German tunic over her. He drew the flap to and sat facing it on the bench at the table. His mind had gone numb.

The camp began to stir. One or two people patted his shoulder as they passed. There was some excited chatter but he hushed it. He wondered how they knew. Then he saw that Maro had also come back here. He nodded acknowledgment to her. And sensed the intake of breath from the now-wideawake crone.

As usual he'd acted without any clear idea of the consequences. Saving Eleni was all that had counted. He supposed he'd had an ulterior motive but dismissed the thought. Why should that matter? Yet the guilt lingered, perhaps pricked by her unfinished accusation.

Shying from such thoughts only reminded him of Dancy. And made him groan inside. He couldn't be bothered with that pain-in-the-neck now. His only hope was that Andonis would lead the Major up the long way round and allow them some additional respite.

The tent flap shook. Eleni ducked out, glanced around the camp and lowered herself onto the bench opposite him. She stared at her hands, clasped on the table.

'You want some coffee?' he asked.

She shook her head then looked up. The fierceness in her eyes alarmed him. But her words came as a surprise. 'I'm sorry for my rudeness last night. It was... shock.'

'The whole day was a shock... And it was my fault. I should have broken the news to you more carefully.'

This did bring a faint smile. 'I'm not sure you can break that kind of news carefully. It's not what anyone wants to hear.'

'No, I suppose not. Never had much experience of it, myself. Did a good night's sleep help?'

The frankness of her laugh disconcerted him more. 'You think I had a good night's sleep?'

'You were out before you hit the bed.'

'Was I? I remember nothing.'

It was his turn, and a relief, to laugh. 'Doesn't that constitute "good"?'

'Until I woke up. The dark seemed to last a long time. It reminded me…'

'Yeah…'

He reached for her hand but she moved it aside and gave a nervous glance past him. He'd forgotten the crone.

'What do you want to do now?' he asked.

'I don't know. Do I need to do anything? It's not the first time I've been separated from Petro.'

The comment hit him like a smack. Yet what had he expected? That she'd also have made the break, as Petros had? Since emerging from his tent he felt she'd closed the gap between them. Now she'd reminded him it was a gulf. He tried to sound calm. 'Isn't it a bit different this time?'

'I won't know that until he returns, will I?'

Returns? Shit. So she still wouldn't believe…? Hadn't she once told him you had to make the best of a marriage? He saw Petros again on the beach and his anger flared at the thought of her deluding herself. But if that's how she wanted it… He realised he'd not been listening. 'Sorry. I didn't sleep much, either. What did you say?'

'I said it's unfortunate I didn't see him last night.'

'What would you have gained from that?'

'I'd have known.'

'Why won't you just be told?'

That had come out too stark. Her face clouded. 'I know you wouldn't exaggerate…'

'No, I wouldn't. And you heard Costi…'

'The Party doesn't always arouse sympathy in others.'

'Eleni, listen. All he had to do was say nothing. He wasn't expected to come with us...'

'He was right not to allow the personal...'

'He's your husband, for God's sake.'

'Yet, if you, too, had been captured, or...'

'He didn't even want us to try. To go and look. To assess the chances. If you'd been surrounded by a regiment of the Waffen SS...'

'You'd have done what? Meekly walked away?'

'Thought of something.'

'Not hurled yourself at them in a futile gesture..?'

'It wouldn't have been a gesture.'

'But it would have been futile. It wouldn't have saved me and it might have destroyed the cause.'

'It wasn't like that. You weren't there. On the beach.'

'I know my own husband.'

'I'm not sure you do.'

'I beg your pardon?'

This was spiralling out of his hands. He didn't care. She had to face the truth. For her own sake. 'Petros doesn't trust you.'

'If I've given him cause...'

'You've given him no cause. It's all in his head.'

'Then I must be more careful. I told you...'

'It's too late for that.'

'Too late? Just because, in the heat of the moment...'

'No, not there...'

He let all his anger go with a sigh. She wouldn't be beaten down. He closed his eyes then looked her full in the face. When he spoke his voice was hushed. 'In the pit. When he came round and saw it was me, he asked why I didn't finish him off. He said no one would know.'

Her eyes regarded him with a steady stare.

'Then he said to me "You think I didn't notice?" I pretended I thought he'd banged his head, had gone crazy. But he carried on. He reminded me "Your ways are not our ways". He'd told me that after the sheep ambush. When he appeared. We were laughing... You remember?'

From the flicker in her eyes he saw she did and wondered if she, too, recalled the shared confidences from earlier on that walk. He kept his eyes on hers, afraid that if he looked away his nerve would go. 'Yes, "Your ways are not our ways", he said. Then he added: "With us, a woman who strays chooses death."'

She struggled to hold his gaze then looked down, starting to shake. He put his hands on hers and when she tried to draw them away again clamped them. 'No. Just think about it. Not now. Not all at once. I expect nothing out of this. I just can't bear the thought of you deluding yourself. D'you understand?'

She flicked a glance at him. He glimpsed the tears. She nodded. Her voice was flat and dull. 'I don't delude myself. I know… But it can't make any difference.'

He removed his hands and stared at the top of her head. The bleakness of it appalled him. He thought of his mother's self-denial and his father's unforgiving God. Beside this, their obduracy seemed inconsequential.

She was holding herself tight to control the shaking. Even so he caught a sob.

'Sorry,' he shrugged. 'I was never any good at understanding people. Too impatient for anyone's good.'

She gave him a weak smile. 'No, you were trying to help.'

'My dad always said good intentions weren't enough.'

'You're not going to blame everything on your tortured childhood again?'

He saw her spirit reviving and played up to it. 'You do know how to hurt a kiwi "oddy".'

'No more demonstrations, please?'

'Is there nothing I'm allowed to do?'

'Defeat the Germans and set my country free.'

That suddenly reminded him. He swung round, peering to see if Yiannis had stirred. 'Yianni!'

He regretted his abruptness as he saw the alarm flood back across her face.

'What's the matter?' she asked.

'I'd forgotten about the Germans.'

'Because you were too busy rescuing me?'

He could feel her slipping back into resignation. He tried flippancy.

'Blame Alec. He wanted to dress up as a German.'

'Alec was with you?'

'He led us in. But when you weren't in the cells below, I sent him away. With the others.'

He realised too late his mistake.

'To the beach?'

The doubt in her eyes unnerved him. 'There might still have been time. Then. But by the time we'd…'

'Don't you ever fucking sleep?' A bleary-eyed Yiannis stood by the table, the shadows on his face deeper.

'Too much. Where's Andoni?'

'Above Souyia. With the machine gun. Where'd you think? He says the fuckers are in no hurry to come out and bury their dead. Lucky that, because I sent twenty men down there to strip them.'

That reminded him of something else he'd forgotten.

'What about our casualties?'

'Seven dead. Ten wounded. They'll bring them up. We'll be rolling in rifles and boots. Let's hope there's ammunition left. The bastards always fire off too much of it. Now, can I go back to sleep?'

Feeling small, he watched Yiannis return then risked a glance at Eleni. Her puzzled frown brought back his unease. However, her confusion this time came from elsewhere. 'If it needs twenty men to bury the bodies..?'

'They lost a hundred and fifty. More.'

'How? When the grenade blew up we were in trouble…'

'That was Alec, too. With his secret weapon.'

'Secret weapon?'

'Though it wouldn't have been a secret to you.'

'Stop playing games. Please.'

'The machine gun. The one you faced in the square in Koustoyerako. Alec turned it on them.'

She looked pensive. 'I see.'

He tried to drag a smile from her. 'Mind you, that wasn't what caused the rout.'

'No? What was it?'

'My kiwi impression.'

She laughed and slapped his hand. Then started. She stared past him.

'Ignore her,' he said. 'She can't report to Petro anything he hasn't already dreamed himself.'

She shook her head and continued to stare. 'You have a visitor. And by the look of him I'd guess he's not the type to appreciate kiwi impressions.'

He resisted the urge to turn round, keeping his eyes on Eleni's face. Damn the bastard. He cursed himself, too. Unprepared again. He gritted his teeth and waited for the command. But the first words – English – made him grin.

'I walked in here unchallenged.'

'Bloody sentries. I'll kill 'em,' he replied, also in English. 'They had instructions to shoot on sight.'

'You were ordered to leave.'

He watched Eleni scan Dancy and pulled a face at her.

'Had a prior appointment.'

'I won't stand insubordination.'

He laughed. He could hear people coming out to see.

'On your feet when I'm addressing you.'

He yawned and stretched out his arms. 'I'm too bloody tired.'

He saw the fear in Eleni's face. Heard the pistol cocked. He raised his eyebrows at her, kept his arms raised – in surrender now – and swivelled on the bench.

The sight of Dancy surprised him. The major had lost weight, though his red face and dishevelled uniform suggested the ascent from the coast had affected more than his temper. Dancy extended his arm in the air and fired.

Kiwi flinched from the sound of the shot, arms still raised. More people tumbled out of tents and shelters. Yiannis and Andreas had rifles. He glimpsed Yiorgos and Costis hurrying across.

Dancy called out to the assembling crowd, still in English. 'I'm dismissing this man.'

Kiwi shrugged at the puzzled faces regarding him. Dancy shouted at them. 'Take him and place him under guard.'

No one moved. Kiwi folded his arms. 'Want me to translate that, Major?'

Dancy ignored him and glared at the crowd. 'Does anyone here speak English?'

'What the fuck's he saying, Kiwi?'

'He wants you to lock me up, Yianni. For insulting his grandmother.'

'You didn't try to flirt with her?' Andreas called.

The crowd laughed. Dancy waved the gun at Yiorgos.

'You. Georgios. Come out here. I know you speak some English. Tell them I'm arresting Watkins.'

'But forgive me, Kapetan…' Yiorgos began, in Greek.

'Major. Speak English.'

'Bloody hell, Kapetan, no know what are Ouatkiss. That Johnny not bloody Ouatkiss. Oh, no.'

Kiwi leaned back to savour Yiorgos' impression of a Cairo spiv. Dancy wasn't amused. 'Stop playing the fool with me. Tell them to do as they're ordered, you hear?'

The tone drew an angry growl from the crowd.

'Who is this fucker?' Yiannis called.

'The new Aleko,' Andreas laughed. 'The one who cut off our supply drops.'

'Then I say we fucking lock *him* up.'

Yiannis stalked forward. Dancy raised the gun. The next moment he staggered back holding his cheek. Kiwi stood, snatched the gun and tossed it to Andreas. He steadied Dancy then sat back down and sought for Costis in the crowd. He hadn't seen the pebble coming, either.

Dancy stared at the blood on his hand and felt his cheek again. Then the Major turned on him. 'You'll pay for this, Watkins. Inciting mutiny.'

'They're Resistance. Independent.'

Dancy swung back on them. His courage was admirable, even if it was brainless. The Englishman sneered. 'They're still under your command. Ill-disciplined rabble. Worse than a bunch of... Turkos.'

They may not have understood Dancy's English but the name of their hereditary enemy didn't need translation. A roar growled from many throats. They crowded in on him. Two men seized his arms from behind. Yiannis whipped out a gleaming knife. 'No fucker calls *me* that and lives.'

With a deft flick Yiannis slit Dancy's tunic to the throat and held the point to the Major's neck. It was tempting to let them have their way. He felt Eleni's hand grip his arm and heard her voice, urgent, at his back. 'Kiwi!'

He knew Yiannis was only playing with Dancy but the force of Eleni's plea made him intervene. 'OK. Enough, Yianni.'

Yiannis shrugged at him, grinned at Dancy and stepped back. Then with a sudden lunge he slit Dancy's shirt, too, in one swift move. The crowd gasped with delight.

The two men released Dancy. Yiannis spat on the ground. Kiwi felt Eleni let go his arm and glanced to see her stand up and step back. She looked appalled. He frowned a question. Her eyes guided his to the right, where the crowd was parting. 'Kiwi, look...'

Sifis was at the head of Petros' men. Two of them were setting down the litter. His mind struggled to make sense of the sight. His eyes sought out Yiorgos for an answer. Yiorgos shrugged and looked away.

Hands were helping Petros struggle upright. The injured man snatched his crutch and limped through the silent people, his eyes raking them. His glance flicked from Dancy to Eleni with the old, disdainful air. 'What's going on?'

Yet when Kiwi met Petros' glare he saw the bravado of a man who knew his moral authority had gone. He breathed out in relief and tried to sound nonchalant. 'Petro? How was Cairo? We came back from Souyia...' He indicated Eleni. '... As you can see.'

Her face was stone. For a moment he feared he'd said the wrong thing. Again. Nor did her husband recoil. 'I can see you've wasted no time..,' Petros said, then turned to the crowd and waved to dismiss them. 'This is over. Sifi, look to the English.'

Kiwi's gaze followed Dancy being helped away. That breach didn't take long. And had been predictable. At least he'd never counted on a resumption of air drops. Even if their dependence on the enemy for supply would now become total.

People drifted off. He waited for Petros to follow but the man made no move. Eleni stood looking down. He couldn't see her face. He sensed he was in the way.

'You can leave us, too, Neo Zealandi.'

"Possession is nine tenths of the law" went through his head. Why, he didn't know. Where had that come from – the university law course? It was about to be demonstrated, if she persisted with her perverse notions of duty. Her lowered head only increased his dejection. She was about to submit to servitude. He pushed himself up.

'No. Stay, Kiwi.'

He looked at her in surprise. She was staring at Petros. 'I've heard one side of the story, Petro. Now I want to hear what you have to say.'

He sank back on the bench and studied the floor. Why did she want him here? To leave him in no doubt?

The suppressed fury in Petros' retort was unmistakeable. 'I have nothing to apologise for.'

'Who claimed you had? But things have been said.'

'And you were fool enough to believe them?'

Kiwi glanced up in alarm but her face was set.

'Don't treat me like a child, Petro.'

'I'm your husband.'

'And since yesterday I've fought a battle, been taken prisoner and had to resist a drunken German commander. Oh, and been rescued, too. Which is the only reason I'm here. So I think I deserve some respect.'

He glimpsed Petros' dismissive wave. And her puzzled frown. 'But why have you returned, Petro? Your foot...'

'Isn't it fortunate I have?'

'Now *you're* being a fool. Did the submarine not come?'

'I needed to know if you were safe.'

There was a pause. 'You were concerned for my safety?'

'You know why I thought they were mad to try. Have I taught you nothing?'

'You've taught me a lot.'

'But not, from the sound of it, that the control of personal emotion is most necessary when it is most painful.'

'Your pain was apparently less than evident.'

'What do they know? They're ruled only by sentiment.'

'Yiannis said you didn't even want them to try.'

'Because I didn't dare hope. Logic told me... If I was wrong...'

'No, Petro, your logic was sound...'

But, Kiwi wanted to shout at her, it wasn't like that. It wasn't about logic.

'... and you know I share your principles, even in their severity. How else could I have borne the hardships, or supported your difficult decisions taken for the sake of the Struggle? So why should I be surprised by your consistency, now..?'

Was she really going to concede? He listened, with the same furious helplessness as at their first parting.

She paused. Kiwi stared at her, waiting for the word of forgiveness. The surrender. But that flash of hardness crossed her face, as she added: '...towards any woman who strays?'

For a moment he didn't realise what she'd said. Petros' face flushed with fury. 'If I made a misjudgement...'

Her voice was taut. 'You didn't misjudge, did you, Petro? I could forgive you for that. As I forgive you for the pitilessness of your political doctrine. But it was neither of those, was it? You know what it was... And what it was cancels my vow.'

She worked the ring from her finger. Petros looked like thunder. 'You can't make that decision.'

For answer she held up the ring. 'Once I couldn't. But I've heeded your lesson. Wasn't it you who said that, in fighting for People's Democracy, women fight also to be equal and free of the constraints of the past?'

Petros' face twisted. Eleni put the ring in her pocket.

'From now on, I shall sleep in my own hut.'

'Do you want to humiliate me?'

'Don't sound so pitiful.'

'You still belong to me.'

'No, I've become free, Petro. Free. Because you yourself broke the tie.'

She held his gaze. Petros tried to sneer. 'Don't imagine I'll forgive you for this.'

He swung round on the crutch and limped away.

Kiwi rested his chin on his fist and avoided looking at Eleni. He realised he was breathing in short gasps.

Her voice rang in his ear. 'Go! Go away. Now!'

He looked round with a start. To see the old crone scuttling off. When he turned back Eleni shrugged at him. 'Isn't that what you call "burning your boats"?'

'More like blowing them to pieces, I think.'

She gave a heavy sigh. 'He should have been more honest with me…'

'Are there degrees of honesty?'

'But was I right?'

'You don't need me to tell you.'

'Don't I? Don't over-estimate me.'

'Over-estimate you? I felt roasted alive just listening. I'd have surrendered on the spot.'

She managed a wry smile. 'I had a good teacher. Once.'

He didn't want to know. His mind couldn't take in what she'd done. And hadn't he, too, just broken his own bonds? But where did these reckless acts leave both of them? Petros' earlier conclusion – 'reduced to dust'– came back to him.

He gazed round the camp. The people were still fugitives, still denied their own homes. Even after yesterday the Germans held Souyia and dominated the South. The only redemption lay in ending that injustice. But how?

Fifteen

He struck the table with the flat of his hand.

'Offensive.'

'I'm sorry,' Eleni said. 'I wasn't thinking...'

'No... What am I doing? Why am I worrying about Dancy? And Petro. We should be stepping up the attack ourselves.'

'Isn't everyone worn out?'

'So what state must they be in? In Souyia they're leaderless. It's our move. I've been so used to hitting and running. Now we should have *them* on the run.'

'With the numbers they still have?'

'Numbers are less use in the mountains. If we can keep pressing them down here...'

He leapt up and set off for Yiannis' tent. His legs felt stiff. Eleni wasn't wrong. They *were* exhausted. But if they let the pressure off... He could imagine in Souyia the effect on the Germans of finding Bortmann's body.

When he'd roused Yiannis and Andreas he returned to the table. Maro placed two coffee cups on the table, nodded to him and slipped away. He called to her. 'Maro. Thank you. We couldn't have done it without you.'

She pursed her lips. She'd been crying.

'Are you all right?'

She glanced at Eleni and then gave him a faint smile.

'Friedrich. My... contact... in Souyia. Yesterday I came across his body with all the others on the beach.'

'Not before we...'

She nodded and walked off. He stared after her.

'Jesus Christ.'

'I don't understand,' Eleni said.

'Twice in getting to you we were only able to fool the guards because Maro played the part of a victimised woman. Yet she'd just found the body of the man, the enemy, she'd let herself fall for. And she said nothing about it. The things this war does to people...'

'It's what *we* do to people that's worse, Kiwi.'

'I didn't mean to get at you.'

'She'd broken the rules. The rules were clear. And had to be enforced. They were all that held us together.'

'Like I said, this war...'

'It's not the war. I was at fault. I shouldn't have swallowed the rules so completely.'

He recalled her submission to Petros at Koustoyerako.

'Did you have much choice?'

'I didn't even try.'

'Don't blame yourself for it. Anyway, those rules don't apply here. Fortunately.'

His attempt at humour didn't work. Her eyes flashed.

'Doesn't that just make me a hypocrite?'

'Things change. And if you'd stuck up for her, she'd never have met her... Friedrich.'

'For all the good it did her.'

She looked drained. He felt ashamed of himself. He'd forgotten how much she'd been through in the last twenty-four hours. While he was trying to make jokes.

The arrival of Yiannis and a sleepy Andreas forced the focus onto practicalities.

'What now, then? No fucking rest for the wicked?'

'We're going to hit them while they're down.'

'That's more like it. Where?'

'Everywhere.'

'Fuck me. Sorry, Eleni. Ain't that a bit ambitious?'

'It's their nerves we're working on. If we shoot up Souyia and their outposts...'

'We'll be out of ammo,' Andreas yawned.

'Not with that collected from the beach. We have to make them think we're more than we are. So, groups of five, to Moni, Linoseli and Souyia. Hit and move.'

'Andonis is at Souyia.'

'I want the machine gun moving up to Epanohori for an ambush. Anything coming south from Hania. I'll take a party to do the same for Omalos at Agio Theodoro.'

'No, you fucking won't.'

He raised his eyebrows at Yiannis. Yiannis glanced at Eleni. 'You'll stay here. It's the fucking enemy within we have to watch. You should have let me slit that Dancy fucker's throat while I had the chance.'

'The British tend to take offence at that sort of thing. It's against their rules.'

He felt Eleni stiffen. Yiannis snorted. 'What'll they do, stop dropping us supplies?'

He held up his hand to calm Yiannis, but he was grateful for the injection of commonsense. 'You're right, Yianni. I need to stay. I ought to make my peace with Major Dancy.'

'Want my knife?'

'We may need his help sometime.'

'What fuckin' use will he be?'

'The radio, Yianni. He's our only link with Cairo. Yes, I know, but even so... You and Andreas set the ambushes. Tell the men to show themselves as much as they dare.'

He watched the bustle of departure. Eleni grimaced. 'I suppose you won't allow me to go with them?'

'No.'

'You don't believe in equality for women?'

'You're too tired.'

'And the men aren't?'

'They haven't been taken prisoner.'

'You're avoiding the issue.'

'That's what my ma always said.'

'Now you're making it a joke!'

'After we'd recovered the sheep, Petros lectured me about how he didn't allow women on raids in case they were captured.'

'That would never happen to me.'

'Who's making jokes now?'

But he was pleased to see her spirits revive.

The pleasure was soon doused. Dancy stalked across the camp towards them. Kiwi felt his jaw clench.

'Don't forget you're making your peace with him, Kiwi.'

'I should have taken up Yianni's offer.'

'Yianni's knife's effect on him yesterday doesn't seem to have lasted.'

'In Cairo he never struck me as the sensitive sort.'

'Unlike you, then?'

He snorted at her and, without rising, saluted Dancy.

'Morning, Major. Sleep well?'

'What are you trying to do, Watkins?'

He gave Dancy a puzzled frown. He *was* puzzled. 'Win the war?'

'Don't try to be clever with me.'

He sighed. This was going to be hard work. 'Look, Major, you're not in Cairo, now. So can we get a few things straight? I appreciate we started off on the wrong foot, but…'

'Insubordination, insults, a knife to my throat?'

'Our nerves were on edge.'

'Save it for the inquiry.'

Kiwi glanced at Eleni. Dancy's tone and body language seemed to be enabling her to catch the drift.

'Why are you persisting in offensive operations,' Dancy went on behind him, 'when the explicit orders from Cairo were to avoid confrontation?'

'They started it.'

'I've warned you, Watkins. You've despatched men to attack German posts now, haven't you?'

'What? Oh, those men? No, they've gone foraging for food.'

'Don't take me for a fool, man.'

'Me, Major?'

'Petros told me what your orders were.'

'Petros? How?'

'Didn't you know he speaks English?'

This news, and Dancy's old supercilious manner, jolted him. He frowned at Eleni and asked her in Greek: 'Petros knows English?'

'Perhaps. Some. I think he learned in Athens. Before the War he had books. Politics.'

'The deceiving bastard.'

He turned back to Dancy, his mind still struggling with the revelation. He tried to recall any conversations with Alec that Petros might have overheard. Dancy smirked. 'So don't bother to pull the wool over my eyes, will you, Watkins? Petros can be very enlightening.'

No doubt. And would lose no opportunity to poison Dancy's mind. Not that it needed help. He tried to brush past Dancy's complacency. 'So you're in the picture about the situation here? Good. You'll know the tide's turning. You've arrived at just the right time.'

'Indeed. But as you deployed those men without consulting me…'

'Consulting you?'

'I am your superior officer. You may have been given undue leeway by Fielding but from now on the irregular forces are under my command and will be used only on my say-so. Is that understood?'

'They won't go to Leros, whatever you order.'

Hesitation flickered in Dancy's face. 'I won't be ordering them to Leros.'

'No? All going smoothly without us, eh?'

'Leros has been evacuated.'

Sfakia flashed across his mind. He gaped at Dancy.

'Evacuated?'

'The enemy counter-attacked in overwhelming strength.'

'Jesus. And the losses?'

'Heavy. But that has nothing to do with…'

'Of course it has. If only we'd had some of those losses. And all the more need to exploit our success now. Don't you see? They're on the back foot here. If we keep up the pressure. And if the British switch their focus…'

'Calm down, Watkins. A re-appraisal is taking place…'

'Taking place? Over how long? The chance will be lost.'

'And it's very likely,' Dancy continued, 'that the new priority will be to consolidate Rhodes.'

'Rhodes? Are they mad? Can't they see, can't you radio them and make them understand that the best opportunity is here? We're close to forcing them back north. If we hit them now...'

Dancy's airy wave of the hand cut him off. 'Aren't you forgetting something..?'

He was remembering how frustrated their first meeting in Cairo had left him. Now the self-important prick had got under his skin again.

'...You've been recalled.'

Dancy stood there smug and composed. Oh, for Yiannis' knife. Elbow on the table, Kiwi rested his head on his hand and closed his eyes.

Even after the 'welcome' from the Cretans, was Dancy really too dense to accept the reality of the situation? He might have expected that. Now, Petros' support must have emboldened the fool. Very well. If Dancy refused to face facts, they'd have to be spelt out.

He looked up at the Major. 'Let's get some things straight. Sir. Your strategy may have failed on Leros but it's not going to ruin things here. If you try, I have to warn you, and you know it's not an idle threat, the Cretans will kill you. They're fighting to liberate their homeland and no amount of your petty bureaucracy will stop them. D'you understand?'

'They remain junior partners in the alliance.'

'It's their country! Look around you. Junior partners? They're on their own. Abandoned. Where is your bloody alliance? It's a fiction. A lie.'

This did make Dancy quail but the Major's change of tone still surprised him. 'I'm not a vindictive man, Watkins. I am willing to compromise.'

'Compromise? Doesn't that mean we all share the bits we don't want? And guarantee more failure?'

'I am prepared to consider the wishes of the Cretans.'

Kiwi glanced at Eleni and saw she regarded Dancy with scorn. He called over his shoulder in Greek. 'He says he's prepared to consider your wishes.'

'As a guest, and an unwelcome one, that's very generous of him.'

'Is there some problem?' Dancy asked.

'She wonders what the trick is.'

'I will be doing you all a favour.'

'Great. How soon can they arrive? The reinforcements.'

'Don't be immature.'

'That's all the favour we need.'

'All you need to do, Watkins, is hand over command…'

'Hand over command? Ha!'

'… to your co-leader…'

'To Petro?'

'Isn't that what he is?'

'You want me to hand over… to the Communists? Didn't you tell me..?'

'And I will overlook your insubordination and other, more serious, offences.'

'So Petros can have me shot, instead?'

Eleni prodded him in the back. 'What is this about Petro?'

'It's Dancy's generous offer. If I surrender to Petro, all is forgiven. We might even receive supply drops.'

'You're not serious?'

'He is. Shall I ask if Petros gets you back, as well?'

'Just pass me your gun.'

'Well?' Dancy said.

'I need time to think it over. Sir.'

'Don't take all night. I have to leave for HQ. You can provide me with an escort for that, can't you?'

'Yiorgos will take you. He knows how to avoid trouble.'

'I don't like his attitude.'

'I'd keep your prejudices to yourself. You wouldn't want him leading you into a German ambush, would you?'

'Don't push your luck, Watkins. I'll start as soon as you've made your decision.'

'Yiorgo!'

The lad's startled face popped out of his tent.

'There's a donkey needs leading up to HQ.'

'His or the Germans'?'

'What's he saying about Germans?' Dancy asked.

'He said he'll make sure you avoid them.'

Dancy turned away with a snort. Kiwi called after him.

'Major. I have thought. About your compromise.'

He savoured the surprise on Dancy's face. 'Yeah. Long and hard…
Stick it.'

Dancy seemed to absorb this in slow motion. Then turned on his
heel and stalked off towards Petros' hut.

All afternoon the sound of distant gunfire had flickered. It was early
evening when he watched Yiorgos, with a jaunty step, lead Dancy away
up the valley. He indicated Petros to Eleni with a smile. Her husband
leaned in his doorway and glared after the departing pair.

'Petros doesn't seem happy to see Dancy leave. What do you think
they found to discuss? The benefits of Communism for the English
middle class?'

'Dancy represents everything the Party despises.'

'Maybe. But they've both smelt some advantage in getting
friendly.'

'I don't want to think about Petro.'

'If I'd agreed, we'd be under arrest by now.'

'Can we talk about something else?'

'Ever had a shaved head?'

'That's not funny.'

'Don't worry. He'd probably just have had both of us shot. D'you
think we'd have been allowed to hold hands?'

'Don't you ever listen, Kiwi?'

'Non-stop.'

'You're incorrigible.'

'I'm what? That's another Greek word I've never heard of. Should
I be pleased?'

'You should be locked in the coal shed. I can understand your
brother's actions now.'

'Fine. Find a coal shed. Lock me in.'

It was a relief to see her amused. And to be free of Dancy. Several dull explosions made him glance south.

'Is that Souyia?' Eleni asked.

'Yeah. Not sure what. Maybe Andonis got lucky.'

'You're lucky we have no coal shed here.'

'Wouldn't bother me.'

'Really?'

'After that pit, the dark holds no fears.'

Her face clouded then she grinned. 'You've outgrown your childhood nightmares at last?'

'Stop mocking me.'

'You deserve it.'

'You sound just like my ma.'

'You mean I'm a scold?'

'Did I say my ma was a scold?'

'Among other things. None of which was very pleasant. And I'm not sure that being compared to somebody's mother is particularly flattering anyway.'

'I've not had much experience of flattering women.'

'You haven't denied thinking I'm a scold.'

'I blame all that communism.'

'You do like to live dangerously, don't you?'

'I told you, I'm unused to women.'

'You surprise me. You mean the women in New Zealand are not constantly demanding to be insulted?'

'It was usually the other way round.'

'Ah, like Mina Sfinx?'

'Muriel Spink.'

'I can see her point.'

'Well, she was almost your age. Fourteen.'

She slapped his hand and laughed. 'Fourteen? That *is* more flattering. To be compared to a fourteen year-old instead of your mother.'

'Even if she was a scold, too?'

'I'm beginning to think this is a cross I have to bear. Though I don't know what I've done to deserve it.'

He wanted to stop the banter and bring her close.

'Hiding that sweet, innocent girl under a mask of hardness and duty?'

She tried to laugh this away. 'What makes you believe I was ever sweet and innocent?'

'I saw your eyes when you first offered me the drink. I thought I was in paradise. Now I know I am. Almost.'

She looked away. Her voice was flat. 'You can't talk to me like this, Kiwi.'

'Why not? Aren't you a free woman? Isn't that what you told Petro?'

Her harsh laugh took him aback. 'Free? Yes, but I'm like your bird that can't fly.'

'A kiwi? You're one of us at last?'

'No, I'm not. I've made myself an outcast.'

'Most people will understand.'

'Not here, they won't.'

'They know what happened.'

'That'll soon be forgotten. A woman's place is with her husband. Even if he has wanted her dead.'

'So I can't even tell you I think you're…?'

'Please, no…'

'Where's the harm in it?'

Her eyes stared. Their depths frightened him. 'The harm,' she said in little more than a whisper, 'is that I might listen.'

He shivered. And tried to laugh it off. 'If you're an outcast, what more is there to lose?'

'I'm only doing what I think best.'

Her crestfallen face made him back away. 'Yeah, sorry. I know. I shouldn't have pushed you.'

She forced a smile. 'No, you shouldn't. And anyway, your brother, the priest. What would he call a woman in my situation?'

'With wild eyes and a fierce sense of independence?'

'Kiwi…'

'Who'd left a husband that wanted her dead? Yeah, he'd know immediately what to call you.'

'What?'

'Australian.'

There was a moment's pause. He saw censure but she couldn't hold it and her face broke into a grin. 'Kiwi, you are impossible.'

Relief mingled with his disappointment. He shrugged and gave her a sheepish grin. 'I'm not arguing this time. But, to put the record straight, you don't remind me either of Muriel Spink or my ma. I mean it.'

He watched her weigh up whether he did mean it. And felt closer to her than he'd ever been.

Before she could reply a cry went up from the darkness.

'Kiwi!'

The voice was Ari's. Kiwi rose to see the boy scurrying across the camp. The two collided and he had to disentangle himself from the gasping lad. As he did so he scanned the sweat-soaked face. To his surprise it was struggling to smile at him. 'Souyia, Kiwi,' Ari got out.

'Yes, Ari, calm down. What's wrong?'

Eleni had come round and supported Ari's shoulders.

'Nothing, Kiwi, nothing's *wrong*.'

'Then why all the panic?'

'No panic. I just had to run all the way. To tell you.'

'Good. Then tell me, Ari.'

'Kiwi,' Eleni said. 'Let him speak.'

'I'm trying. Ari?'

The lad gave him a broad grin. 'It's the Germans. They're leaving.'

'Leaving? Leaving Souyia? You're sure?'

'Andonis had us firing all day. Changing our positions. Making them think they were surrounded. In the early afternoon a large caique appeared from the west. It had been spotted passing Lissos and we were waiting above the harbour. We fired and threw grenades. All of a sudden there was a huge explosion and a sheet of flame.'

'Yes, we heard explosions up here. So what was it bringing, ammunition?'

'Gasoline, Andonis said. There were more, smaller explosions from in the town. We didn't know what from.'

'Not burning oil from the caique?'

'Andonis thought they were setting fire to the town. As it grew dusk they put up a terrific barrage of firing on every side. We had to keep our heads down. When it stopped, a convoy of lorries and jeeps raced out and off north. Then all was quiet again. Like a dead place.'

'The entire garrison has fled?'

'It seems so.'

'Has Andonis gone in?'

'He's waiting until daylight. The men were eager but the fires are burning and there may be mines.'

A crowd had gathered and an excited buzz spread through it. He waved them to calm and disperse. 'Tomorrow. Look after Ari. He's brought great news.'

He sat down and stared up the valley in the direction Dancy had gone. A welter of thoughts whirled in his head. He pulled a face at Eleni. 'I wonder if this would have made a difference to Dancy?'

'You think it might?'

'Probably not.'

'Should you send after them?'

'Only Ari could catch Yiorgo but I can't expect him to, now. I can hardly believe it myself. Can they really have abandoned Souyia?'

'You suspect it might be a deception?'

'It's certainly unlike the Germans to run.'

'So they may be back?'

'Not if they've burned it. Shit...'

'What?'

'If they've burned it, there won't be much left for us, will there? We'll have a celebration on an empty stomach. And an offensive that can't take off.'

'We'll be a whole bunch of kiwis?'

'It doesn't bear thinking about.'

'As long as you don't give a demonstration...'

He didn't want to joke about it now. 'Then clear off and sleep before I start.'

'You'll sleep, too?'

'I'll use Andreas' tent.'

'Make sure you do. Good night. And thank you, Kiwi.'

'For what?'

'For making me laugh.'

'Yes, Muriel. Good night.'

He watched her close the flap and sat on, staring at it. He should feel glad. The last two days had brought a transformation. Yet what had he really gained? Eleni had let slip the mask on her feelings but the woman in the tent remained out of his reach.

And the Germans. Could they really have pulled out of Souyia? The term "pyrrhic victory" came into his mind. From school? Latin? A victory that wasn't a victory? How appropriate, if the enemy had laid it waste.

He recalled Galatas and the wild, exhausted ecstasy in the Square after the bayonet charge. There was no elation this time, just exhaustion. And a foreboding that once again exploitation of their success might elude him.

Yes, just like bloody kiwis, Eleni, he thought as he heaved himself to his feet. What had Danna compared them to, headless chickens?

His impression two years ago may have made Eleni laugh but the image didn't brighten his mood now.

Sixteen

A heavy pall of smoke hung above Souyia. The oil tanks still burned. The air stank of gasoline and greasy black flecks settled everywhere. Apart from the noise of fires and the occasional crack of a small explosion all was quiet.

Kiwi and Andonis proceeded side by side down the main road and halted at the perimeter gates. These swung open on the breeze. He suspected the Germans' precipitous withdrawal made it unlikely this route had been mined but he'd advised caution.

Behind, two lines of men followed, rifles at the ready, eyes flitting from the ground ahead of them to the devastation either side. Almost every house lay in ruins. Some burned or smouldered. Others had been dynamited. In haste perhaps but with effect nevertheless.

A light breeze made him gag and holding his arm to his face he peered into the small enclosure on his right. Whatever its crop had been was now singed and dark. An oil drum had been punctured, rolled across it and then set alight. What sort of mind had cared about such petty destruction? The oil wasn't the source of the stench.

The donkeys must have been machine-gunned. He stared and tried to block out the smell of burning flesh. There *were* only donkeys. Any relief was jolted by the sight of a movement. He squinted. The twitching belly was no death-thro. His stomach heaved. 'Wait, Andoni,' he said.

He stepped through the mess, arm pressed hard to his face and came up behind the shuddering animal. Its legs were broken and half its skin charred. As he held the revolver to its neck a red socket flicked upwards. He shut his eyes and pulled the trigger.

'It had to be done, Kiwi,' Andonis smiled.

He shivered. 'They've brought lessons from the Russian Front. Scorched earth. Leave nothing usable.'

'Let's hope the people had the sense to flee.'

Not all had had the chance. Bodies in the dirt looked as though they'd been shot from passing lorries. As the long main street wound down to the shore, the level of destruction both increased and appeared more systematic. Only here and there had doors been spared.

'No, don't go in,' he called as one of the Cretans went to open one. 'It's too neat. Sifi, prod it open with that plank.'

The door groaned and gave way a little. Sifis pushed harder. The door swung. A cloud of dust swept out on the muffled thud.

'See? Treat anything that looks untouched with care. The only thing they'll have left here is death.'

'And stay off the beach,' Andonis ordered. 'Until we can clear the mines.'

For an hour they probed among the rubble. The most complete devastation had been wreaked, as he'd guessed, on storerooms. The HQ building was a shell, a litter of burnt paper blowing around it. The greasy, oily sheen lay everywhere.

Andonis had tried to keep the squatters in the Lissos valley, the former inhabitants forced out of their homes by the German occupation, from coming back in to scavenge. Many had been unable to resist. With predictable results.

A group of old women knelt and wailed over a dead boy. A man stared at the blackened skeleton of his house. And a woman held up ruined fruit and berated them as they passed her along the shore road. 'What have you done? How are we to eat, after this? Eh? Is this what victory looks like? At least before we could scrape a living off them. But now? We'll starve.'

Andonis shooed her away. 'Mind your tongue, woman. You're alive, aren't you?'

'She may be right, Andoni,' he said when she'd gone. 'My plans to re-supply ourselves from the enemy just fell apart. And if Jerry's got any sense, he'll let hunger mount his counter-attack for him.'

'We've got sheep. And we can fish now they're not here to enforce their ban.'

'But we've inherited more hungry mouths.'

'You worry too much, Kiwi. God will provide.'

'Will he? In the meantime, find me five of the most cool-headed men.'

'To teach you patience?'

'To dig up mines on the beach. We'll need them to block the road in case the Germans do decide to return.'

Briefing the five, fashioning wooden probes and emphasising the need to keep strictly in line abreast all took time. The Cretans' natural impulsiveness strained his patience. 'No!' he called out as the line sagged. 'Keep together. Or you risk stepping on one.'

The problem of transporting the mines to the periphery of their liberated territory was another headache but he left that for now. He realised he didn't know how far the German withdrawal had gone. To the west he could make out smoke above Paleochora but it seemed less than here. If only he had Yiorgos. He alone was capable of covering the distances required. In Yiorgos' absence Ari offered himself. 'I can match Yiorgo for speed any day.'

'It's not speed that counts, Ari, you hear? It's care. Don't run into any ambushes. Take the coastal path to Paleochora. If there are Germans there, come back. If they've gone, follow the road north and try to find where they're dug in. Then hurry back. OK?'

'Don't worry, Mr Kiwi. You won't miss Yiorgo now.'

'He'll be all right, Kiwi,' Andonis laughed when Ari had gone. 'He's got a wise head on his shoulders.'

'I know. I remember when I landed...'

That seemed a long time ago. Yet it was only months. He surveyed the blackened wasteland. 'The Brigadier wants some hell raising,' Dancy had said. The order had sounded futile then. He hadn't expected to be standing in the middle of it.

A shot from inland cut his day-dreaming. He ran back along the shore road to the foot of the main street and peered up it. Was it more mercy killing or worse?

'What is it?' he shouted to the guard posted at the top of the hill where the road disappeared from view.

'Vehicle coming,' the man called back.

A dust cloud rose before the jeep careered over the crest. He took out his revolver. If it was Germans they were either mad or drunk. He stepped back and took aim.

Its brakes screeched. The jeep threw up a swirl of grit as it slewed to a shuddering stop. He choked and peered into the cloud. Something made him hold his fire. Two figures staggered out towards him.

'Fine welcome, that is,' Andreas laughed, pointing to the gun. 'When we've brought you a present.'

'Andrea, what the hell are you playing at? A German jeep? You could have been shot.'

'No chance. Only Costis could hit such a target and he's back at Epanohori. You want a ride? It'll impress the women.'

'If you hadn't kicked up so much dust, you'd see there's no one here to impress. How did you get it?'

'Ambush. The old log in the road trick. Costis took out the driver and officer before they'd stopped. We'd have had a lorry, too, but the tank exploded. The ones behind managed to turn back. Still, the lorry's blocking the road. Until they return with lifting gear.'

'Your jeep'll help prevent that.'

Andreas looked horrified. 'You don't want to waste this beauty on a roadblock?'

'I want it to transport mines up there to complete the job. Especially if they can stop some heavy stuff. Did you lose anyone?'

'What do you take me for? We were well hidden.'

'And Yiannis? Have you heard from him?'

'He sent a message. They burned the post above the Gorge and blocked the west road out at Agio Theodoro. A big convoy came across the plain but when they fired on it it stopped and turned back. It's camped in the village but there's no sign of any further attempt.'

'So they are going to let hunger take us first?'

'Hunger?'

'Look around you. We've liberated Souyia and there's nothing left. Including petrol. So mind how you drive that thing. When it runs out of gas, you'll have to get out and push.'

'You're a killjoy, Kiwi, you know that?'

'My pleasure. Were you actually driving or was it…?'

'Course it was me. Don't you recognise style? I bet you've not seen driving like that before.'

'Only once… I attended his funeral.'

They packed the floor and back seat of the jeep with salvaged mines, laying them on sand for stability. He leaned on the windshield as Andreas started the engine.

'You know the expression "she goes like a bomb", Andrea?'

'It describes New Zealand women?'

'Fast cars. Because if you go above walking pace, you may come to understand it in a more personal way.'

'Kiwi, I will treat her as a woman.'

The car revved loudly, juddered forward and shot up the hill. The sound of the jeep faded. He closed his eyes and waited for the explosion.

When he opened them Andonis was regarding him with a grave expression. And nodding towards the terrified-looking young boy standing further off. Kiwi recognised Fotis, from the camp. His heart jumped. 'What is it, Andoni? Not the camp?'

'The sheep.'

'The sheep?'

'They were grazing east of Kaloyeros, above Tripiti…'

'And..?'

'Stolen. Most of them. We left only boys on watch.'

'Surely not Germans? Out there?'

'No, sheep stealers. Though the Germans'll probably end up buying them up north.'

'Shit… And the boys? Are they OK?'

'Aye, though they shouldn't be.'

'Don't blame them. Any point in pursuit?'

'Only Yiorgos would have a chance of tracking them.'

For the second time that day he cursed Dancy for taking Yiorgos away. Until he remembered he'd offered him.

'Anyway, there were many of them,' Andonis went on. 'And they were heavily armed. We could nick sheep back from German thieves but if these are our lot...'

'They're worse than Germans. Where are the remainder of the sheep, Foti?'

'At the camp, sir.'

'OK. You get back now. And don't worry. We all get caught out some time or another.'

The lad ran off. Kiwi shrugged at Andonis. The fruits of winning were already tasting sour. He affected calm.

'Let's finish here for now and follow him. We'll send people down tomorrow to carry on. If anything can be rebuilt, we'll start on it then. As for feeding ourselves, *that* might need a miracle.'

He sent messengers to summon Andreas and Yiannis back to the camp to review their situation. And Costis, too, to work on the radio. Now they were on their own, they'd need any help they could get.

Yiorgos, newly back from delivering Dancy, tried to lift spirits around the table with jokes about the major.

'Slower than an old woman, Kiwi.'

'I hope you didn't get too friendly, Yiorgo.'

'Whenever we saw Germans he was shitting himself.'

He frowned, at the mention of Germans, not Dancy. 'Was that often? That you saw Germans?'

'More than it used to be on Omalos. But they aren't venturing into the mountains. We went up through the pass of Stephanoporo.'

'So Dancy's settled in the cave above Drakona?'

'You wouldn't say settled, Kiwi. A bag of nerves. And he's there on his own for the next week.'

That *was* a surprise. 'On his own? Where's the radio operator?'

'My cousin took him to Amari. Radio problem there.'

'Huh. He should have brought him here. No joy, Costi?'

Costis looked up from the table and made soothing gestures. 'S-soon, may-b-be.'

'He treats that thing like a woman, Kiwi,' Andreas laughed. 'And see what reward he gets. Sorry, Eleni…'

Before she could retort Petros levered himself on his crutches onto a bench at the table. The others edged away from him.

'So how bad is it, Kiwi?' Yiannis growled.

'You've heard about the sheep?'

'Thieving bastards. It'll be those Viglis boys. When I fucking catch up with 'em…'

'Never mind that. But because of it our store position's going to become critical…'

'What do you expect, Neo Zealandi, when you take on the protection of the whole world?' Petros put in.

'Shut the fuck up, you,' Yiannis said.

'Both of you. Listen. German small arms and ammunition we're OK for. Machine gun ammo is low. And the British ammo is almost gone.'

'Fucking bastards.'

'The food situation is the worst. The Germans have left nothing behind…'

'So we're free – to go hungry, Kiwi?' Andreas said.

He nodded and felt the stab of guilt. Hadn't he led them on into this? Muttered curses broke the silence.

'There are fish in the sea,' Sifis offered.

'And what would you catch them from, Sifi?' Yiannis snorted. 'The fuckers burnt all the boats.'

'You could send the families back to their villages,' Petros suggested.

'Spoken like a true Communist, Petro,' Andreas scoffed and indicated the radio. 'Pity you can't call your mates in the Red Army to drop us some stuff.'

'I wish them here as much as you.'

'I bet you do.'

'Then there's the problem of the winter,' Andonis said.

Andonis was ever the practical one. Without British drops or German supplies they already faced starvation. With the loss of the sheep the threat loomed close. Kiwi affected a nonchalance he didn't feel. 'Got an answer to that, Andoni?'

'If we could continue to attack, Kiwi… Force the Germans to retreat back down to Hania before the snow…'

If only it was that simple. Andonis must have glimpsed his impatience because the Cretan went on quickly. 'It may take less than we think. They're under pressure from all sides. After their losses here they'll fear a winter in the mountains, too.'

Petros butted in. 'And what will we pick them off with, Andoni? Almonds? Walnuts? Air?'

'I was asked for the answer. Of course there is a short-term problem.'

'That just happens to be insurmountable.'

'Don't sound so fucking pleased about it, Petro,' Yiannis said and turned to him. 'So, Kiwi, we're fucked?'

He shrugged his shoulders. For the first time since the night he landed he struggled to see an answer. Surviving the winter looked hard enough as things were. And if the Germans weren't dislodged and counter-attacked in the Spring…

'Our only hope is the British,' Eleni said.

She held her gaze steady as the men stared at her.

'K-kiwi,' Costis interrupted.

The radio crackled. The high pitched whine of the valve made him wince. His eyes followed Costis' hands as they twiddled the knobs. For a moment his spirits rose.

'Can you get us some dance music?' Andreas laughed.

The crackle died. There was a communal groan.

'Is that it?' Yiannis asked.

'It's c-coming,' Costis muttered. 'D-does any w-w-one know m-morse?'

'I do, a bit,' Yiorgos piped up. 'If you make it work, Costi, I can ask Aleko in Egypt for his help.'

'And give away our position to the Germans?' Petros sneered.

Kiwi bit his tongue. 'Well done, Costi, keep trying. Though without the code Cairo would probably assume we were Germans anyway.'

'Perhaps we could listen in to the Germans' messages?' Yiorgos offered. 'And intercept a food convoy somewhere.'

'Only if you can learn German, Yiorgo. Without Aleko we're stuck for the language, aren't we?'

'Another little problem, Neo Zealandi?'

'I'm sure we can overcome it.'

But he felt the gloom pressing down on him.

'We're all waiting to hear how. What a pity you treated Dancy so well,' Petros said. 'Now that you need him. With the code book he could make Cairo listen.'

'Except that he won't. Dancy cut off our supplies, remember?'

'Perfectly. And that was even before you treated him like a dog. Clever, wasn't it?'

'I ought go up there and cut his fucking throat like I should have done when he was here,' Yiannis said.

'That'll produce food, will it?' Petros gloated.

Kiwi held up his hands to stop the arguing. Eleni was looking down, her face grim. At this rate they'd be at each others' throats before long. Petros coughed. 'He might listen to me.'

'Listen to you? Why?'

'I wasn't in your lynch mob.'

'What's made you so fucking keen to help all of a sudden?' Yiannis sneered.

'I'd be starving, too.'

Kiwi glanced at Eleni again. She stared with narrowed eyes at her husband, as if she also sensed something wrong. He couldn't keep the barb from his tone. 'You'll manage the journey, will you, Petro?'

'I'll write.'

'And that bastard will understand?' Yiannis sneered.

'Petros knows English,' Eleni said.

Petros glared at her. The others seemed to regard this news as a further betrayal. Petros shrugged. 'Please yourself. Sifis can deliver it to Dancy.'

'No, Yiorgos will take it.'

'You don't trust me, Neo Zealandi?'

'Yiorgos knows the fastest way through.'

'What if the fucker still doesn't listen, Kiwi? Even to this slimy bag of shite?'

He studied Petros. The man's scorn was a goad. 'I'll go up there myself and kill him.'

The cloudless sky made a mockery of the shadow over them. His doubts wouldn't ease but he decided it was unwise to share them. All he could do was wait. Eleni returned to Souyia to help with the work and after a day of moping he went down to unburden himself.

He found her inside a small house, supervising its renovation and shared his anxieties. She paused from her work and frowned. 'I'm sure Petros had some other motive.'

'It was the only choice we had.'

'Did you read the letter?'

'I offered to but he accused me of interfering.'

'I don't like the sound of that.'

'It took him so long to finish I just wanted Yiorgos to be on his way with it.'

'Yiorgos will be back tonight?'

He nodded and surveyed the almost completed repair with grudging admiration. In less than a day and a half in Souyia she had some buildings habitable. Yet it was a day and a half when he hadn't seen her.

'You've made a lot of progress.'

'It helps if I keep busy.'

'And away from me?'

'Don't worry,' she laughed. 'I can defend myself even from the Minotaur.'

'That's what I'm afraid of.'

'Hey, Kiwi,' Andreas burst in. 'You heard there's going to be a celebration here tonight? Of the liberation.'

He glanced at Eleni but replied to Andreas. 'Bit early for that, isn't it?'

'Here we go again. Your opportunity to dance.'

'Have you seen him dance, Andrea?' Eleni asked.

'You don't mean you have?'

'A long time ago. He won't have improved.'

'You need lessons, Kiwi?'

'I need to return to the camp. To wait for Yiorgo.'

222

'You chicken.'

'I recall now,' Eleni said with a smile. 'His dance had similarities to a chicken.'

'So you won't persuade him to stay?' Andreas grinned.

The hesitation in her eyes fanned his annoyance. 'Have you both finished? Andrea, I need you at the camp, too.'

'Killjoy. God, your father would be proud of you.'

Andreas stomped out. Eleni's smile became a question.

'Would he be? Your father?'

'At me avoiding dancing? He'll be turning in his grave. With horror that it was even mentioned.'

'He has more to be proud of than that.'

'He'd have found some objection.'

'I don't think so.'

'I can think of plenty, myself. Like, what have I achieved?'

'A great deal.'

'Of raised hopes that I can't fulfil..?'

'In time...'

'But as Andonis said, if we could just keep this going. If we don't seize this opportunity...'

'Another will come. We've lived under occupation for two years, don't forget. Longer under dicatatorship...'

'All the more reason to get it finished.'

'And for centuries under the Turks. Why must you be so impatient?'

He let out a sigh. And tried to affect unconcern. 'In that case perhaps I should stay to dance?'

'I shan't be taking part, either.'

'All the better.'

'Kiwi, stop it.'

'There's no one spying on you here.'

'Just give me time. Please?

'Do we have time?'

She rushed to help an old woman staggering in with a mattress. He chafed at the evasion. She frowned at him.

'Petros is taking it all too calmly.'

'Think he'll give me some tips?'

'He never just accepts defeat. You must be careful.'

'I'll try to be.'

'You're not taking me seriously.'

'I'm deadly serious.'

'You're becoming distracted.'

'I think I know the solution to that.'

She ignored the taunt. 'Petros spent too much time with Dancy. Doesn't that worry you? What were they up to?'

'Discussing British–Russian collaboration?'

'Petros will have some plan. He always takes the long view.'

'He'll be after his own supply drops.'

'He'd prefer revenge.'

'So what's he written to Dancy in his letter? Send us supplies and he'll get rid of me?'

'You're making a joke of it.'

'Why not? Would anyone lift a finger to support Petro now? If he made any attempt he'd be dead on the spot.'

'I'm just telling you not to underestimate him.'

'OK. For you, I won't.'

'Not for me, for yourself.'

'I'm not worried about myself.'

'You should be. All these people depend on you.'

'Even you?'

Exasperation flashed in her eyes. It gave way to the old look of concern. 'Would you really go and kill Dancy? You know what it would mean for your future if you did?'

The boast had been provoked from him. He'd thrown the same remark at Alec. He shrugged at her. 'Never thought about it. As Petros was so quick to point out, it won't help us eat. Let's just hope his letter succeeds. If it doesn't, well…'

He was brushing away the question again. But he knew that if it came down to a choice between Dancy and the Cretans, the present and the future, he wouldn't need to think.

Seventeen

'You're like a donkey with a sore head, Kiwi,' Andreas laughed.

'Shouldn't that be a bear?'

'We have no bears in Crete. They all died of a broken heart.'

'Yiorgos should have returned last night. D'you think Dancy's arrested him as well?'

'Mightn't Dancy be waiting for orders from Cairo?'

'Perhaps. And Ari? Where's he gone? I told him to hurry back but it's more than two days. If he's been captured, I'll never forgive myself.'

'Stop worrying. Ari is a survivor. He's too smart to get himself caught. You're just finding anything to fret about.'

'Then tell me some reason not to.'

Andreas rolled his eyes and began to whistle. 'She's making it easy for you, Kiwi.'

'You could have fooled me.'

'Staying down in Souyia, away from prying eyes?'

'It's not prying eyes that are the problem.'

'You're not being too timid, again, are you?'

'No, I'm not being too timid.'

'But you've not caught the worm?'

'Don't be disgusting.'

'Clearly you need some brotherly advice.'

'My brother's a priest. What sort of advice do you think he'd give about pursuing a married woman?'

'I'm hurt, Kiwi, that you don't see me as your brother.'

'You can be my brother any time, Andrea. It's your advice that scares me.'

'Even if it wins you the prize?'

'She needs more time. To get over Petros.'

'Pff. She got over Petro months ago.'

'Know that for a fact, do you?'

'Call it intuition.'

'Lying, then, is she?'

Andreas' arm wrapped his shoulder and drew him aside from the stir of the camp. 'Kiwi, brother... How little that small, provincial place of New Zealand prepared you for the wiles of women in this great island of ours.'

'My military training did have other priorities.'

'I'm not talking about military training. Though didn't that teach you the value of taking the initiative?'

'It taught me that most of it was bullshit. Like what I'm hearing now.'

'Ouch. My own heart, Kiwi, is being lacerated by your ingratitude. But am I deflected from my course?'

At least Andreas had now made him laugh. 'You poor, wounded soldier.'

'Exactly. But what does the poor, wounded soldier do?'

'Find a nurse to treat his wounds?'

'Counter attack.'

'So I should return to Souyia and attack Eleni?'

'You're catching on.'

'Not very subtle, is it?'

'Where's subtlety got you? You mope about like a motherless lamb. She says wait and you bleat your life away. Seize the initiative. Beat down her resistance.'

'I respect her too much.'

He was jerked to a halt. His shoulders shaken. Andreas' face blazed at his own. 'When my grandfather was a young man he stole my grandmother from a neighbouring village. He seized her in the night and carried her away in his arms. She made no protest as he ran.'

'Doesn't sound much like Eleni.'

Andreas punched him on the chest. Hard. 'Listen, you fool. When they reached the river, he waded in. Halfway through he stopped and asked her if she wanted to go back. Know what she said?'

'"Will you punch me if I say yes?"'

'Nothing. She said nothing.'

Andreas folded his arms and stared at him. Part of him wanted to laugh but he was also touched by the passion.

'It's a moving story, Andrea. But I can see one problem in its application to me.'

'What? That you're too feeble to make the attempt?'

'At Souyia the river is dry.'

Andreas glared at him then stalked off. After several paces he stopped and turned back. His face was pained.

'How can a *pallikari* like you be so utterly stupid? I don't understand. Why won't you get it? She's crying out for you, Kiwi. And no *pallikari* should refuse that cry.'

He studied the stony ground. Words. 'Fine words butter no parsnips', his mother used to crow. He never did know what it meant. Until now. It meant feeling even more depressed than you had before.

Ari's return did bring some relief. The boy strolled in as if his trip had only been up to the spring. Kiwi was sat hunched at the table, watching Costis fiddle with the radio. He swung round in fury on the lad. 'Ari, what the hell happened? I expected you back two days ago. Are you all right?'

'I went to Kastelli.'

'Kastelli? They haven't abandoned Kastelli, have they?'

'No. I used my initiative.'

He heard Andreas laugh and softened his tone. 'Good. Tell me what I asked you to find out.'

'Except for Omalos, the Germans have pulled back to the northern foothills.'

'They've given up Paleochora as well?'

'With less destruction, but they still cleaned it out.'

'And Kantanos?'

'The military presence has gone though as you know there was little left to destroy.'

'So the whole of the south west is free?'

'But like us with nothing to eat. Manoussas' band has occupied Paleochora but they have few weapons and may not stay.'

'They fear counter attack?' Andreas asked.

Kiwi caught the knowing glance in his direction and carried on before Ari could reply. 'Why did you go to Kastelli?'

'Manoussas sent two men there, also to see where the German line was. And to check on the food situation. I asked to go with them and he agreed.'

'What is the food situation?'

'Hopeless. Whatever there is the Germans take. Our people are starving there, too.'

'So what's Manoussas going to do?'

'He told me to ask if you can call for supplies from the British.'

'He'll be lucky.'

'I understand the logic to this withdrawal, now, Kiwi,' Andreas said, becoming serious. 'They've ceded us the unproductive land. That's why they must be staying on Omalos. The plain feeds Hania.'

'And that's why a further push now, would make all the difference. I wonder if Dancy knew that before he came. In order to stop it.'

Andreas' frown become puzzlement. 'Don't the British want us to succeed?'

'Only slowly. Independence in their allies worries them. Especially when they can smell communism.'

'So we're stuck?'

'It does happen, Andrea… In lots of different ways.'

He sent Ari off to eat, remembering to thank the lad again for his initiative. There was still had no word of Yiorgos. An increased German presence shouldn't have delayed him. Yiorgos was too experienced for that. The problem could only be Dancy.

In late afternoon Yiannis returned with a grim face from checking on his men up at Omalos. 'The fuckers are moving the garrison from Lakki up there. Basing it more in the centre. With a very wide defensive perimeter…'

'So no creeping up unawares next time?' Andreas said.

'Only if you want to do a Pavlo. But that's not the fucking worst of it…'

'Go on.'

Yiannis looked hard at him. 'They're levelling the fields. You know what that fucking means, Kiwi?'

He felt the pit opening before him again. Before he could reply the radio crackled into life. Costis frowned at him and held up his hand for quiet. A German voice barked out at them in a rapid stream of orders. Costis looked up in consternation.

'Fucking hell,' Yiannis glowered. 'Are they fucking coming for us already?'

The voice cut. Costis turned the dial but the radio only crackled. He switched it off, abashed. 'At l-least we may b-be able t-to reach some d-distance now.'

'Don't be too fucking sure, Costi…'

Kiwi waved Yiannis quiet. 'How far? Cairo?'

'Or out to s-sea. A s-submarine?'

'Kiwi…' Yiannis began.

'Wait, Yianni.' He was clutching for hope. 'You might get a message to carry that far, Costi?'

Costis shrugged. 'B-but w-without the codebook…'

'We may have to try.'

He turned back to Yiannis with reluctance. 'Yianni, sorry… I know what you're saying. Are you sure?'

'You can tell from the fucking shape.'

'It's more than the foundations of buidings?'

'It's a fucking airstrip.'

He stared at Yiannis. Gasps told him one or two others had caught on to the implications.

'Why the panic, Kiwi?' Andreas laughed. 'It's not like you. There are planes at Maleme.'

'From Omalos they'll be able to sit on top of us. All day. Track our every move. And call in the heavy stuff whenever they want.'

The silence hung. So this was the real reason for the German withdrawal? Starvation might be the enemy's longer-term strategy. In the short term the means would now be more direct. The whine of stukas drowned out all thought for a moment. Seeing desperate faces snapped him alert. 'How long have we got, Yianni?'

'Before the fucker's operational? A week? Two? It's only the perimeter defences that'll take the time.'

And which they had no means to stop. He shuddered again at the memory of close-range attack aircraft. It was their lives, now, that hung on Petros' letter to Dancy.

'Let's hope that Petros' magic words have worked their charm on Dancy, then,' he muttered, moving away.

'D-do you b-believe they w-will have, K-kiwi?'

He made no reply. As he walked into the trees the answer "Not for a minute" rang in his head.

By the time he watched Yiorgos stumble into the camp an hour later Kiwi had realised what he'd have to do when Dancy said no. The threat from the airstrip changed everything. He forced himself to sit still and wait.

Alerted to the messenger's arrival, a crowd escorted Yiorgos in. The lad looked subdued.

'You have a reply?' Andonis called.

Yiorgos waved a letter as he approached the table.

'Tell us what it fucking says, then,' Yiannis growled.

'It's sealed. I was ordered not to read it.'

'Well, give it Kiwi, for fuck's sake.'

Yiorgos looked down. 'I was instructed to hand it only to Petro.'

'That fucker Dancy doesn't give us orders.'

'Sit down, Yiorgo,' Kiwi said with a calmness he didn't feel, desperate to get this over and move on. 'Andrea, fetch Petro.'

Yiorgos seemed relieved to sit and gulped tsikoudia. Kiwi made conversation to shut out his tumbling thoughts. 'Was it difficult coming down?'

Yiorgos nodded but still averted his gaze. 'There are more patrols out in the foothills. But they don't seem to be around Stephanoporo.'

Kiwi only half-listened. He waited for Petros to clump across the camp at a pace designed to irritate.

'I was ordered to place this in your hand,' Yiorgos muttered.

Petros took it with a grunt and turned to go.

'Hang on, Petro,' Yiannis said. 'Open the fucker here. Not got any fucking secrets from us, have you?'

Petros balanced himself on the two crutches and slit open the letter. The man scanned it for what felt like an age, face expressionless. Twisting the knife.

'D'you need it translating, Petro?'

Petros flashed him his old look of scorn. And held out the letter. He read it then stared at it without seeing, weighing up its purpose, trying not to betray his shock. Hadn't he half-expected this?

'Well, Kiwi? Don't fucking keep it from us,' Yiannis groused. 'I take it it's a fucking no?'

'Not exactly.'

'Can't the English ever fucking talk straight?'

'Read it out, Kiwi, please,' Yiorgos asked.

He nodded. It *was* clever. And typical of Dancy. Could it have been all his own idea? He glanced at Yiorgos. 'Did he radio to Cairo before giving you this?'

'I don't know, Kiwi. He sent me down the hill to wait.'

'Just read us the fucking thing, Kiwi.'

'Yeah, OK. He doesn't say much.'

'It's taking fucking long enough to do so.'

'Yianni, shut up!' Andreas shouted. 'Kiwi..?'

He perused the message again and felt a strange calmnesss. This answer made no difference. In fact...

'Kiwi...' Andreas repeated.

'Yeah, sorry. Major Dancy says...' His voice sounded detached and distant. "'Cairo orders Sergeant Watkins... on pain of court martial... to surrender himself to me."'

He waited for the uproar to subside and went on. "'If he does so, in person, I am permitted to radio for the resumption of supply drops."'

It took a moment for this to sink in. Then the outrage burst out with renewed fury.

'The fucker dies,' Yiannis cried.

There was a chorus of agreement. Fists thumped the table. Several knives waved. He seemed the only one to remain calm. He held up his hand. 'There is some good news. He wants an answer by tomorrow night.'

'That's good news? Tomorrow night?' Andreas protested.

'It'll take you all day to get there,' Yiorgos said.

'Neat, though, isn't it? A simple choice.'

'We might as well all surrender,' Andreas said.

Something still puzzled him. Why not a straight "no"? He might have expected a devil's bargain from Dancy, but surely Dancy knew he wouldn't agree to this condition?

Yiannis turned on Petros. 'Was this your fucking idea, you...?'

'I merely put in your request...'

'Well, write back and tell him to fuck off.'

This, too, brought shouts of approval.

'The Neo Zealandis can tell him that himself,' Petros said, his tone matter-of-fact.

'He'd get more fucking notice taken than you did.'

'Shall I return and say no?' Yiorgos asked.

He stared at the ground. That was it. Of course Dancy knew he wouldn't agree. Dancy *wanted* refusal. Refusal meant a court martial. And the entire blame for the Cretans' starvation and failure. It was the perfect trap. He looked up and shook his head. 'No.'

Andreas gaped at him in horror. 'You're not going to obey?'

'What choice is there?'

'Have you gone mad?'

'If I don't obey, you'll lack the arms to stop them completing the airstrip at Omalos.'

'Without you we'll lack the strength.'

'Not necessarily.'

'Yes, absolutely definitely.'

'I don't fucking see how not, either,' Yiannis said.

He glanced round each of their faces. 'Dancy's doing us a favour.'

'You could have fucking fooled me.'

'We urgently need arms, don't we? Heavy stuff.'

'True, Kiwi, but...' Andreas began.

'What better way than for me to tell Dancy in person?' He smiled at Petros. 'As Petros suggested.'

'Aren't you forgetting something, Kiwi?'

'Oh, the bargain? That won't be a problem.'

'How exactly do you hope to manage that?' He glanced round the taut faces. 'Souyia?'

Andreas still looked baffled. 'What do you mean?'

'He didn't say I had to come alone.'

Behind him Costis chuckled. Yiannis' scowl gave way to a slow grin. 'You fucking sly bastard...'

'You have the advantage of me, Neo Zealandi,' Petros said. 'I don't know what masterstroke you propose.'

'No, we know you weren't in fucking Souyia, don't we?' Yiannis spat.

Kiwi met Petros' puzzled look with an even stare. 'We'll sneak in unseen. I'll present myself to Dancy. I'll ask that he makes the radio call for heavy weapons...'

'And then I'll cut his fucking throat.'

Petros didn't join in the laughter and cheers but seemed unmoved, even by the reminder of his abandonment of his wife.

'You don't object, Petro?'

'Would it make any difference if I did?'

'I might fucking slit yout throat, too,' Yiannis said.

'My people also have to live, Neo Zealandi. No, I have no objection. I'll be glad.'

'You fucking liar,' Yiannis said.

He pulled Yiannis away. Costis was frowning now.

'What's wrong, Costi?'

'It m-must...b-be a trick, K-kiwi.'

The others went quiet. He let Costis struggle on.

'Even if you w-went...alone... H-how could he en-force your s-surrender? It d-doesn't make s-s-sense. W-why s-send so foolish a d-demand?'

'Because he's a self-important fool,' Petros snorted. 'We all saw that with our own eyes.'

'You more than most,' Andreas said.

Petros' face remained emotionless. 'Maybe he thinks that away from here you'll be unable to refuse the order of a superior officer.'

'You're very keen that I should go all of a sudden?'

'I told you, Neo Zealandi, we have to survive, too.'

'Why should he expect me to come alone?'

'You'd have decided to surrender, wouldn't you?'

'Better make sure I get there, then. Costi, you, Andreas and Yiannis can come to protect me. We'll leave in the morning. That make you feel any easier, Costi?'

Costis muttered something inaudible and peered at the radio. Petros raised a finger. 'One more thing, Neo Zealandi. If he does make the call to Cairo, will you still need to kill him?'

'For the fucking insults,' Yiannis said.

Petros grunted and turned away. The man's lack of feeling chilled. How did he always find it so easy to sacrifice those for whom he no longer had a use?

Kiwi's eyes followed Petros across the camp. The summons did provide the perfect cover for going to coerce Dancy. But would Dancy give way? His earlier obstinacy didn't bode well. And if they were sent the arms, was there still time? Once in operation, an airstrip would be fatal. Then there was Costis' fear of a trick…

Andreas' voice broke into his misgivings. 'Sounds as if you should take a walk, Kiwi – to Souyia.'

'Eh? Why?'

Andreas laughed. 'I hear the river's in flood.'

Shadows lengthened in the dusk. He sat on a rock beneath the clump of tamarisk trees on the edge of the beach. To the west, above the headland, the deep red of the autumn sunset had become a pale glow. Before him the darkening sea stretched wide. Only some low flat rocks just off the shoreline broke up its emptiness.

If he'd hoped coming down to Souyia would calm his mind, he'd been mistaken. The chance to dwell on the implications of the airstrip only undermined his resolve. Hadn't it been an airfield that had undone them in '41? Was this new one going to bring him full circle? Unless they could stop it happening. Some hope…

The sight of Souyia's perimeter wire reminded him how little success they'd achieved against that. Even if he did force Dancy into calling for heavy weapons, their chances of destroying the airfield were slim. And he could guess what a few stukas would do to Eleni's renovations. Unable to face her, he veered left to seek refuge on the beach. Recriminations – and regrets – swarmed after him.

Wasn't he the one to blame for their present plight? Petros' accusation was just. If he'd not persisted in defying Dancy, they might already have had the means to attack. To have prevented its starting. Whereas now… And when they killed Dancy, his own future would stop, too.

A cough made him turn. Eleni picked her way slowly towards him – across the river bed. It had been dry since March. She indicated the sea. 'Waiting for a submarine?'

'I needed to think.'

'You've had a reply from Dancy?'

He gestured to her to the adjacent rock. She sat with her head bowed and listened, hands clasped before her. When he finished she looked up in surprise. 'What is there to think about if you've decided..? Oh, the consequences?'

'Damn the consequences,' he lied. 'It doesn't matter that I've decided. It's probably all too late.'

'For you? I seem to recall your timing…'

'It's because of me it's too late.'

'Then tomorrow you can put things…'

'No. I lost it for us months ago. I always think I know best. I have to push too far. I asked for trouble.'

'From…?'

'Isn't it obvious?'

'I suppose so. But you do have a chance to put it right. At least it's not your father this time.'

'That's not funny.'

There was silence.

'What did you write on the wall of the graveyard?'

'What's that got to do with anything?'

'Was it a bigger crime than offending Dancy?'

'You're… oh, shit… making it small, I don't know how to say it.'

'Trivialising?'

'If you like. All this is a different scale.'

'How should I know?'

'It's not worth knowing.'

'Obviously not.'

The flat rocks stood out darker now against the sea. He took a deep breath. '"Clifford Steel loves Susan Cross."'

'I don't understand. What is "Glifford"? Or "Steel"?'

'"Clifford." They're names.'

'Whose? Of some important people?'

The fading light gave little shelter from her scrutiny.

'Kids. In my class.'

'At your school? When you were ten?'

'Twelve! Satisfied now?'

A faint slap of water was the only sound.

'How big were the letters?'

He stuck out a finger and thumb in the gloom. They almost touched. He caught a stifled laugh. 'And this was your great offence?'

'I still don't find it very amusing.'

She stood up. He let himself be pulled to his feet.

'It could have been worse,' she said.

'Think so, do you?'

'If you'd done a kiwi impression.'

The full moon must have risen behind them. Its light picked out the broad smile on her face.

'Kiwis are nocturnal. Shall I do one now?'

She grabbed his hand and jerked him onto the sand. 'Good God, no. Dance with me instead.'

Tugged forward, he stumbled after her over the yielding ground. 'Dance? Are you sure?'

'What are you afraid of?'

'My dancing ability. And…' He waved a hand at the expanse of beach. The moonlight gave everywhere a bright silver sheen. 'Aren't you a married woman?'

She stopped and dropped his hand. The next thing she was pummelling his chest with both fists. Fast. He staggered back. Her smile had gone. 'Everyone keeps telling me what I am,' she shouted. 'I'm *me*…'

She went to beat him again. He grabbed her forearms and clutched them to him. She pushed and pulled then suddenly gave up and subsided on him. He put his arms round her. He could feel the beating of her body and smell the scent of her hair squeezed against his cheek. He couldn't take in the fury he'd unleashed.

'Sorry,' he said. There seemed no other words. He listened to the sea, not wanting this to end.

She eased herself loose. He raised his hands to plead.

'Please don't beat me again…'

Her eyes flashed wide, with laughter this time. 'You poor little worm.' She seized his wrists, pushed them apart and gazed at him. Then took a step forward and planted a kiss on his lips. He stared at her. She stepped back, dropping his arms. 'You remember old Manoli?'

'At Koustoyerako? Before the machine gun?'

'Yes. And his shout?'

'"Freedom or death".'

'Our traditional Cretan cry of freedom.' She turned to walk away. 'That's the only slogan that matters now. And the only thing you need to ponder.'

He couldn't move. She looked back at him: 'If you won't dance, I'm going to run along this beach.'

For a moment he watched as she did then set off in pursuit. When he caught up she was laughing. He ran alongside. 'Eleni, have you gone crazy?'

'Yes. Catch me if you can.'

She dodged away from him and doubled back. He followed and let her evade him again. She began to slow. He jogged beside her and feinted to catch her but held off. A weight had somehow lifted from him. 'You know… there's a game we play… in New Zealand… It's called… rugby.'

'Ragby?'

'**Ru**gby. It's our kind of dancing.'

She stopped, panting, and regarded him. 'Dancing? In New Zealand? That I must see.'

'You sure?'

'Yes.'

She started to run again.

'I should warn you…'

'Just show me.'

His tackle sent both sprawling in the sand. She landed on him and he lay winded as she scrambled to her knees. He cowered from the sand and pebbles she flung at him and heard her incredulous laughter.

'That's New Zealand dancing?'

'I did try to tell you…'

'You're barbarians. And your women have to do this dance, too, do they?'

He clambered up and gasped, hands on his knees. 'No, you're very honoured.'

She flung another shower of grit. 'Honoured? At least a Cretan man just beats his wife. Is this New Zealand a completely insane place?'

He inclined his head at the shoreline. 'Come and look for yourself.'

Her puzzled frown brought a flutter in his chest.

'Look? How?'

As she hesitated he swept her up into his arms and staggered towards the darker line of the sea. She struggled to free herself. 'Put me down.'

'Only when we reach New Zealand.'

'Kiwi, if you throw me in that water…'

'What will you do, kiss me again?'

He splashed into the sea. She gave up struggling. Her shriek in his ear deafened him. 'Where are you taking me?'

The cold water made him catch his breath. He stopped. It was up to his thighs and soaking the trailing edges of her dress. He turned her to face the flat rocks ahead.

'I told you. New Zealand.'

'That's New Zealand?'

'I've always thought it looked familiar.'

He ploughed on. She laughed and clung to him. 'There won't be more ragby, will there?'

'No, I promise you.'

'You sure you're not going to drown me instead?'

'Would a dancing kiwi let you down?'

'And I thought Cretans were mad.'

The water passed his waist. He had to hold her higher. In a few more strides he'd be out of his depth and she'd be soaked. And he didn't know if she could swim. Perhaps it had been too stupid a stunt. Like all the rest. Then the seabed began to shelve upwards and give way to layers of rock. He breathed out. Maybe recklessness was his natural guise after all. 'We're almost there.'

She smiled at him. 'Will I like it?'

He stumbled out of the water and set her onto her feet. She was shivering. He wrapped his arms around her and turned her to face the dark wall of mountains inland.

'Like New Zealand? I'm sure you will. Look…'

He swung her round under the immense sweep of sky.

'Mountains… sea… and sheep, too.'

'Yes? So what?'

'New Zealand. It's just the same as here.'

She laughed and snuggled into his embrace. He listened to the gentle lapping of the waters against the rock. Beams of light played on the surface of the sea. And when he glanced up, an enormous moon held steady above.

Eighteen

On the long trek back up to the camp he laughed at himself. It shouldn't have been his father he blamed: his self-pity on the beach had sounded more like his mother. He pushed both of them aside. And thoughts of the future. There were more pressing things now. His exhilaration calmed. He slept a deep and dreamless sleep.

But woke with stiffness in his limbs. That jolted him into the day's task. The airstrip. Dancy. Today shouldn't have been necessary. And Dancy was the one to blame, not him. If the man hadn't set out to be obstructive... He told himself to forget that. Their only chance was to get the request sent fast as possible. Time was everything.

He sat and laced up his still wet boots. The memory of their soaking did bring back a smile. He ducked out of the tent buttoning his shirt. To see Andreas look up from pouring coffee. Grinning. 'Clean shirt, eh, Kiwi? And pants?'

'My others got wet.'

'I thought the river in Souyia was dry?'

He pulled a face. No distractions... 'It was the sea, if you must know...'

Andreas laughed again and handed him the cup. 'The sea? Don't do things by halves, do you, Kiwi? My grandfather waded across a river but for you it has to be the sea. And you look as if it took all night to cross.'

'Can we talk about something else?'

'You are allowed to enjoy success.'

'The one success I'm interested in is with Dancy.'

'Of course, Kiwi. Ha, ha, ha. I hope you're not going to be too preoccupied today?'

'Only by him. And the damned airfield.'

His chest thumped. Eleni strode through the camp towards them. Conscious of Andreas, he put down the cup and felt himself tense. 'I didn't expect to see you this morning.'

She blushed. 'I had to come up from Souyia for some things.'

'Lucky Kiwi overslept or you'd have missed him,' Andreas said with a straight face then put on a show of remembering something before hurrying off.

Kiwi shrugged. She gave him a shy smile. He drank in the intensity of her eyes, the pale brightness of her skin, her dark hair. Then stopped himself. What had he vowed? 'I'm glad to see you.'

His pretence hadn't fooled her. 'No. I shouldn't have come. If you're late…'

'That's just Andreas…'

'It was thoughtless. But I wanted to see you.'

'There'll be plenty of time for that. After…'

'Yes.'

He caught her uncertainty and knew why. Yiannis was twiddling his knife. They did have to go. He didn't want to part from her like this and cursed his inarticulacy.

However, she was smiling. 'Perhaps I ought to come with you?'

'No.'

He said it too quickly. Her eyes showed the hurt. 'It is my war, as well.'

'I know, but…'

'I'd be in the way?'

'Not at all…'

'Liar.'

The accusation came with a twinkle. He sighed. 'I just want you to be safe.'

'I'd feel safest beside you.'

He saw she'd given up and grinned back at her. 'Look where it landed you last time.'

'That was your fault. For not reacting fast enough.'

'I was distracted.'

'There. You've admitted it.'

He raised his hands in defeat. And relief. 'I'm beaten. Again.'

His eyes held hers. Their sparkle made his heart lift.

Costis heaved the radio onto the table and broke the spell. 'One f-final try b-before we go, Kiwi?'

They ought to be off. 'Have we got time?'

Costis' sad eyes looked so downcast that he shrugged assent. At his back Petros' voice snapped 'I can't imagine what good it will do, either.'

He swung round. Her husband had turned to Eleni. 'You seem pleased with yourself.'

'Things are progressing well in Souyia.'

Petros stiffened. 'You are still my wife. Whatever you think.'

'I'm not your property, Petro.'

'Nor anyone else's, remember that.'

'Calm yourself, Petro,' he said. People were gathering to hear the radio. He hadn't time for a scene.

'Calm myself? I warned you once, Neo Zealandi. Do you really think you can humiliate us with impunity?'

The tone of the question took him aback. Before he could retort the radio crackled into life. In morse. 'Damn the thing! Yiorgo..! Where's Yiorgos?'

'Here, Kiwi. Shh…'

The tapping stopped. What the hell was this distracting them now? He glared the question at Yiorgos. Yiorgos frowned. 'I think it's English.'

'English?' he heard Petros exclaim.

The shock on Petros' face surprised him. But he shared the disorientation. English? How could it be? He groped to make sense of it. Petros remained pale.

The radio crackled again. Andreas set a pencil and paper on the table. Yiorgos waved it away. The tapping stopped.

'It's being repeated… It is English. But odd…'

'Odd? Why? Yiorgo…?'

'It just repeats "Send… only… code."'

He screwed up his face. '"Send only code"? What the hell does that mean?'

'It's the Germans, trying to confuse us,' Petros said.

'In my case, they've fucking succeeded,' Yiannis put in.

'It can't be the Germans. They'd want *un*coded,' he said, trying to shake off the confusion.

'You surely don't think your own side would send uncoded messages, do you, Neo Zealandi?'

Damn the man. Speculation was futile. And the delay was dragging on too long. He rounded on Petros. 'I'll leave you to work that out. Switch it off, Costi. OK, everyone, show's over. We have to go.'

He seethed as the crowd dispersed. Costis packed up the radio, still fretting over the message. 'W-what if it *was* being s-sent to D-dancy?'

'Why would Dancy need reminding about that?' Petros sneered. The whole thing seemed to have thrown him off balance, too. 'Doesn't he have the code book?'

'He'd fucking better,' Yiannis growled.

Petros hesitated then stumped off. Kiwi watched him stumbling on the crutches. Too many things didn't add up. Yet he shouldn't be letting them rattle him.

Eleni was also frowning. He raised his eyebrows at her.

'What's got into him?'

'You can't guess?'

Petros limped away without a backward glance.

'He can't know, can he? It was the radio that panicked him.'

'Yes, the English. Did you notice how..?'

A whining voice cut her off. 'Where are you going?'

He wheeled round. The old, black-clad crone pointed her finger at him, fierce eyes flashing from a wizened, leathery face. 'You must not go. Not today.'

This was all he needed. 'What? Kyria...? What do you say?'

'I've told you. You must not go.'

The crone spat and then scurried away. He glanced at Eleni. Her frown had become shock. He forced a joke.

'Nothing beats a bit of kiwi optimism.'

'Don't laugh about it.'

If he didn't, it threatened more delay. 'You don't expect me to take notice?'

'I don't know... Old women like her...'

'Can see things? You don't believe that?'

'Some of them have a sixth sense...'

'So you think I shouldn't go?'

'I think we should... Oh, I can't accept...'

'This is no time for doubt.'

'Maybe she's heard something?'

'Like voices in her head?'

'Don't mock me, Kiwi.'

'I'm sorry, it's just all becoming too...' Then a thought struck him. 'Maybe you're right.'

'About what?'

'Why is Petros so keen to see me gone?'

'I don't follow.'

'Has she overheard him plotting something? While I'm away?'

'About what?'

'About you.'

'Me?'

'There was something he said back there. About impunity...'

He struggled to recall the exact words. His fears brought a smile from Eleni. 'You don't need to worry about me.'

'I can't help it.'

'No one will take his side now.'

'Even so...'

She squeezed his arm and smiled. 'You concentrate on what you have to do.'

It was becoming more difficult by the minute. Though what she'd said about Petros' isolation was correct. And he knew she could look after herself.

Costis was returning, and Yiorgos, with a rifle. Eleni frowned again. 'And make sure you come back. Please?'

'You just watch out for Petro.'

He felt a sudden, irrational urge to stay. His fear for her had touched a raw nerve. Then Yiorgos was pleading with him. 'Let me come, Kiwi. For security. To scout ahead for Germans. I know the way better than...'

'No, I want you to watch out for Eleni.'

'Kiwi,' she protested.

'Don't argue. Either of you. Yiorgo, this is the best way you can protect me.'

His eyes met Eleni's and he looked away. They had to go. He picked up the bren from the table and checked it again. He patted Yiorgos' shoulder. 'I'll give your regards to Kapetan Dancy.'

He remembered something and took the piece of blue cloth from his pocket. It was still damp. He offered it to her. 'Can you dry this for me for when I come back?'

'No.'

The fierceness in her eyes shook him. 'Why not?'

'I want you to return it yourself.'

He felt himself blush and pocketed it. They'd delayed long enough. He nodded goodbye and strode off.

The early part of the trek wound up through the pines. His mind fretted over the airfield but Andreas kept breaking in. 'Don't woods like these make you recall your bayonet charge at Galatas, Kiwi?'

'No. Why? At Galatas we were in olive groves.'

'Trees are trees if you're trapped in them. That's what I remember. And hearing your battle cry. The...?'

'Haka.'

'Like the thrill of a thousand women in your veins.'

He repeated Yiorgos' response in the *Eleftheria* to this: 'I have no desire for a thousand women.'

'Shall I tell you a secret, Kiwi? Me neither.'

That did jolt his attention. 'What? You could have fooled me.'

'Yes. I, too, want only one woman.'

The absurdity of it made him stop. Andreas shrugged. 'But she has no dowry.'

He stared to see if it was a joke then began to laugh. 'I'll send her a sheep from New Zealand.'

'Kiwi, you're a heartless bastard. Where's your soul?'

The fierceness in Eleni's parting glance slapped him. 'I left it back at the camp.' Then he felt a pang of guilt. 'Sorry, Andrea. Tell me about your fiancée.'

'Not until you're ready to take me seriously.'

He'd have preferred the diversion. The more he thought about an attack on Omalos, the more hopeless it appeared, even if the Germans hadn't already mined outside the perimeter. He made himself concentrate on the immediate task. If he failed in that, the rest was irrelevant.

The slow going up the steep track over Strifomadi fuelled his impatience. Potential complications with Dancy crowded on him. What if Dancy wasn't alone? What if the fool refused to comply? Costis' claim that it was a trick nagged away. Could Dancy have some reception planned?

The old crone's cries also kept repeating in his head. *Had* she been warning them about Petros? But why should she? She owed them nothing. Or was it her guilt? Had she heard Petros planning some revenge on Eleni that had pricked her conscience?

The lack of answers only fed his urge to move faster. While his mind kept picturing Eleni, wondering if she was safe and what she was doing…

Sitting beside the spring she listened to the trickle of water and tried to take comfort from the previous night. Too many shadows intruded. Petros' claim to Kiwi in the pit that 'a woman who strays chooses death' churned. It puzzled her. They *must* be empty words. She heard herself reassure Kiwi 'You don't need to worry about *me.*' Then felt a sudden chill. 'Oh, God,' she muttered and stood up.

Kiwi chafed as they rested after midday on the saddle above Linoseli. He glared at the granite bulk of Gingilos to his right, irritated by Costis' continuing speculation behind him over the meaning of the radio message.

'It c-can't be a g-general warning, Yianni.'

'I don't know why the fuck not.'

'T-then it w-would have been… *in* c-code.'

'I can't see what fucking difference that makes.'

Nor could he. They were wasting time. He stood up. 'Come on. We should move.'

'I w-wonder if it w-was *t-to* Dancy after all?'

Despite himself, the question made him start. 'How? As you said, Dancy has the codebook.'

'N-no, Petros s-said that. W-what if he's l-lost it? Or the r-radio operator has t-taken it to A-Amari?'

'That's all we fucking need,' Yiannis said.

Indeed. If Dancy had no a codebook, they were in deep trouble. But it was all supposition. And only promised more delay. His impatience seethed. Get on, do it and return were what mattered. He helped Costis up. 'Forget it, Costi. Whatever it was can't stop us now.'

'Fucking sense at last,' Yiannis muttered.

The path down to Xiloskala required close attention, with the gorge on their right falling sheer for a thousand feet. The north wall of Gingilos was already in shadow. Its darkening clefts made him shiver.

Although they were behind schedule, he paused on the eastern flank of the plateau for a closer look at the building works.

'I wasn't fucking seeing things,' Yiannis said.

'I know. I just want to get an idea of the scale.'

It was impressive. The Germans must have brought large numbers of forced labourers up to work on it. They'd also dynamited their former barracks and the houses around. Someone had clearly planned the defensive fields of fire.

'N-not an easy t-target, K-kiwi,' Costis said.

He grimaced at Costis' understatement. Had he the resources now, and assuming there wasn't yet a minefield, a night attack might just seize it. If that caused the enemy to flee back down to Lakkoi, the plateau – and the pass leading up to it – would be theirs. They'd be saved.

He cursed Dancy. Since the earlier cutting off of supplies had drained their reserves, the scale of the drop needed now was huge. Time was running out. And the bastard would probably still continue to be obstructive…

247

'How much longer, Yianni?' he snapped.

'Four cigarettes to Stephanoporo...'

'In time, not damned cigarettes.'

'Six more to Zourva. Drakona another six.'

'Four hours? Shit. So we'll arrive in the dark?'

'All the better if the fucker can't see us coming.'

'I'd prefer to see if we're expected.'

Because it *was* all too simple. He brooded on Costis' original doubts. Dancy must know that if he came, he wouldn't come alone, or to obey. With a start he remembered what had led to the summons: Petros' letter. Could Petros have put the idea into Dancy's head, to remove him and expose Eleni to his own revenge? In which case Dancy must have something planned.

He tried to dismiss the fears. Lack of certainty was fraying his nerves. At least it had stopped him worrying about the future. When Yiannis halted below the Pass of Stephanoporo he slumped down against a boulder that still caught the warmth of the late afternoon sun...

He was back in the camp hearing Eleni insist to Petros that she wasn't his property and Petros retort that nor was she anyone else's. Her husband had said 'Remember that.' Then added what had sounded like a threat: 'Do you really think you can humiliate us with impunity?'

He went cold. *That* was where the answer lay. But he still couldn't make out how or where. His eyelids felt heavy. It was all too confusing for him. Maybe Eleni would be able to figure it out...

She stood with hands on hips and scrutinized Petros. He lay slumped back in the chair before the table outside his hut, his injured foot on an upturned ammunition box. She could feel no connexion to him now.

'Petro, what did you mean by "Do you really think you can humiliate us with impunity"?'

He barely deigned to glance at her. 'I warned the Neo Zealandi before but he didn't listen, did he? He still had to betray me.'

The tone of injured self-justification grated on her. 'You betrayed yourself, Petro. When you wanted me dead. If you hadn't done that...'

He cut her off with a wave of his arm. 'I'm not interested in excuses. Just don't expect me to take you back, after...'

'Don't delude yourself, Petro,' she began. Her days of being patronised were over. The word "after" made her stop. Kiwi had used it earlier. 'Take me back after what?'

'Ha. Wouldn't you like to know.'

'After what, Petro?'

He made no reply. She leaned forward on the table, pressing her hands on it to steady herself against the rush of foreboding. 'And who's the "us"...? Petro, what have you *done?*'

He avoided her gaze. She stepped back with a start.

'Oh, my God. You've set up something with Dancy?'

He shrugged. Her mind wanted to scream. 'In that letter. What did you put in the letter..?'

'You think you're a clever bitch, don't you?'

'Answer me.'

'I hope you enjoyed your night of betrayal.'

'My what..?' She shook off the diversion. 'What have you told Dancy to do?'

All her question provoked was a dismissive laugh.

'You heard... On the radio... The message...'

'Did Dancy send that?'

'Dancy..? No... Ha, ha, ha. *He* didn't send it...'

'Then who did...? Petro, who did?'

'It was in English. Who do you think?'

Her thoughts whirled. 'The British...? *They* sent it to Dancy? Why? What had Dancy done?'

Petros stretched back and sneered again. 'You thought you were in control, didn't you? Isn't it obvious what he'd done?'

Her nerves strained to see. The message had said 'Send only code.' If the British had sent that from Cairo to Dancy, what must Dancy have been sending previously to them? At once she understood. The

249

full implications. The horror of it swung her round. 'Yiorgo!' she shouted. 'Yiorgo, here… Quickly!'

Could Yiorgos catch them up in time? She tried to think. Her head was too fuzzy. If he couldn't…

A further, terrible realization hit her. She stared at her husband. 'Oh, God, Petro… it was you who gave Dancy the idea, wasn't it? How could you…? You poor, deluded, treacherous fool.'

Her eyes fell on the rifle propped beside the table…

Yiannis was poking his arm. He blinked up in alarm. 'How long have I been asleep?'

'Don't panic. Not long.'

They had to move. As he scrambled up, Costis grabbed his arm. The Cretan's usually sombre eyes blazed. 'K-kiwi… W-w-w…we… sh-should… t-turn back.'

'Turn back? What? You know we can't…'

'But th-th-they're… w-waiting… for us.'

'Who?'

'The fucking Germans,' Yiannis butted in. 'Costis thinks he's worked out that fucking radio shit.'

He shivered. The sun had gone. 'The "Send only code" message?'

'It *w-was* to D-dancy.'

'So what?'

'It m-means D-dancy had s-sent an unc-coded message, to C-cairo…'

'Yeah, OK, if you say so…' Where was this getting them? They'd had enough delays. 'What's that got to do with the Germans waiting for *us*?'

'T-think, K-kiwi.'

The chill he felt wasn't now from lack of sun. 'Because the message was about me?'

'And y-you know what t-that c-c-could only be?'

He stared at Costis' anguished face. 'That he'd ordered me to come up and surrender?'

'B-by t-today.'

'Deliberately for the Germans to hear.'

There was silence. He glanced at the others. If Dancy had sent to Cairo, uncoded, the details of his order, including the date, he could have had only one purpose. But surely even Dancy wouldn't have gone that far?

Yiannis broke into his bewilderment. 'I told you I should have cut fucking Dancy's throat.'

He felt the world sliding away from under him. It wasn't just Dancy, was it? Petros' offer to send the letter – which no one else had read – seared his brain. He grasped now the man's panic over the English on the radio that might have given him away. Still he struggled to believe they would stoop to this. Until he remembered Petros' "With us, a woman who strays chooses death." Eleni had been right about her husband.

'S-so you'll t-turn back, K-kiwi?'

The Germans would be waiting for them, would they? He glanced up at the pass. It appeared quiet. If Costis' theory was correct, turning back had to be the wise, the only option. And months back, Andreas had warned him 'If Costis speaks, do what he tells you'.

Yet if they did turn back, their future was gone. A supply drop might still make a difference. It wasn't just success or failure. It was life or death. He shook his head at Costis. 'If we turn back…'

'W-we c-can t-try *our* radio.'

'It's too uncertain. We don't know if it'll work. Or reach. And we have no codebook. We have to see Dancy.'

'We could wait,' Andreas said. 'If no one comes, the Germans will think Dancy's message was a trick on them.'

'The airfield's taken away that choice. You saw how it was at Omalos. Every day lost could be fatal.'

'B-but… what if the G-germans are already there..?'

'Where? Already where?'

'If th-they picked up the m-message, w-won't they h-have been s-searching for Dancy's r-radio, too?'

The ground gave under him again. Costis and Andreas were right, too. He ground his teeth in frustration. Then had a sudden thought. 'Costi, you've just clinched the argument for going on.'

'I h-have?'

'If the Germans have already found Dancy, our hopes are done, aren't they?'

'And we'll walk into a trap,' Andreas said.

'In th-that c-case, K-kiwi, doesn't th-that c-clinch the argument – f-for n-*not* going on?'

His pulse was racing. 'Unless they *haven't* found him. In that case we have a chance. Our only chance. We have to check. If we don't…'

'We've fucked ourselves before we start?' Yiannis said.

'You could put it like that, Yianni.'

For a moment no one spoke.

'Better keep our eyes open, then,' Andreas said.

He glanced round them. 'Are you sure?'

Costis smiled. 'F-forewarned is f-forearmed, Kiwi.'

A surge of humility swept over him. He sighed at Yiannis. 'The damned radio, eh, Yianni?'

Yiannis slung a bandolier across one shoulder and grimaced at him as he lifted the other. 'What did I fucking tell you last week? About the radio.'

'That they *had* sent a repair man after all?'

'Good job they hadn't.'

'And if I had been one? At the start.'

'I'd have fucking sent you home again.'

'No problem there, now, Yianni,' he laughed. He knew he was letting the relief go to his head but couldn't resist.

'Why the fuck not?'

He waved an arm at the trees, hills and still blue sky.

'I am home.'

'You're fucking crazy, Kiwi, wherever you are.'

'It's my best quality.'

'L-let me lead, though, K-kiwi,' Costis asked.

'I prefer your marksmanship guarding my back.'

'The mad fucker has to lead,' Yiannis muttered. 'It's the only fucking way he understands.'

For the first time today his head felt fully clear. He smiled at Costis. 'Just for you, we'll spread out.'

He adjusted his pack and waved the bren. Andreas waited to give him ten yards start. The old crone's warning flipped back. Danna shouted in his ear: 'You always were too bloody reckless.' He shrugged the voices quiet. Wasn't this at least a more calculated risk?

He glanced back at their spread line. Logic urged against going on. The Germans could be waiting anywhere. But logic would have blocked everything he'd done. Koustoyerako, the pit, the rescue of Eleni. Logic told him outside the burnt-out house at Askyfou that Eleni was dead. And as for the mad bayonet charge at Galatas… Sometimes there *was* no choice.

'Kiwi!'

He turned at Yiannis' shout and stopped. 'What's the matter?'

'After what the fucker Dancy's done, when I kill him, will the British give me a medal?'

Of course – why hadn't he realised? – Dancy's betrayal wiped clean their own slate. But he called back: 'Don't build up your hopes.' If they couldn't stop the airstrip the rights or wrongs would all be academic.

Andreas caught him up and grinned. 'I'm going to lead.'

'What for?'

'I can see you're too busy brooding.'

Before he could protest Andreas had gone on ahead up the track.

'Anyway,' Andreas called back, 'after your cruel mockery of my distress, it's the least you can allow me.'

'I didn't mean to laugh. Really…'

'The Germans burnt her dowry, if you must know…'

'God, is she all right?'

'Haro. I think so. Her uncle smuggled her to Kassos.'

Kassos. He remembered now. Andreas' fury that night on the deck of the *Eleftheria*…

'I'm glad. And sorry I…'

'Don't think about it. No distractions, remember…?'

'Andrea, s-stop. L-listen.'

He swung round to see Costis' anxious face. The Cretan scanned the hill. He followed the mournful gaze and listened. Only the loud droning of bees. Costis gave an apologetic shrug and waved them forward.

He turned and moved off behind Andreas. All their nerves were stretched now. The sooner they got this over the better. It *was* only a prelude. The real ordeal was still to come.

He kept his eyes on the trees but his mind skittered. Had Costis heard something? It was a Cretan art. Yiorgos' ability to pick up sounds in the gale on the beach when they first landed had astounded him. And the old witch, what had she sensed? He felt a surge of fear for Eleni. At least he'd left Yiorgos to watch her. As for Petros, the reckoning would follow...

The bird lifted without his remarking it. Costis' second cry of alarm even stirred a flash of irritation. Was it going to be like this all the way? He also registered surprise. Costis hadn't stammered.

'Andrea, watch out. Ahead...'

There was a single shot. In a dream he saw Andreas stagger. He stumbled forward. Trees and sky swept at him in a headlong rush. He caught Andreas as his friend fell, sinking to his knees supporting him, searching the trees up ahead.

'Kapitulieren! Surrender!' bounced off the hills.

Behind him he heard Costis' shouts. 'Kiwi, r-roll away. G-get d-down.'

But he couldn't move. The German command re-echoed.

'Komm. Kapitulieren.'

Andreas went limp. With his left hand he eased the body down while fumbling with the other for the bren, his mind stuck on cursing the lost dowry.

He scoured the trees. A blur of green then bright blue sky swirled in his face, brushing it with the fragment of blue cloth. Once more he was back at Askyfou. And a German voice booming. 'Das letztemal! Jetzt!'

But this time there would be no surrender. In fury he scrambled up, swinging the bren to fire, and shouted his defiance at the sky.

'No! Freedom or...'

A roar cut everything to black.

High above, a lone eagle began a long sweeping glide across the face of the stark granite peaks beyond.

Late May 2011

The road up to Omalos, Western Crete

The chilled spectators began to disperse. Several bowed to the black-clad old lady in the wheelchair. She gestured at the middle-aged woman pushing her to take her towards the memorial. 'I want to touch the marble again.'

'Mama, must you? The steps. I can't support you.'

'No, but someone else will.'

She met the fierce eyes of the tall, upright old man.

'One last time, Ari?'

He offered his hand and she stood, taking a stick from her daughter. She straightened and walked with deliberation on his arm along the tarmac road. He laughed. 'You say that every year, Eleni. Is it hope?'

She paused at the foot of the rough stone steps up to the memorial and indicated it with her stick.

'The date on that slab ended my belief in hope.'

'Not only yours. If he'd lived, I've always said the Germans would have given up a year earlier, like on the mainland.'

The pair began the laboured climb. Ari glanced back.

'You've still not explained to her? Chryssoula?'

'Why should I? She was born long after.'

'You never wanted to tell her? About any of it?'

'Like how I shot my first husband, you mean?'

'Or killed the British major for his part in the betrayal?'

She shook Ari's arm and stopped to catch her breath.

'How many times do I have to tell you, Ari? I did not kill that man Dancy. He simply disappeared.'

'With a price on his head.'

'Which I didn't place there. And which no one claimed. He must have fled, got lost and blundered into a pit.'

She jerked Ari's arm to move up. They gained the space below the slab and stared at the words she knew by heart:

1600 Metres
To the place Stephanoporo
Where perished in a German ambush
The fighters of the Resistance
Andreas G Vandoulas
and
the New Zealander
Dudley Watkins, Kiwi.
Your heroic death is an example to us all

'He made me believe I could do anything,' Ari said.

Eleni sighed and rapped her stick on the slab. 'Yes... You bloody fool, Kiwi.'

'You haven't started to blame him?'

'I never did. But he was too brave. Too independent. Too committed to our cause. Yet if he hadn't been...'

'We'd not be standing here, now?'

She edged round and stared across the telephone wires down the V-shaped valley, to the round hill in the middle distance. She shook her head.

'No, it's not that. I meant I wouldn't have shared with him the most unforgettable few days of my life.'

Bibliography

Any historical novel is informed by the accounts of those who were there and the research of later historians. So while the characters and events in this novel are fictitious, the books listed below have provided invaluable background detail and insight.

Antony Beevor	Crete – the Battle and Resistance
Christopher Buckley	Greece and Crete 1941
Alan Clark	The Fall of Crete
Murray Elliott	Vasili, the Lion of Crete
Dominique Eudes	The Kapetanios
Roy Farran	Winged Dagger
Kimon Farantakis	The Leaden-Sky Years of WW2
Patrick Leigh Fermor	Roumeli
Xan Fielding	Hide and Seek
Nicholas Gage	Eleni
C Hadjipateras)	
M Fafalios)	Crete 1941 Eyewitnessed
Yiorgos Harokopos	The Fortress Crete
	The Abduction of General Kreipe
Nikos Kazantzakis	Report to Greco; Freedom & Death;
	Zorba the Greek; The Fratricides
H D F Kitto	In the Mountains of Greece
G C Kiriakopoulos	Ten Days to Destiny
Callum MacDonald	The Lost Battle
Mark Mazower	Inside Hitler's Greece; After the War was Over
George Psychoundakis	The Cretan Runner
Tim Saunders	Crete, The Airborne Invasion 1941
I McD G Stewart	The Struggle for Crete
W B 'Sandy' Thomas	Dare to be Free
Evelyn Waugh	Officers and Gentlemen